INISH CARRAIG
BY
JO ZEBEDEE

ENJOYED 'INISH CARRAIG'? PLEASE LEAVE A REVIEW:

https://www.goodreads.com/book/show/25952789-inish-carraig

THIS ONE'S FOR BILL.
WE MISS YOU.

ACKNOWLEDGEMENTS

I wish I could say this, my second book, wrote itself. In truth and as ever, I needed wise heads to help me.

Once again, my family. My daughters, Becky and Holly, who are so proud of their writing mum and never jealous of the time it takes from them. My husband, Chris, for an insane amount of support, for brainstorming, for cups of tea and being able to find the laugh in things. My mum, for endless support. Graham, for lending me his boating knowledge.

Also, the readers: John J Brady, whom I owe at least six books to, the best-humoured of betas; Paul Dee, always supportive and fair; Sue Jackson for those nit-picky things I miss; anyone else who has contributed to Inish in any way, including the writing community of the sffchronicles. As ever, you are all thanked.

J Scott Marryat, who did a fabulous edit when Inish was a baby and who patiently supported me during its growth and was one of the first writers to give me encouragement.

Finally, a big thank you to Gary Compton, of Tickety Boo Press, for the cover design, and to Sam Primeau for a fantastic final edit.

CHAPTER ONE

John got up from the bed as quietly as he could, making Stuart stir before settling again with his thumb stuck in his mouth. John paused – he should probably take it out. Their mother had said, to the day she died, that only babies sucked their thumbs. He didn't, not wanting to disturb the boy, but gently wrapped their Da's winter coat closer around his brother, tugging at a loose piece of the furred lining until it came away. He straightened, shivering. Wind whistled through the hole in the ceiling, but at least the room was safe. Well, as safe as anywhere in Belfast.

" 'Night, Stuart." John tiptoed to the door and pulled it closed behind him. It was no warmer in the hall, but the roof was intact. He crossed to the window and looked out over the city. All was quiet under the curfew. The only thing moving was a cat crossing the yard below. It padded carefully, keeping its distance, and no wonder: there were a few recipes for cat stew doing the rounds. Further away, on the lough, the sewage farms' floodlights lit up the night skyline. A low anger started, and he found his fists clenching. He bet the aliens' kids didn't wake up freezing and hungry, like his wee brother and sister did. A door closed and he turned to see Josey coming out of the girls' room.

"Is Sophie asleep?" he asked.

She nodded, and she looked tired and older than her thirteen years, her face wan, her blonde hair lank and dirty. "Yeah."

"Stuart's settled, but he was asking for his night-light again. You're sure there's nothing we could take batteries out of?"

"No, I checked everything I could think of."

"I told him he had the moon instead." He half-smiled at the silver lining of a hole in the roof. "I'll keep an eye out for batteries. I have to go out and see what I can scrounge, anyway."

"If you could get some sort of heater, it'd be good," said Josey. Her voice didn't hold out much hope.

1

"I'll see what I can find." He brightened. "I could nick a barbecue."

"We could get some furniture from downstairs. The kitchen table is wood."

"Maybe. I'll see if I can get a barbie first."

"Okay." Her voice was small and he put his arm around her, feeling how thin she was through her fleece. She'd lost so much weight it worried him. He pushed the thought away; it was no more than he'd lost, and there was nothing more sinister behind it than hunger. He let go and climbed onto the window ledge. "You know the drill: if anyone comes near the house, the three of you get under cover, right? Don't come out until I'm back."

She nodded, her eyes resigned to his nightly instruction. He put his hands onto the wall at each side, bracing himself for the jump down.

"John?"

Her quiet voice stopped him. "Yeah?"

"Be careful. And stay away from McDowell – he's dangerous."

John didn't reply. McDowell *was* dangerous. He was also the person with the best access to food, medicine and water in North Belfast. All of which they needed. He took a deep breath and jumped onto the flat roof below. He stepped onto the wall of the yard and ran along, his arms out for balance. At the end, he climbed down the iron supports Da had put in. Christ, he wished his da was here and in charge.

The sound of flapping made him jump and press against the wall, heart somewhere in his throat. A ripped poster opposite caught in the wind, and he relaxed. Nothing but the usual promises of food-drops, hospitals, reopened schools....

A lot of shite. His old school was a dent in the ground, the only upside of the invasion. The hospital, shut down in the war, hadn't reopened. There were rumours – good rumours, too, from different sources – that the cops and army were working with the aliens now, and things were about to get better. His mouth pulled into a sneer. He'd believe it when he saw it. The Earth-Committee leaders, pulled from the governments that had made it through the invasion, might have time to drag their feet: they weren't starving their arses off in the ruins of Belfast. It didn't matter a damn to him that working with the Galactic Council meant liaising with the Zelo, or the never-seen Barath'na, it just mattered that someone, somewhere, turned up with some food. And a roof, that'd be good.

" 'Supporting Earth to a better future'," he muttered, straightening. "There was nothing wrong with it before the bastards invaded."

He hugged the wall until he reached the end of the back lane, and darted across to a wider alley, the first of a series. The authorities could say what they liked about the war being over. He was taking no chances until someone proved it.

A hand slapped down on his shoulder. "Got you!"

John reached for his knife, but stopped at a laugh. He croaked, "Taz, you *bastard*."

"McDowell wants us," said Taz, his voice hushed. His jacket was denim, not nearly thick enough. He hunched into it, so the only parts visible were his nose and dark eyes. His clothes were clean and well patched, though, proof of having a mum who took care of such things. John swallowed a sharp wrench of jealousy. He was nearly sixteen, he shouldn't be yearning after his mum. He put his hands in his pockets and slouched. "Why?"

"He says he has a job, and we'll get food if we do it."

"Christ, for that I'd take on a Zelotyr patrol single-handed."

"Yeah, right."

They stopped where the alley opened onto a courtyard, once part of the council's sports-ground where he'd tried out for the first team. Da had stood on the touchline, screaming for John to get the ball over the line. His celebrations when the try had been allowed had almost got him thrown out for incitement. Now, the courtyard was weed-strewn and garbage-clad, and his da six months dead.

"Get back." Taz grabbed him, and they pressed against the wall as a platoon of soldiers crossed. Human, not Zelo – the lack of stench told him that. Not that it made any difference. They'd still lift him and Taz for curfew violation.

The platoon left the courtyard, and John ran across, through a hole in the fencing, and down the final alley skirting the playing field. Taz, quick and wiry, soon passed him. They reached the rubbled remains of the peace wall. John smiled as he stepped through the gap; it was easier getting across the city now the Zelo had trashed it. He relaxed as they entered his old estate and passed the gable end mural. Its slogan, *We'll fight for Ulster*, had been replaced with the promise to do the same for Earth since he'd last been here.

"Let's hope it's only McDowell," said Taz as they reached McDowell's familiar terraced house.

"Oh, Junior will be here. His da isn't taking a piss these days without him in attendance."

"Just keep your distance if he is," said Taz. "Don't rise to him – that's what he wants."

"Okay." Taz was right, but John hated Gary McDowell knowing his business. The latch turned, and he put his shoulders back. If the cost of a meal was toadying up to Gary, so be it. He'd kick a few walls on the way home to feel better.

"All right, lads. You took your time." It wasn't Gary, but Demos, one of his cronies.

"Patrol," muttered John, eyeing Demos' fat belly hanging over his trousers. He'd no problem getting food, evidently. His own stomach clenched, but he stood straight and waited while Demos made a show of checking were they to come in, all the time holding a pistol by his side. After a few moments, they were led into a room off the hall, where a group of men were gathered close to a fire. The men turned, their eyes more dangerous than any soldier's.

"You wanted us," said John, keeping his voice steady.

"Aye." McDowell stood, his tall, rangy frame dwarfing John. A scar, running from his left eye to his ear, stood out against his skin. His badge of honour, he called it, given to him by a Zelotyr he'd fought with an iron bar and balls of solid rock. The sort of balls that earned so much street respect John's hands shook, and he had to stick them in his pockets to hide it.

"John Dray and Taz Delaney, I'll make a deal with you," said McDowell.

John swallowed and hoped his voice held. "Go on, then."

McDowell didn't answer, and John made sure to stand straight. He focused on McDowell's leather jacket – it may be battered, but it was thick and warm. On his wrist, a designer watch could be seen.

The silence stretched until Taz drew in a loud breath, making John want to thump him and tell him how to face someone like McDowell: by embracing whatever he issued and coming back for more, knowing you'd either grow or die from it, until you were strong enough to protect your own. He glanced at Taz, decided his friend was in danger of passing out, and said, "All right, what can we do for you?"

"Good lad, right to the heart of it. When you've got a bit of flesh around your scrawn, you'll go far."

John fought the urge to smile. It wasn't the first time McDowell had hinted he might take him on. He looked at McDowell's boots - new, thick soles, real leather - and down at his own trainers, their uppers parting from the sole. His mouth went wet and spiky with desire, but he didn't say anything. *Stay cool, like it's just another job...*

McDowell reached into his jacket, and John held his breath. Weapons? He'd done his first delivery across town about three weeks ago, and had been terrified: not just for himself, but for Josey and the kids if he got lifted. The payment for it had been a coat for Sophie, though.

McDowell brought out a tin box, just small enough to fit into his inside pocket. He held it up, displaying it. "You can take yourselves to the top of the Cave Hill and open this," he said. "Give it a shake, make sure you empty out what's in it. If you do, and come back to me, I'll see you get some food." His eyes narrowed, and he nodded at John. "Maybe some fresh fruit for wee Sophie and Stuart?"

The boys exchanged glances. That was it? John took the box and stuck it in his pocket.

McDowell went back to where he had been sitting, popped a beer and nodded to the door. "Best get going, boys."

They backed out and headed up the street, onto the bottom of the Cave Hill. They followed the path up the hill, and the stench from the sewage farms hit John, even worse this high up. He pulled his scarf off and tied it so it covered his nose.

Taz gave a short laugh. "You look like a twat."

5

John felt himself go red, and pushed the scarf back round his neck. They kept going, the hill getting steeper now they were away from the streets. They climbed in near silence, taking their time to pick their way over the rocks in the dark, until they reached McArt's fort and sat for a minute, getting their breath back. From here the city looked tiny.

"What d'you reckon is in it?" asked Taz.

John shrugged and shook the tin. It made no sound. "The ashes of the last poor fucker to piss him off?"

Taz shook his head. "His finger."

"No, an eyeball. We'll open it and it'll be looking at us –"

"Both of 'em – he wouldn't take one and leave the other."

John shook it again, and it didn't *feel* like eyeballs. He glanced over at Taz.

"We don't need to," said Taz. "We could just say we did."

For a moment John was tempted, but the thought of going home with no food strengthened his resolve, and he shook his head. "You must be joking."

He edged to the cliff face. From here, it was like being king of Belfast. He cast his eyes over the lough. What was left? He knew Glasgow had been wiped out – it had gone early – and it would be years before London would be rebuilt. New York, too – everywhere. He shivered, and bile rose up in him. It wasn't their planet; what right had the shit-eaters to destroy it?

He opened the box – it took a bit of work, the lid was on tight – half-closing his eyes, sure it would be gruesome. Instead, all it contained was dust, fine like ash, sparkling very slightly in the moonlight. He touched it with his finger, tracing a pattern in it, and it felt like fine sand.

"It's drugs," he said, a little disappointed. "It must be a bad shipment."

Taz leaned over and put his finger in the sand. "Weird – why not tip it down a drain and have done with it? Why here?"

"Who cares? It'll get us food, and I'm starving. You're so skinny, you'll slip through a crack in the road soon." John reached the tin out. "Want some?"

Taz shook his head. "Go fuck yourself."

"Chickenshit."

6

"Bollocks I am." Taz traced a line in the dust and put his finger to his mouth. He licked it. "That's not drugs; it tastes like sand or something."

"You could be eating someone's body," said John.

Taz rubbed his hand over his mouth, and paled a little. "It's not a body, you arse."

John reached out his hand, holding the tin tightly. If McDowell wanted it sprinkled over Belfast, that's what he'd do. Hell, if the big man wanted him to piss off the side of the cliff, he'd do it. He shook the box into the wind, watching the dust lift into the breeze. He put the tin in his pocket and clapped his hands to get rid of the sand. "Let's go."

They hurried down, skidding on the scree, half on their feet, half on their arses. They'd got partway down when Taz doubled over with a grunt. His face curled into a grimace. Sweat beaded his forehead.

"Jesus," said John, reaching for him. "What –?"

Taz screamed.

"What is it?" John shook Taz.

"It hurts!" yelled Taz. He slumped to the ground. "It fucking hurts everywhere!"

Waves of panic thudded across John's head. Taz rolled onto his side, shaking. John knelt and put his hand on him, not knowing what to do. There was no one to get help from, not this deep into the curfew. He stood and pulled Taz up, fumbling in the dark, almost dropping him, until Taz was draped over his shoulders. He had to get the pair of them back to Taz's house and let his ma see to him. He took a first step, grimacing at the dead weight on his shoulders, but forced another step, and then another. There was nothing else for it. Taz needed help, and Josey and the kids were waiting for him.

CHAPTER TWO

ohn staggered to the garden wall, Taz draped over his shoulders. Christ, for a skinny guy he was heavy. John took a breath and his chest burned; he had to stop, just for a minute. He propped Taz against the wall, but his friend slid down and curled up on the ground. He rocked back and forth, moaning. At least he'd stopped yelling.

John leaned forward, put his hands on his knees, and took gulps of air. A year ago, he'd have managed Taz's weight easily, but that was when he was getting ready to try out for the trials, not when he was half-starved. He straightened, looking down the length of the Ballysillan Road, and saw streaks of light in the sky. It had taken them all night to get this far. Josey would be worried, and Taz's mum.

Maybe he should hide Taz? Shove him under a bush and go for help? He'd be in the Oldpark in about fifteen minutes if he did.... A long groan from his friend convinced him not to. He took another deep breath and tapped Taz's shoulder.

"Come on, mate," he said, trying to haul Taz upright. His friend fought against him, but John managed to hoist him up, using his belt for leverage. He managed to get Taz draped over one shoulder. John gritted his teeth and headed down the road. "Taz, try to walk a bit."

Taz nodded against him, and his weight lessened a little. Not enough, though – they'd never make it. There was a rumble in the distance, coming nearer. John cocked his head. An engine, somewhere to his left, probably a patrol; no one else would be out before curfew ended. Taz had slumped again, his full weight across John's shoulders, making them ache. The noise came closer, really close now – it must be in the next street. John kicked open a garden gate to his right, cursing as he tried to manoeuvre both of them through. He

8

tripped and they went down in a heap, Taz screaming as he fell on him. John clapped his hand over his friend's mouth. "Shhh - patrol."

Taz groaned and nodded. John held his breath. *Fuck.* He looked around; there was nothing in the garden other than a kid's slide, purple and shaped like a bear. Totally crap.

"In the corner," he said. At least they'd be shielded from the road by the hedge. He glanced at the house; it looked empty, its windows dirty with thin curtains drawn. The engine stopped.

Taz crawled, John behind him. A door slammed. He pushed Taz into the corner of the garden and ducked down, pulling the slide in front of them. Voices came from the street: Belfast accents, not Zelo translators. John pulled out his knife, flicking it open, and put his head against the grass, watching through an arch beneath the slide as the tip of a rifle touched the gate, pushing it open. Beside him Taz had collapsed and was breathing too heavily, half moaning.

"Shhhh," he said, but Taz didn't respond. He looked terrible, pale and sweating, his eyelids fluttering.

The gate opened fully and someone stepped into the garden, their cargo trousers tucked into a pair of heavy boots. *Shit.* The feet stopped. John huddled beside Taz, holding his head, and his friend was hot, really hot.

The slide moved. John held his breath. *Could he run?* He tightened his grip on the knife.

"Don't even think about it."

He looked up into the barrel of a machine gun. He followed the line of the gun, up past a burly chest, to see a soldier of about forty, his face stern.

"The knife. Hand it over."

"Right."

John got to his knees and handed the knife to the soldier, who snapped it closed and put it in his pocket.

"Captain!" the soldier yelled. He gestured to the boys. "Stand up, hands in the air."

John got to his feet, slowly, keeping his hands high.

"And your mate."

"He's hurt."

Taz moaned, a long moan, and the trooper frowned. He really was big, like a rugby player or something. His cheeks were flushed; John bet his hair was red under his helmet. "How did he get hurt?"

"I dunno. Maybe he ate something."

The captain came into the garden. "Bring them in, Peters; they're out after curfew." He cursed and turned away. "They're the last thing we need on top of what's happening to the Zelo."

John tried to protest, but two of the squad stepped forward and grabbed his arms. He twisted, trying to get away, but his wrists were pulled behind him. A circle of cold iron encased them, snapping into place.

"You can't cuff us! We haven't done anything!" yelled John.

"Save it." Peters jerked his head at the gate. "Let's go."

Another pair of soldiers pulled Taz to his feet, and he gave a long shriek. John glanced back at him; he was sweating and pale, his face scrunched in pain.

"My mate – Taz – he really is sick," said John. "Look at him."

"If he is, we'll get a medic for him." Peters pushed John out of the garden and up against the wagon. He patted John down, his hands hard and impersonal, and stopped at the tin in John's pocket. "What's that?"

"Nothing."

The soldier pulled it out and turned it over in his hand. He looked up at John, and his eyes were shrewd. "Doing a run tonight, were you?"

"I don't know what you're talking about," said John. Behind him, Taz screamed, and a voice said something about the boy telling the truth, he *really* wasn't well. John, his head held against the vehicle, said, "Taz – he is sick."

"How?"

"I don't *know*."

The soldier let him go. "Get in, lad."

John clambered in, struggling with his hands cuffed, and the soldier leaned in, giving what looked like a sympathetic smile. "If he's taken something, you'd best tell us. The sooner we know, the better for him."

Taz was ushered into the vehicle and collapsed onto the bench opposite. His eyes were wide and scared.

"You think we've taken drugs?" John asked the trooper. "You must be thick. We don't have money for anything like that. I don't have a clue what's wrong with him. We were up on the hill, and then he doubled over on me. I know it was after curfew, but you want to see where we live. It's such a dump, you have to get out sometimes."

The soldier paused a moment, as if considering this. He looked back down at the tin in his hand, and up at John again. "What's your name, son? And there's no point lying to me, we'll get to it one way or the other."

John took a deep breath, looking at his sympathetic face. "Piss off," he said, and kicked out. Sympathetic, hell. No one cared about the people left in the estates. His kick didn't get anywhere near the trooper, who shook his head and slammed the door, leaving John in the dark, his hands pulled behind him, the only noise Taz's soft groans. He put his head back as the engines started. *Shit.*

CHAPTER THREE

The door to the office opened. "Inspector!"

Carter set down the overnight report he'd been reading, smirking a little; it appeared there were worse jobs than being the Zelotyr liaison officer in Belfast. In Derry, some residents had taken to chucking rocks off Butcher's Gate, proving Zelotyr skulls were close to impenetrable. Since the Galactic Council had ruled humans were sentient, the Zelotyr couldn't retaliate by razing the Bogside, a point O'Leary, his counterpart in Derry, had spent the night making. Apparently, even the aliens were finding Ireland a bastard to conquer. "Yes?"

Sergeant Sanderson, short, squat and scowling, looked more bad-tempered than normal. Just. "One of the Zelotyr is downstairs – he says there's an emergency."

Carter rubbed his mouth with the back of his hand, but stopped when he saw Sanderson's slightly raised eyebrows. It wouldn't do for the aliens' liaison officer to admit that the Zelotyr still turned his stomach. Not given what the rest of the station thought of him: an efficient turncoat and traitor were the most generous comments he got these days. That he'd been ordered into the role when Bar-eltyr, the alien commander from the Cave Hill, had requested him as part of the deal for peace didn't make any difference – he'd still been tarred as a collaborator.

"Thanks." Carter grabbed his jacket and was halfway down the hall when he heard shouting. He took the stairs two at a time and burst into reception. A male Zelotyr – a senior, judging by its armour – was cradling the body of a junior, its eyes blank and silvered over.

Carter took a moment, not sure what to say, and raised his eyes to meet the Zelotyr's, at the same time managing not to look in its maw. It had taken weeks to learn that trick. "What happened?"

"Dying," said the Zelotyr, in flat, electronic tones.

Carter touched the child, careful to be gentle. "Yes, I see that. I'm sorry – what can I do?"

The Zelotyr owned the hospitals, they controlled what remained of the transport network... there was nothing Carter could offer that they didn't already have.

"All dying..." The Zelotyr gave the child to Carter and stumbled back. "Dying..."

Carter handed the baby to the receptionist, too quickly for her to realise what it was and refuse. He darted forwards, put a hand on one of the huge arms and nodded at Sanderson to do the same. A look of disgust swept over the sergeant's face, but he took the other arm and held it firmly.

"Who are dying?" asked Carter, straining to support the alien.

"The Zelotyr. All of us."

"How?"

The Zelotyr dropped to its knees and cast its eyes between the two policemen. "You must ensure we are avenged."

It pitched forward, its body emitting a stench like Carter had never smelled before: worse than the sewage the aliens harvested or the mucus oozing through their plating. He covered his mouth, fighting not to gag, and stepped back.

"Sir." Sanderson pointed at the screen above the reception desk, broadcasting the news. The receptionist had set the baby's body on her desk and was backed against the filing cabinet, watching the screen, her eyes shining with what looked like tears.

Carter read the words scrolling along the bottom of the screen. It was true: the Zelo were dying. Sanderson's face cracked into a grin.

"Yes!" said the sergeant. "Someone had the balls to get rid of the shit-eaters. About bloody time."

"It says it's happening all over the world," said the receptionist. The reception filled with officers and station staff. One of the cleaners wrinkled his nose and asked who'd died. Carter winced and tried not to look at the Zelo's body.

On the screen, a spaceship leaving Earth caused someone to start a round of applause, and it spread through the room. A whistle pierced the air and the caretaker jumped onto a chair, punching the air. "Don't bloody come back!"

There was a cheer, and Carter added his voice to it - he might have had to work with the Zelotyr, but he'd never wanted to. The screen changed, showing their little scene being played out in a darkened Times Square, followed by a snow-covered Russian vista. A human presenter appeared on screen, and the information band along the bottom announced the retreat of the aliens. The picture changed, highlighting the locations - worldwide, filling the screen with red dots - where the poison had already taken effect. It plotted the spread of the virus, showing how it would cover Earth in a maximum of two days. The picture changed to another departing ship; it appeared the aliens weren't going to wait around. Judging by how fast the alien had died tonight, Carter didn't blame them.

"They're gone!" Sanderson's voice carried over the cheers, reigniting them, and the noise went on for a few minutes before quietening again. Now the initial excitement had passed, it felt strangely flat, like Christmas after dinner, with all the presents opened and the T.V. still crap.

Carter watched for another moment, until the screen started to show repeats of the same pictures. His gaze fell on the body of the baby Zelo, its silver armour - not armour, not yet, more like scales - dulling as the body stiffened.

He turned and pushed open the door to the car park, welcoming the air on his face. The Zelotyr were gone. It was a good thing; the best thing. He tried to regain the excitement, but it felt like icy tentacles were reaching into his stomach.

"Sir?" asked Sanderson, behind him. "Are you okay?" His voice changed, took on an edge of a sneer. "Aren't you pleased? Earth is free."

"Is it?" Carter stared at the housing estate opposite. What happened when the residents found out? Or the Barath'na? The second alien race had tried to force the Zelo off the planet when Earthlings were declared sentient. It was one of the reasons the Zelo had started to work in partnership with Earth, to appease the GC and allow them to stay. Carter hadn't met a Barath'na, but the Zelotyr enmity to them had been openly evident. Whether it was long-standing racial hatred or based on truth, he'd prefer not to find out. He remembered the horror of the Zelotyr attack, the smart mines – there were some still scattered around the city, waiting for poor sods to get close enough to set them off – destroying the city. The last thing they needed was another lot of aliens deciding to try their luck.

Or, for that matter, the first set wanting revenge. His blood chilled; the Zelotyr didn't have to be on the ground to attack. Last time, the first waves of bombs had come from space.

"Don't you see?" he said to Sanderson. "We need to find whoever has done this, before it causes another war..."

Sanderson cleared his throat. "About that, sir." He nodded at the station's barred gate. "You might want to hang around – they've lifted a couple of lads.

***

At the sound of a door closing, Carter turned to face the army sergeant, Peters, who'd brought the two bedraggled lads in. One was sitting in the interview room next door, looking fairly stunned. Carter crossed his arms and leaned against the observation window which dominated the small room. "Well? Ours or yours?"

"Yours." Peters dumped his paperwork on the table in the centre of the room. "It lies under police jurisdiction." He set a clear bag on the table, and pointed at it. "We thought they were drug running at first." He lit a cigarette, making Carter cough.

"There's a smoking ban, you know," he said.

Peters gave a short laugh. "You want to arrest me?" He leaned back and blew a series of perfect smoke rings at the ceiling. "You know what's happened to the Zelo. In fact, you probably know more than I do; you're the shit-lover, right?"

Carter took a deep breath, trying to hide his annoyance. "If you mean I'm the Zelotyr liaison, then yes."

"Whatever." Peters nodded at the window. "We're waiting

for forensics to confirm what was in that tin, but I'd put money on it being the virus."

"That's a hell of a jump – from drug running to xenocide?" Carter turned to the observation window. The lad was sitting on a wooden seat, arms on the table in front, chin resting on them. He looked young, maybe about fifteen, his hair long, falling into his eyes. "He's just another street kid."

"You didn't see his face when he heard the Zelo were dying. Or how sick his friend is. He told us the other lad ingested whatever they released, and he's ill. Really ill. It doesn't take a genius to make the link." Peters walked across, his footsteps loud in the empty room. "Any idea who'll be behind it?"

"Not him." Carter thought for a moment. "Locally, there're a couple of possibilities. When we get confirmation from forensics and know what we're looking at, I'll get someone on to it."

Peters threw down his cigarette, grinding it out, and Carter glared at him. The sergeant ignored him, crossing his arms, muscles standing out against his black t-shirt.

"What will happen to them, if they did release it?" he asked. "I was told you knew the Zelotyr better than anyone."

Carter walked back to the desk and picked up the custody form, checking the details. "Hard to know for sure; they're odd, the Zelotyr."

"We noticed."

Carter signed the sheet, separated the duplicate, and checked the report of the arrest. "A year ago, I was with an army captain – a guy called Nugent. We were cornered by a pack of Zelo teenagers."

"I heard. He got killed, they say. Eviscerated."

The sergeant's voice was clipped, and Carter looked down, studiously reading. "Yes, it was... it wasn't quick." He swallowed bile at the memory. "When an adult Zelo came across what was happening, he let me go. He didn't support the killing; it went against their culture." And yet the Zelo had descended on Earth, unleashing an attack across the world that had killed millions. "The problem is, what happens to the lads, if you're right, isn't just Earth's decision. You know why the Zelo came here, right?"

"The three bears' porridge was good for their babies…"

"Yep. Their planet's overheating – they can't breed on it. Earth matched what they needed."

"It's our planet." Peters frowned. "Just because their technology is a bit more advanced than ours –"

Carter snorted. "A bit? We've managed to get a couple of probes into space, walked on our satellite; they have faster-than-light technology, and weaponry that could blow Earth out of space. I call that more than a bit."

"So?"

"So, they were working with us. Rathcoole, for instance: they funded all the new housing." Carter ducked his head, not able to meet yet another stare branding him a conspirator when it was the only way to save the little people. Lads like the one in the room next door, abandoned in the ruins of a dying city. "Look, I know what everyone thinks of me, I'm not stupid. Or deaf…. But, we're wrong about the Zelo. They made a mistake on Earth and they're committed to rectifying it."

"A few billion deaths is more than a mistake," spat Peters.

He was right: it was a fucking tragedy. But so was a few billion more. Carter set the report down and rubbed his forehead. God, he was tired. "I don't believe they knew we were sentient." Unless the aliens had completely duped him, of course. "In fact, I think since they found out, they've been trying to atone for their sins. They are unbelievably moral, in their own way –"

"What's moral about destroying a planet?" The soldier started to pace. He pulled another cigarette out. "What's moral about killing kids and families who were in the way of where you wanted to put hatchlings?"

"Nothing." Carter pushed his hair back. "Nothing at all. And they would agree with you. That's why their technology is running our hospitals. That's why they provided the transports and weaponry you need to do your work. Without them, Earth will take decades longer to rebuild."

Peters shook his head in disgust, and pulled the papers to him. "Right, which copy is mine?" He took the lid off his pen, his movements jerky and angry.

"I'm not defending them," Carter said, frustration creeping into his voice. "Christ, of all people I'm not going to do that. What they did to Nugent...." He wiped his mouth. "I think we can say I'm no lover of the Zelotyr."

Peters shrugged, and Carter wanted to tell him that every night he'd gone home from working with the aliens and scrubbed himself in the shower, only the belief he was doing the right thing getting him up each morning. Instead he said, "In another couple of weeks, this lad would have been off the streets before the winter set in. We'd have pulled Belfast back from the brink."

Peters shifted, his stance relaxing. "We'll have to agree to differ." He nodded at the boy. "You didn't answer my question: what happens to him?"

"The Zelo will believe whoever did this must be punished. An eye for an eye." He paused. "How many Zelotyr are dead?"

"Thousands."

"When they let me go, they said their teenagers would face three deaths each, the same as Nugent."

Peters paled and glanced at the small figure in the interview room. "Shit."

"Yes."

"But they must know the virus didn't come from the streets of Belfast. It could have come from anywhere; the Barath'nas won't exactly be sorry about it."

"And I'm sure if they find a Barath'na is behind it, they'll murder him a thousand times over, too." Carter knocked on the window, a rat-tat-tat of nerves. "If these lads released the virus, under galactic law they'll be found guilty of..." He shook his head. "I don't know; accidental xenocide, I suppose. Alien-slaughter?"

"What will you do?" asked Peters, after a moment.

"What can I do? I'm only a policeman, I have no authority over the GC."

"A policeman whose jurisdiction the lads lie under. The Zelotyr have pulled out; our colonel is dealing with the fallout. No one else has claimed jurisdiction."

Carter shrugged, hoping to hide how upset he was. The soldier was right – the boys were humans, they deserved to be dealt with as such, but the last months had taught him his hands were tied when it came to the Galactic Council. He was nothing to them, just a cop buried on Earth.

"It lies with the GC. I'll report the incident to their representative," he said, knowing how it sounded, a Judas taking his silver coins. Peters' mouth tightened into a thin line. Carter crossed his arms. "I don't like it either, but there's not a damn thing I can do about it."

Peters looked through the glass, taking a long moment before he turned his gaze back to Carter. "If it were me, I'd hand in my stripes and walk away." Carter went to cut him off, but his voice rose over Carter's. "Because it's *shit*. He's human, they're the invaders. It's shit."

He turned and walked out, leaving Carter to stare at the boy. Peters was right. It was crap, and there wasn't a damn thing he could do about it.

CHAPTER FOUR

arter walked into the interview room, pulled out the chair opposite the boy and sank into it. It had taken him a bit of time to find out who he was, but finally a constable had come up with a name. The boy ignored him and Carter watched for a moment, letting the silence stretch. John was holding something in his hand, a rag of some sort, and his hands were clenching and unclenching around it, as if it was the only thing he could sense or control.

"John." No response. Carter rapped the table. "John Dray!"

This time, John lifted his head. "What?"

"Do you know where you are?"

"The station. Antrim Road station."

"Good lad. My name's Henry Carter, I'm an inspector based here." The boy nodded, and Carter went on, "Now, since I already know your name, could you confirm it for the record?"

"No."

Carter took a deep breath. "John Dray," he said. "Your mate is Terence Delaney. Living somewhere in the Oldpark. Parents died about three months ago, foraging for food. Got some siblings." He laid his hands on the table. "That's all I know about you, John. Can you help me out with some more?"

"I haven't done anything," said the boy. "You've no reason to hold me."

He clenched his fist around the rag and Carter pointed at it. "What's that?"

John looked at it, and his eyes seemed to soften. "It's nothing. Just something I carry around with me."

"Whose is it?"

"It doesn't matter."

Carter waited, thinking. The siblings, apparently, were younger. "What will happen when you don't get home?" The

20

lad's head came up, and Carter shrugged. "Because you're not going anywhere." Carter leaned forward. "You weren't the only one who carried out a job tonight: Baltimore, Rostov, Marseilles, Istanbul, Buenos Aires and Mombasa, they're the ones we know of. All the other runners who let the virus go are dead." He paused, but there was no answer, so he pushed again. "All the Zelotyr are dead, John. That's what the job was, to kill them."

John's eyes hardened. "I don't know what you're talking about."

Carter smiled at his bravado. "You know we picked up two men waiting at the edge of the estate? They had guns." The boy paled slightly at that. "Now, what were you doing on the hill?"

"Nothing; I told the patrol that."

"Spare me." Carter nodded at the rag. "So, whose is it? Since you've nothing to hide, why not tell me?" The boy's hand clenched around it, and Carter softened his voice. "I'm here to help, John."

The boy looked up, his eyes hard. "Like hell you are."

"Well, no one else is," said Carter. He leaned back in his seat, looking at the ceiling's pattern of cracks from the Zelo bombs. He waited.

"It's my little brother's – from his coat," said John, his voice hesitant. "That's all."

Carter stifled a smile of relief. "What's his name?"

"Stuart."

There was a clatter from the corridor and Carter got up to open the door and take a tray from Sanderson. He set it on the table, picked up a mug of tea, and pushed another mug towards John. "Hot chocolate. I thought you must be cold. Biscuits, if you want any."

The boy's eyes went round at the sight of the biscuits and he reached out and took one, nibbling at it for a moment before his hunger got the better of his manners and he devoured it in two bites. Carter pushed the plate over to him.

"Help yourself," he said, and waited while the boy did just that. After, John picked up the mug and huddled over it, his face pinched and dirty, his too-long hair falling over his face, hiding his watchful eyes.

21

"Any other brothers?" asked Carter. The boy shook his head. "Sisters?"

A slight nod. "Two."

"Where are they?"

The boy's shoulders stiffened.

"At home."

"Where's home?" The boy shook his head, and Carter moved back to safer ground. "How old are they?"

John pushed his hair back. He looked younger. More vulnerable. Slowly, he said, "Josey's a couple of years younger than me – the other two, they're just kids. Josey'll look after them until I get home."

Carter leaned forward until his hand was nearly touching the boy's. "Look, John, you're in a lot of trouble, do you know that? It's just – you won't be getting back to them anytime soon."

The boy blinked before he looked back at Carter and nodded. He looked like he was scared to speak in case he cried, and Carter didn't blame him.

"Can you tell me anything? Who gave you the tin?"

"We found it." John's voice was a whisper and his eyes didn't meet Carter's.

"Where?"

"On the ground."

"So you found a tin, and decided to risk the patrols – leave your kid sisters and Stuart alone – to climb up the Cave Hill?"

"Yes."

"Oh, come on. If you're going to lie, at least make it convincing." Nothing. Carter fought to keep the frustration out of his voice. "John, I don't know where you live, but I bet whoever set you up does."

There was a rattling noise, and Carter looked around, trying to tell what it was. He looked back at John and realised the boy's feet were drumming off the ground and he was shaking, his shoulders shuddering as if he couldn't stop.

Oh, hell. Carter got up and draped his jacket round the boy's shoulders. He pushed the table back and crouched down, putting his hand on John's chin, tipping his face so they were looking at each other.

"John, things are really bad, okay?"

John's eyes didn't waver, even though his teeth were chattering.

"I need you to tell me what happened, and who was involved." No response. "If you don't, John, you'll be taking the rap for it. You'll get sent to the Zelotyr and they'll..." He stopped. He couldn't tell this kid what he faced. He had to. "They'll..."

"K - kill me," whispered John. "Like they say, on the street – they do it more than once."

God help me, he knows. "Yes. Unless you tell me who set you up for this, John, that's exactly what they'll do."

"I *can't*. You're right, he – he – knows where the kids are. If I tell you..."

"That's right, John, he does..." Carter looked into the boy's eyes – they were older than they should be – until John nodded.

"He won't hurt them," said John. "He knows if they're gone, there's nothing to hold me."

Carter fought the urge to thump his fist on the desk and point out that the bastard, whoever it was, didn't need more than one of them. He saw the boy was still shuddering, and held his tongue; threats weren't going to work here. Especially since he suspected the boy knew the truth, but was too scared to admit it.

"John," he said, picking his words carefully, "the word will be spreading that the Zelotyr are gone." John watched him, his pupils huge, making his eyes seem like dark pools. "I'm expecting trouble once people realise the patrols are gone. Does that sound right?"

"I suppose."

"Good. The thing is, when that trouble comes, there's not enough police or army left to stop it." He waited until the boy nodded his understanding. "People will get hurt and angry and they'll turn on the people who can be blamed. Once they realise the Zelotyr were keeping them safe, they'll blame you for changing things. And if they can't find you... even if whoever you are working for doesn't go for your family, someone else might."

The grey eyes closed, stayed shut for what seemed like minutes, and Carter snaked his hand out until it covered the boy's.

John's eyes opened. "Ten Shannon Road," he whispered.

Carter squeezed his hand. "Good lad. I'll go and see myself, and then I'll come back and we can talk some more."

"If you get my family in front of me, I'll tell you everything you need to know. The kids need me, I can't be sent away..." John looked down at the desk. "You might want to check number six as well, that's where Taz and his mum live."

"Right." Carter stood to go.

"Sir?"

"Yes?"

"I didn't mean it. Nor did Taz. Is he okay? He seemed really sick."

Carter paused. In some ways, the other boy might be the luckier; he was still unconscious, and not aware of the mess. He nodded. "He's still very shocked."

"Please, can you help?"

Carter paused, looking at the boy. What had he survived: a year of a bloody war, hiding, foraging food by night? And he'd ended up here, doing someone else's dirty work.

"I'll do what I can, John," he said, choosing his words with care. There was no point promising the earth, not if he couldn't deliver it.

"You promise?"

The too-old eyes searched him, as if grasping at the hope in front of them. Carter took a deep breath. "Yes. I promise." He turned away before the boy could ask anything more.

CHAPTER FIVE

osey sat at the top of the stairs, in the spot where John stayed when he kept watch. A shaft of daylight crawled over her foot, warming it, and she bit her lip. Where *was* he? He'd never been so late back, and he knew she had no food. She glanced at the two empty water bottles – she'd had to give the kids something to fill their stomachs – and over at the dwindling supply in the corner. Tears pricked her, but she bit down on her knuckle, making sure no noise escaped and woke the kids.

She looked over at the closed bedroom doors. The layout was the same as in their old house, and all it took was a slight narrowing of her eyes to imagine she was back there, a year ago. There'd been no way to know 2014 was going to bring an invasion worse than any in the comics John and Taz used to buy. She shifted on the step and stared at what would have been her parents' bedroom. What she wouldn't give to push open the door and find them sitting there, cups of tea in hand. Or go to her room and get into a bed that wasn't mouldy and manky, but clean, its covers just off the line and smelling of fresh air.

Some hope. Useless daydreams, nothing more, like the dreams of the family who'd lived in this house at the start of the war and who'd been in it the day the Zelo bomb had brought down the roof. Their kid had died in the house and they'd fled Belfast afterwards.

She got up and paced the landing, not able to sit any longer. Her CD player sat in the corner beside her bedroom door. She'd love to turn it on and dance to Jessie J. She'd done that with the kids to keep them from crying after Ma and Da died, until the batteries had given up. She wanted it to be the old days when John annoyed her and it was easy to

25

hate him, not sit and pray he'd get home, and he hadn't been caught, or....

She leaned her head against the door. He *couldn't* be dead. He was too smart. He was quick, like a shadow in the streets. He'd be fine.

A soft noise made her start, and she strained, listening, but there was nothing except the kids' soft snores, and a whistle of wind.

Another noise came, louder this time, from downstairs. She went to the top of the stairs and looked down into the darkness. It had been ages since she and John had barricaded the door and told the kids it was going to be a grand adventure camping on the landing. Neither of the little ones had been fooled, not really. They knew aliens weren't the only danger in Belfast, that hunger made people desperate.

There was a crash, making her jump. A splinter of light appeared where the front door was. She wanted to scream, to run, but stayed still, not daring to give away they were in the house. A second thud and the damage widened to a crack.

That got her moving. This was no looter, trying for an easy break-in. She ran to Sophie's bedroom and kicked the door open. "Wake up! Hide in the wardrobe and don't come out unless me or John tells you to."

Sophie came awake immediately – she might be only eight, but she'd lived through the invasion, too – and darted into the wardrobe. Josey ran into the boys' room. She picked Stuart up, struggling a little, her hands slippery from fear. She managed to pull him onto her hip and ran into the biggest bedroom, the one that had no roof at all left, not daring to look downstairs. As she shut the door, there was a splintering noise, followed by the sound of men's voices.

"Wha...?" asked Stuart, still sleepy.

"Shhhh," she said. "It's hide and seek, okay, Stuart? You have to be quiet."

He, too, was a veteran, and crawled under the big bed. She joined him, pulling boxes around them, ignoring their musty smell. Her ma had used the same sort of boxes to store shoes she'd never wear again. Josey choked back something –

not quite a sob, more a strangling fear. There was no time to mourn Ma, not when she was busy trying to be her. Footsteps sounded on the stairs, more than one pair. Josey closed her eyes and prayed: *be John.* It wasn't, of course it wasn't. A plastic bottle was knocked over, dully bouncing on the landing floor, and she had to bite back a yelp. She wished she hadn't separated Sophie, but the wardrobe was too small for all of them.

Wardrobe – who was she kidding? Whoever this was, they were going to find them. She groped around, trying to find anything to use as a weapon, but there was nothing. She kept her other hand on Stuart's back. He squirmed and she didn't blame him – the stench of mould from the carpet was thick, clogging her throat.

The door was kicked open and hard footsteps crossed to the wardrobe. The door opened, followed by a loud tut. Josey fought the urge to wriggle away, and pulled the terrified Stuart close. He was too warm, his skin sweaty. The footsteps came over to the bed and stopped. She could see boots, leather and shining. Top of the range. No one she knew had new clothes.

"Josey Dray, is that little Stuart you have there?" The voice was broad Belfast, harsh, not at all safe. "Come out before I drag you."

She didn't move. Another tut, and he got down on his knees. His face appeared at the edge of the bed, looking at her from a sideways position, and her breath caught: Gary McDowell. He was a good four years above her at school, but she knew about him. He'd taken one of the boys from her class, who'd called him Graham instead of Gary, and flushed his head down the toilet. He'd left the boy in the cubicle for an hour, telling him if he called for help he'd spend every day facing more of the same.

"There you are," he said, and gave a mock wave. His mouth tightened, and his eyes flashed anger. "If you don't come out, I'll kick your arse from here to Derry."

She had no option; he was between her and the exit.

"I don't want to," whispered Stuart.

"It's all right," she said. She backed out, pulling him with

27

her, and stood. Her heart was hammering in her chest, making her a little dizzy, but she lifted Stuart onto her hip and faced Gary. She daren't show fear; his sort loved people to be scared.

"What are you doing here?" she asked.

He came to the end of the bed, blocking her way past. "Where's the wee girl?"

He was close enough to smell beer on his breath, and her fear deepened; drunk and looking for kicks was never a good combination. She stopped meeting his eyes - she couldn't afford to anger him. She tightened her hold on Stuart, trying not to frighten him. "She's in the next room. I'll get her."

He grabbed her arm. "Let's do that." He pushed her towards the door.

She stumbled, barely keeping her grip on Stuart, and hurried next door. To hell with pretending not to be scared. She opened the wardrobe where Sophie huddled, her eyes huge and staring.

"You need to come out," said Josey.

Sophie hesitated, but at Josey's nod came out, and they turned to face Gary. Another lad joined him, wiry and full of nervous fidgeting.

"Is that all of them?" he asked.

"Aye." Gary smirked. "The Dray family, just where they should be."

Josey shivered. She had nothing to offer to make him go away. He was watching her, his eyes sharp, and her legs started to shake. She'd heard what some of the lads on the streets were up to since the invasion, how girls had been brought into the gangs and made to do what the blokes wanted. It was why John didn't like her going out to scavenge, even in the daytime. She backed away. "John will be back in a minute."

"I don't think so. John's been detained."

Detained? Who by? Sophie pulled against her leg. Stuart froze, numb with terror, clinging to her top. She tried to stop her legs shaking - she couldn't fall apart in front of the kids - and lifted her chin. "What do you want?"

"Put the kid down." She tried, but had to uncurl Stuart's

hands first. Gary indicated the stairs with a jerk of his head. "You're coming with me." He nodded at the other man. "Deal with the kids."

"That wasn't what your da told us. He said to get the older girl."

"Are you arguing with me?" Gary's voice was low, threatening. He grabbed the other lad's collar. "Because if you are, we can take it to the Big Man and see who he backs."

"All right. Calm down, eh? You take the girl and leave the kids to me. No problem."

Josey moved in front of the other children. *Deal with them?* She shook her head. "No, please, they're only kids..."

Gary grabbed her. "Let's go," he said.

She fought him, scratching at his jacket. Sophie yelled for her; Stuart was crying.

"Stop that, you little bitch." Gary tightened his grip, digging his nails into her skin.

"You're hurting me!" she yelled.

"I'll hurt you some more if I have to." He pushed her into the hall. "Downstairs. Go."

Stuart screamed for her. She tried to turn back but was pushed down the stairs and through the splintered door into the street. Taz's mum approached, leaning on her stick, escorted by a bloke so fat that rolls of stomach hung over his belt. Liz's eyes were red, and there was a bruise starting along her cheekbone.

A hard shove sent Josey towards a car. "No!" she shouted, but if there was anyone in the street, they weren't going to interfere. Liz was pushed into the car. Gary kicked Josey's legs from under her and shoved her in, too.

"You can't hurt the kids," she said. "They know nothing."

He got in beside her and slammed the door. "Last warning. If you don't shut up, I'll beat you black and blue."

She closed her mouth. He would, and then she'd be no use to anyone. He nodded his satisfaction.

"Good." He leaned forward and tapped the driver's shoulder. "Drive."

arter closed the door and found Sanderson waiting in the corridor.

"Any luck, sir?"

"He's given an address. He won't give me a name, though."

"We think it was McDowell's lot." Sanderson gave a balancing gesture with his two hands. "Dray was a runner for them."

"Makes sense. Get someone to follow it up. Also, I need a car."

"What are you planning?"

They started to walk towards the reception area. "I'm going to head down the Oldpark and check the house."

Sanderson stopped and stared at him. "You missed the last bit."

Carter shook his head, puzzled. "I did?"

"Go down the Oldpark, check the house and get lynched."

Carter paused. Sanderson was right, the Oldpark wasn't somewhere just to walk into. Not in this city of hidden dens and closed-off, half-feral streets. "I'll liaise with the army, get some back up." He smiled. "We may as well go out with a bang."

Later, as they drove up the rubble-strewn streets of north Belfast, he wasn't smiling. The city felt as if it was in stasis: the explosion of fear, held in abeyance for months, close and dangerous. The soldiers sat in silence, their faces closed and grim. Peters, leading the squad, had seemed resigned to the request from Carter for support. They passed no other vehicles, saw no one out on the streets. Below them, deceptively calm, was the lough. One of the old passenger ferries from before the attack was moored at its neck. No smoke rose from the sewage farms, but their smell permeated the van, an accusing reminder of the Zelotyr.

They pulled up outside the house. Carter got out of the vehicle, glancing down the small cul-de-sac. There was no one in sight. He could see the Oldpark Road, just visible through a gap beside number ten, its tarmac filled with weeds. A sparrow chirruped nearby, making Carter jump. He looked at the surrounding houses. Their windows - the ones with glass - were dark and empty. Was anyone there? Peters came alongside, his firearm ready, and Carter pulled his pistol from its holster. Both men walked forward, crunching over broken glass in the small front garden. The rest of the soldiers got out of the vehicle, dispersing into the house and round the back. Carter waited, tight against the wall, his heart hammering.

"Clear!"

He stepped through the splintered gash, Peters close behind. Carter pushed a door to his right and stepped into a small living room. He opened the curtains, ignoring the skittering spiders. Peters sniffed; the room was dank, unused. They moved to the back, into a small kitchen, Peters leading this time. Dishes stood in the sink, mould-covered. There was a stench of decay - not just mould, but foul air merging with it - and when Carter touched the kitchen boards a film of dirt clung to his fingers. Peters pointed to the back door. It was ajar, swinging on its hinges. Peters approached it, Carter covering him, and pushed it open. The only people in the yard were three of the squad, carrying out a search. The back gate to the alley beyond was open, and one of the soldiers had taken up position beside it.

"We'll check the bedrooms," said Carter. He climbed the stairs. A breath of air touched him and he looked up at the ceiling. Peters was right, the boy had lied - no one could live here. He paused at the top of the stairs, listening, and shivered in the cold landing.

"Over there."

Carter jumped at the voice. Peters pointed at a small pile of blankets in the corner. Carter nodded and walked forwards, into a small bathroom. It wasn't clean, exactly, but it was dust free. Four toothbrushes sat on the sink. His breath hitched: the boy had tried to keep going as if it was normal, had brushed the kids' teeth and made them wash their hands. He rubbed his mouth, feeling sick, and turned on the tap.

31

The water came out, rust brown. If they'd been using this for washing, it was amazing they'd survived. He stepped into the hall and saw the empty water bottle.

"They've been here," he said to Peters, who nodded, his eyes troubled.

Carter pushed open the next door, to a small bedroom dominated by two beds. Light flooded through several holes in the ceiling, and a breeze lifted dust motes, making them dance in the air. He touched one of the duvets, and it was sodden. The other bed had a plain blue cover, and draped over the end was a football shirt, worn through and at least three seasons out of date. They obviously hadn't had much even before the war, if the boy hadn't updated it. He took a deep breath and turned round, imprinting the room on his memory. He'd seen many horrors since the war began, but this room, the desolation masking as normality, hit him hard. How had they survived here? They must have been like rats, curled together in a nest. A small noise, like a rustling, made him turn round.

"Peters?"

"Down here! Looks like the parents' room."

Carter crept forward and checked the landing, but it was clear. He'd been spooked, that was all. He spun at another noise and scanned the bedroom again. He walked to a small wardrobe and opened it. From the back of the wardrobe, two pairs of eyes, grey like John's, watched him.

"Peters! Come here."

Carter reached into the wardrobe. "It's okay, I'm not going to hurt you."

The children shrank back from him, and he reached in a little more. His hand touched one of them –

"Shit!" he yelled, pulling his hand back, seeing the line of teeth marks. "You little sh–"

The children darted past. He made a grab for the smallest and caught him, but the child wriggled and pulled away, leaving Carter holding only the coat. He lunged forward, into the hall, and found himself looking at Peters, a child held firmly in each hand.

Carter knelt in front of them. The boy was evidently Stuart, and the girl was young; Sophie, he presumed.

"It's okay," he said. "I'm Carter – John sent me. Where's Josey?"

"Gone," said the girl. Her voice was a whisper but her eyes met his, brighter since he'd mentioned her brother. "The man with us left when he saw your van."

Carter got to his feet. "Take them out to the APC. We'll get them into one of the hostels and cleaned up. I'll arrange someone to keep them safe. I assume whoever was left with them wasn't a babysitter."

"I'd guess not," said Peters. "And then?"

Carter shrugged, helplessly. He walked down the stairs, taking in the house one more time. How many more were like this? He had no idea. The small figures walked past him, each hand held firmly by Peters. He rubbed his fingers along the hood of the boy's coat, seeing where a piece had been torn off. They were too young for all this. He stopped and scanned the sky, taking in that thought. They *were* too young. All of them. Slowly, he smiled.

***

The outside door of the station slammed, announcing a pissed-off Superintendent O'Brien. Carter set his cup down, checked his uniform, and rubbed at a smear of dirt on the pocket. The more he rubbed, the more it spread, and he cursed under his breath. Still, he'd been on duty for the best part of a day and a half; that might give him some leeway.

"Carter!"

Carter hurried to the reception area, where his chief was standing at the desk, her foot tapping with impatience.

"Ma'am," said Carter.

O'Brien looked him up and down, lingering on the stain. Evidently, the dress inspection had been failed. She handed Carter some papers and he scanned them.

"Your office, Carter."

"Yes, ma'am." Carter led the way, swallowing his nervousness. He opened the door to his office with its usual jumble of papers and bin overflowing onto the floor. The superintendent swept past and sat in Carter's seat. Carter closed the door and didn't need to be told to stay standing.

"Enlighten me. Why have I just been given jurisdiction over the biggest pain-in-the-ass problem on Earth?" O'Brien's voice cut through the air like a whip, and Carter fought not to wince.

"Ma'am, the boys didn't know what they were doing."

"That's irrelevant; the Zelotyr have demanded the right to try the boys, and I think Earth has managed to piss them off enough for now. Thirteen thousand dead and all the hatchlings." O'Brien looked tired, her hair lank and needing washed, her face drawn and strained. "I want an explanation. That –" She nodded to the paper still clutched in Carter's hand. "– went above your remit. Juveniles, indeed. The Galactic Council judges puberty to be the age of adult responsibility. I'm assuming your boys aren't falsettos?"

"No, ma'am."

"Then why the request?"

"Ma'am, I understand there has to be a biological standard when governing more than one species. But Earth hasn't ratified the Galactic convention; here, they're considered juveniles." O'Brien's eyes hardened, and Carter took a deep breath before he went on, "I thought it would give you time to assess the situation."

There was silence, and he glanced down at the paper, before looking back at his boss and admitting, "I didn't think they'd agree. Not so quickly."

His words petered out under his boss's glare, but he kept his head up. O'Brien hated people who tried to hide from her flak.

"That's all very noble, Carter. They agreed because no one wants jurisdiction over this nightmare."

"Yes, ma'am." Carter steeled himself –

"But your thinking was excellent." Carter raised his eyebrows as the chief went on, "I don't want to hand the boys over. This is an Earth issue, not the GC's; they're just another set of bloody aliens."

"Thank you, ma'am." Carter hoped he'd kept the surprise out of his voice.

She nodded. "You still overstepped your rank. For that, you can do the shit work on this. Arrange some sort of counsel for the boys and liaise with the GC. Find out what they'll accept." She paused. "It's likely they'll seek a life term."

"Yes, ma'am." *A life term, at fifteen.* His dismay must have shown because O'Brien's eyes softened.

"We have to abide with the GC's ruling on this one." She looked down at the desk and scowled. "You can get in here tidied up, too, Carter; if you have meetings with the GC it can't be a pigsty."

"Yes, ma'am."

"Do it in your own time, Carter." She frowned. "You do know the scale of what these boys have done? You know the Deklon system can't sustain the continuation of the Zelotyr?"

Carter nodded. It was the reason the Zelo had come here: their planet had overheated to the extent where their hatchlings couldn't spawn.

"There must be other planets, ma'am." He looked up at the ceiling, and the bomb-damage crack running across reminded him of the little house earlier. "It's a big galaxy, and they have faster-than-light ships."

"The chance of the Zelotyr finding another planet within this generation's lifespan is tiny. Unless they can find a way to overcome the virus – and to do that, they need access to some quantity of the source material – their species is doomed. They will demand full accountability."

"I understand, ma'am."

O'Brien gestured at the seat opposite. "Sit down. You know how the GC is set up? That it's split between the Zelo and Barath'na?"

Carter brushed some crumbs off the seat and sat. "Yes."

"The Zelo believe the Barath'na are behind the virus; the Barath'na claim it came from Earth. To say relationships are tense makes the worst days of Stormont look good-natured."

Carter took a moment, thinking about that. He'd never met a Barath'na, but knew their reputation: altruistic, cooperative in their dealings with other races, they were nothing like the warrior Zelotyr. He picked up a pen, pressing its nib in and out, the dull clicks filling the room, and asked, "Who do we believe?"

"Hard to say. The means of distributing the virus was low-tech, which makes me think it's from Earth. But I don't believe it came from central government." The chief reached out, took the pen out of Carter's hand, and went on, "You know the sort of military capacity Earth has?"

"I know about Belfast," – *not enough* – "and that our situation is replicated across Ireland," said Carter. "Farther than that I only know rumours, ma'am, and those rumours aren't good."

"They aren't wrong; if there is substantive resistance, Earth can't hold the peace. We don't have the personnel, the hospitals or the people to run them. The army advises they do not have enough troops should civil unrest take hold." She waited until Carter gave a curt nod. "Earth may have to ask the GC to send a peacekeeping force. No one wants that. Especially not if the GC believe the virus came from us. But we might not have any choice."

Carter drew in a whistle of breath. "I see."

O'Brien started clicking the pen. "Any force will be predominantly Barath'naian, which is something. But if it turns out Earth's governing bodies had any connection to the virus, the Zelo will attack. They have nothing to lose, after all." She pointed upwards. "The Barath'na have the weaponry to face the Zelotyr. Earth doesn't. If we get it wrong..."

John's face flashed in front of Carter, followed by the memory of the half-lived-in house. How many other Johns were out there? Many – most, if he was honest – wouldn't survive another war. Carter nodded.

"So, you'll understand why I say I'm glad you kept your boys on Earth, but they must be dealt with accordingly. Whatever the GC want, we must consider it. It won't be capital, I hope, but it won't be youth custody for a couple of years, either. You understand?" Carter nodded. "The lads still haven't said who gave them the virus?"

"Not yet. Dray has said he'll cooperate once we let him see his family, which obviously we can't do."

"The other boy?"

"Recovering." A little, anyway – the last report had declared him conscious, but weak.

His boss leaned forward. "Whoever's behind it in Belfast had to have someone behind them. This was a global attack. Your boys are the first – the only – step on that chain. We need them to talk."

Carter rubbed his forehead. "I'm doing my best, ma'am."

O'Brien tapped the table with the pen. "Keep at it. And make sure the boys are secure; to lose them might be seen as careless. Convenient, even."

"Yes, ma'am," said Carter.

"Good. You can go."

CHAPTER SEVEN

John sat on the narrow cot, chewing his nails. He'd seen no one for hours, not since the cop had said he'd make sure Josey and the kids were safe. It was getting dark now. Helicopters droned nearby. He got up and went to the small window, and watched for a while. There was a lot of activity, police vans coming and going all the time, but nothing he could look at and figure out what it meant.

The lack of information was driving him mad. He didn't know where Taz was, or if he was okay. He had to find out. He went to the door and started to bang his fists on it, but the metal was so thick he only made dull thuds. He stopped banging. The noise continued. *What the – ?*

Yells, and a muffled bang. John stumbled back from the door. McDowell had found out where he was. It was like in Terminator, when the girl hid while everyone who was supposed to protect her got blown away. He glanced around. There was only the bed, and anyone who came in would look there straight away. He backed into the furthest corner, his heart hammering. Another bang sounded – a shot, he was sure of it – followed by a yell. The handle of his door started to turn, the metal bar-lock moving from horizontal to vertical. He looked around for something, anything, he could use as a weapon, but there was nothing.

Fuck it. He stepped into the centre of the room, hands spread in front of him, poised and ready. If they were here for him, he'd go down fighting, not cowering like a dog. The door opened.

"Come on!" Carter looked nothing like he had earlier. His baton was grasped in one hand, and his eyes stared out from a filthy face. Behind him a cop raced past, someone supported across his shoulders. *Taz.* That got John moving, across the cell and out. Carter pointed down the corridor. "Follow Sanderson – there's a patrol car waiting."

Yells sounded through the station and running footsteps came closer. Carter backed away, keeping John behind him.

"Get him!" a voice yelled, close and angry. More joined it, echoing through the tiled corridors.

Jesus, it was a riot. Like in the old days, when trouble sprang out of nowhere. But there hadn't been any since the Zelo invaded – everyone was too busy either fighting them or finding a way to survive. His mouth twisted in sour realisation; now the Zelo were gone, Belfast was back to what it did best.

The sound of a shot got him moving, old instincts kicking in. It didn't matter why the riot was happening, only that he was caught in it. He reached the officer helping Taz, who was at least making an attempt to walk, and took one of his friend's arms over his shoulder.

The officer nodded his thanks. "The fire-escape," he panted. They hurried to the door at the end of the corridor, and the policeman swung out from under Taz's arm. "Take him."

John tightened his grip on Taz. The officer slammed the fire-bar down and pushed the door open. A shrill alarm rang through the air. In the car park a crowd had gathered at barred fencing, shouting and jostling each other for position.

John ducked as something flew past him, something alight. More followed, lighting up the night sky and filling it with the thick smell of petrol. A second group of protestors sent up loud whoops as they broke through the main gates and flooded the yard.

"Bollocks," said Sanderson, reaching for his pistol. He wrenched the door of the waiting police car open.

"Get them away!" yelled Carter from behind. "Go!" Another flaming bottle flew past and smashed. "Now!"

John heaved Taz forward, but one of the rioters had broken from the main pack and was blocking his way. Carter pushed past and faced the man, squaring up to him.

"Back off," said the officer.

The rioter's face twisted. "Fuck me, it's the shit-lover!" he yelled. He lunged at Carter. "Here he is!"

The crowd surged forwards, ignoring John and Taz. Carter stumbled back and brought his baton up.

"Sanderson, get them into the fucking car!" he yelled, the posh accent gone. "Now!"

Taz was yanked away from John and thrown into the car. One of the men in the crowd thumped his fist off the car's bonnet. "The shit-lover's trying to do a runner!"

Sanderson grabbed John's collar and forced him into the car, before bundling in after him. The car revved as he slammed the door closed, and the rioter backed off. The rest of the crowd had gathered at the station's open door – Carter had no hope of getting through.

John grabbed Sanderson's wrist. "We can't leave him."

"We've no option." Sanderson jerked free. He tapped the driver's shoulder. "Put your foot down."

Sirens sounded as three army vehicles tore through the main gates towards them, scattering the protestors. Soldiers dived out into the remaining crowd. Flames framed the melee, distorted in the riot-shields. The troops forced their way through the protestors to be pushed back, then surge forward again, like a dance. At least one gun sounded.

"We'll never get through!" shouted Sanderson. "We'll have to try the back gate."

The driver nodded. The car screeched in a circle. John craned his head to see what was happening to Carter but it was impossible to tell through the mass of bodies. The driver floored the vehicle. There was another crowd ahead of them. Christ, the car was going to hit them. Even Taz had managed to sit up and was staring ahead.

"Holy shit!" yelled John, ready for the thump of a body. The crowd parted at the last second, diving to the side, and the car made it through the gate and out onto the main road. Something hit the back window, giving a dull smack, and a yellowed flash filled the car. The driver kept going.

"Yes!" yelled Sanderson. He looked back the way they'd come. "They're too far back – we're okay!" He paused, and gave a sly smile. "Reckon ol' shit-for-brains *will* get out?"

"Carter?" The driver glanced in the mirror. "He's a lucky enough fucker, all right."

John remembered the rioter's face when he'd seen

Carter. He'd been the target, not John. He frowned. "Why do they call him shit-lover?"

Sanderson made a hacking noise. "He's the Zelotyr liaison officer in Belfast."

It took a moment for the words to sink in. Carter was a collaborator? He looked over at Taz, whose eyes had widened in shock.

"He worked with the Zelo?" said Taz, his voice slow.

The officer hadn't mentioned working with them. His hands closed, into tight fists. *Bastard.* He'd been half-sucked in by him. Hell, he'd thought about giving him McDowell's name to keep Josey safe. Now it turned out the guy had sold out Earth. How did John know he wouldn't sell him out, too?

"What did he do for the Zelo?" he asked. There might be some sort of mistake. Maybe Carter had been forced to take the post and had sabotaged the aliens at every opportunity, like an old-fashioned wartime spy.

"When the ceasefire was agreed, the GC put him to work with the local Zelo command." Sanderson's voice was as sour as John's stomach. "He went for it. It seems he's an ambitious little turncoat – he got a promotion."

They pulled off the main road and sped to the outskirts of the city. Fires burned in the estates either side of them, radiating from the suburbs and snaking a line of orange into the city centre. Would tonight be the end for what was left of the city?

Carter's posh voice came over the driver's radio, ordering reinforcements to the squad trying to hold York Street. He'd made it, then. John felt oddly relieved; no matter what Sanderson said, he was still the only person who'd shown any interest in getting the kids out.

"Where are we going?" John asked.

"Somewhere safe." The cop turned away and John watched out the window. The sky was orange, not black. There were no Zelo anywhere. None of their spaceships lit up the sky; their armoured transports were abandoned by the roadside, one with a figure lying over the control-panel, its armour glistening in a shaft of moonlight. They'd lost a few of

41

the transports in the early days of the invasion, John remembered, booby-trapped by the locals until the Zelo had learned to check before they used them. It had been the subject of jokes, how the aliens were reduced to using mirrors to check any nooks and crannies, all their technology undone by Belfast's determination to piss off the authorities, second only to the city's ability to have a good riot.

His stomach tensed. Was Josey caught up in the riots? He thought about asking Sanderson if there was any news about her, but the cop was ignoring him, his shoulders bunched and tight. John frowned. He might not know what to make of Carter, but Sanderson was obviously well acquainted with his own right hand.

The car pulled onto a wide, straight road. John squinted, trying to read the road sign coming up, but it had been painted over by a crude picture of a Zelo and the message to take their shit and fuck off. He squinted until he made out the destination and his stomach lurched. Moira: near the space port. They were being sent to the Zelo. He nudged Taz and nodded at the sign.

"Ask," croaked Taz.

"Hey, guys," said John, trying not to piss the officers off. "Are we going to be taken off Earth?"

Sanderson's face softened a little. "No. You're staying." He paused for just a moment too long. "For now."

"What do you mean for now?" Taz's voice was shaking.

"Quiet." The officer leaned forward and touched the driver's shoulder. "Floor it."

A crowd had gathered in the middle of the road. Something burned behind them, something big – a Zelo space-transporter, John decided, a proper one with deep-space capacity, not the planet hoppers they used for patrols.

"Hold tight!" The driver floored the accelerator. John was pushed back against his seat. The crowd didn't move. John's mouth went dry and he put his hand on the seat in front, braced for impact. Twenty feet at most. The driver sped up.

"Just like old times!" yelled Sanderson. "Keep going – they'll break up."

The crowd stayed where it was. Sanderson swore. John half closed his eyes. The crowd scattered just as the car shot past, still speeding up.

Sanderson laughed and nudged John. "Didn't I tell you? They always scatter." His eyes were high with excitement. "So, you want to know what will happen to you?"

"Yeah," croaked John. "Wouldn't you?"

"I suppose so." Sanderson was gripping his gun tightly, making John's shoulder itch. The officer didn't look quite balanced. "The Earth authorities will call in the Galactics after tonight. We lost most of our armed forces in the Zelo invasion. Earth needs to be safeguarded."

"Safeguarded from what?" asked John. "Surely once people find out the Zelo are gone, the resistance will end."

"People do know they're gone, and this is how they're reacting. Besides..." The officer pointed at the sky. "The Zelo attacked from space last time. There's no reason they won't again. We need the Galactic Council to hold them off. But if we turn to the Galactics, they'll want justice for the shit-eaters. It might be a choice between giving them that justice, or being destroyed by another attack."

John's stomach twisted, remembering the first day of the invasion, how the smart bombs had fallen through the clouds with no warning. One had taken out a whole street not a mile from his house. He remembered the panic of not knowing where the screaming bombs were going to hit, the scramble to get out the school grounds and home to check his family were safe. He and Taz had taken off from the classroom and split to go to their separate estates, just a quick hand-clasp and good luck to each other, cut off when a bomb hit nearby, denting the air.

Earth would do what it must to avoid another attack like that. He glanced at Taz and knew that if it was a choice between that or handing them over, there'd be no contest. Their fear must have shown because Sanderson gave a grim smile, and a nod.

"Not your best night's work, was it?" he said.

"No." John gulped. "So they'll send us to the Zelo, you reckon? To Deklon?"

43

The soldier shrugged. "I dunno. Maybe." His mouth twisted. "Either way, I wouldn't fancy being in your shoes."

No one would. He saw his reflection in the window, framed against the darkness. He was pale and thin and looked nothing like himself. It was a new face, not the same one as before the war. He'd never get back to that person.

The thought shocked him. All this year, he'd told himself that things would go back to normal sometime. He'd tried to keep up some training, doing push-ups in the bedroom and running instead of walking when he could. He'd told himself that everyone would be thinner and he'd still get a place in the first team. Now, there wasn't going to be any team for him. He'd be on Deklon, waiting to discover how the Zelo would kill him, and how often.

He fought back tears, damned if he'd give anyone the satisfaction of seeing them. He should have left Taz on the hill. It would have been better to die once than face what was ahead. If he had, he'd have got home when he should and McDowell's men would have shot him. He remembered Gary telling him he wouldn't miss him - and he wouldn't have. A single bullet and it'd have been over with.

He wished he could go back to that night and do things over again. He'd have bargained more out of McDowell, he'd have made sure Josey and the kids were safe before he'd taken the job. But he'd still have carried it out. He had no option; McDowell had trapped him months ago, with his errands and food and clothes.

John opened his eyes and forced himself to face the boy in the window. It might not be the person he wanted to be or one he recognised, but it was the one the war had moulded him into. The Zelo had killed his parents because they believed they were worthless; they wouldn't do the same to him. When he died, however many times he did, he'd make sure they knew they were killing a man, not a boy, who'd survived as best he could, and did the best he could. He'd be brave and make himself count; he owed it to the boy who'd been lost in the war.

CHAPTER EIGHT

John sat on a bench just inside a barracks reception hall, somewhere in the back end of nowhere. He looped his hands between his legs and glanced at Taz. His friend looked terrible, pale and strained. Bags were dark under his eyes, and a sheen of sweat across his brow.

"What happens now?" asked John.

"Dunno. None of this is good, though." Taz jingled his cuffs.

"No." John watched the door of the station, ready for it to open and a squad to walk in and escort them to Deklon. Why else had they been taken from their holding cell to here? He bet the Zelo's planet stank like the hatcheries. He let his mind wander, dreaming up more and more alien environments, taking his mind off his shoulders, tight with tension, and how the muscles along the back of his neck ached.

The station's door slid open and a familiar posh accent carried from outside, accompanied by one that was clipped and English. John stiffened.

"Showtime," whispered Taz.

Carter stepped through the door. His uniform jacket was missing, his shirt filthy and torn. His eyes were red-rimmed. A bruise stood out on his forehead. The officer gave John and Taz a brief nod as the second man stepped in. He was tall and thickset, at least in his sixties, with a straight back and steady pace. His jacket – army, not police – was neat. John didn't know what the insignia on his shoulder meant, but he looked important. The man looked him and Taz up and down. Suddenly, John was sure he'd rather deal with Carter. At least he was the devil he knew.

"This is them?" asked the soldier.

Taz leaned close to John and muttered, "Not good, J-Boy."

The use of his old nickname didn't settle John's nerves. He watched, nervous as hell, as Carter faced the older man.

"That's them," he said. "The forensics came through. The tin they had definitely contained the virus."

"We'll take them under our jurisdiction, then, and wait for confirmation of orders from the GC."

John's stomach dropped. He stared at Carter. *Don't hand us over. You might be a shit-lover, but at least you listened.*

Carter met the older man's gaze. His eyes had the same look as when he'd faced the rioter, fixed and determined. "It's a police matter."

"It's a GC matter," said the soldier, "and they're liaising directly with the army until the current crisis is over."

Carter squared his shoulders, and John's respect for the officer went up a little – if he'd been facing that glare, he'd have given the army officer anything he wanted.

"The boys are about to be charged for a crime committed on Earth," said Carter. "I have spoken to Superintendent O'Brien about this and she agrees their case lies with the police, not army. Regardless of what the GC want." He crossed his arms. "She won't stand for me handing them to the GC. I'm sorry, Colonel."

Jesus, a colonel. John gulped. Taz's eyes widened so far they seemed to take up half his face. A colonel, he mouthed. John nodded, and then the rest of Carter's words sank in. They were going to be charged. His cuffs jingled and he had to clench his hands together to stop them shaking.

"You need a secure holding place for them," said the colonel. "The police can't provide that."

Carter said, in a much softer voice, "I hoped we could take a joint approach, to be honest." His posture changed, became more relaxed. "And you're quite right. Police custody isn't secure enough. The Super asked if you would assist us in that matter." He held his hands up. "But we can't give them up to the army – due process must be followed."

The colonel flared his nostrils. His gaze swept up and down John once more. John brought to the fore all his experience of facing the McDowells, and managed not to duck his head. He wasn't going to be cowed. Well, not openly, anyway; inside, he was shitting himself.

"Very well," the colonel said. "We'll cede to the police's authority on the understanding that if jurisdiction moves to the Galactic Council at any point, control reverts to the army. I can't have my lines of authority to the GC blurred." His mouth thinned. "It's confusing enough with the Earth authorities claiming governance of the army, and the GC declaring they hold control for the duration of the crisis."

"It must be very difficult," said Carter. A muscle in his cheek twitched. "I have experience with the GC. They like to pull their weight on local matters." He looked over at John and Taz. "I need a moment with my charges, please."

The colonel motioned for the two soldiers to stand down. Carter crouched in front of John and Taz. "Are you both all right?"

He sounded like he actually cared. John bit back the urge to ask him whether he really was a shit-lover, and gave a curt nod. "Yeah."

Taz shivered. "I feel like shit. Like I have 'flu or something."

"You were pretty sick. It's amazing that you're even up and about." He took a moment, looking closely at Taz, and frowned. "I'll get a medic to check you out, though – you don't look great."

"Thanks." Taz hunched down a little.

"Okay, I need you both to listen to me." Carter's face became serious, and he cleared his throat. "John Dray and Terence Delaney, I'm arresting you for xenocide. You do not have to say anything, but it may harm your defence if you do not mention something when questioned which you later rely on in court. Anything you do say may be given in evidence." He looked between them. "Do you both understand what that means?"

God, yeah. They weren't stupid. John's hands shook again, and he clasped them tighter. He cleared his throat. "You're arresting us."

"Yes." Carter looked at Taz. "You?"

"I get it." Taz's voice was half what it normally was. "What happens now?"

"We'll get some photos taken and have you fingerprinted."

Mugshots, he meant mugshots. John closed his eyes. This

might be the only good thing about his ma being dead: he wouldn't have to explain getting arrested for doing McDowell's dirty work to her.

"After that, you'll get a room here for the time being, and then we'll have to see." Carter paused, and then lowered his voice. "For now you are being dealt with by my officers. I intend to keep it that way if I can. I'll talk to you about appointing a defence lawyer." He straightened, and turned, presumably to go.

"Carter." John's voice was louder than he'd meant it to be and the colonel, standing with his soldiers, glanced round.

"Yes?" asked Carter.

Were you really on the aliens' side? John grimaced; there were more important questions, ones he had to ask no matter how much he dreaded the answer. "What about our families?"

Carter paused for a moment too long. John's stomach dropped. Taz tensed beside him.

"I'm taking care of it," said the policeman, finally. "I'll let you know."

"They'll be all right?" Taz's voice shook and John looked at him, surprised. Taz would rather die than let anyone see weakness.

"I'll do my best to make sure they are," said Carter.

No promise, this time. Taz half-stood, but one of the soldiers brought his rifle round. Taz sat down again.

"My mother, she's all that I have," he said. "And wee Josey..." He glanced at John, and then lowered his gaze. Josey shouldn't be in this mess.

Carter nodded. "I understand." He looked at John and seemed to think for a moment, before saying, "I *can* tell you Sophie and Stuart are being placed somewhere no one is going to find them." He nodded at the colonel. "We're just arranging it now."

"But you don't know about Josey?" Everything felt far away, as if John's mind was keeping things at bay until he was able to deal with them.

"No," said Carter. "I don't." He swallowed, throat rippling. "I'm sorry, for what it's worth."

John glared at him. Not enough. Not nearly enough.

48

John thought of Gary McDowell's dark eyes and smirk, his way of knowing what you were ashamed of and using it against you. He'd keep Josey as long as he needed to, and then he'd discard her. He cleared his throat.

"Carter?" He'd have to tell Carter who had Josey. He had no choice; not to would only delay McDowell's plans. He cleared his throat. "It's McDowell. He set us up."

The cop breathed out, a breath of relief. "Thank you." He straightened. "I'll get onto it."

CHAPTER NINE

az nudged John and pointed at Carter coming through the door of their shared cell. "What the fuck has he got there?"

John grinned; it was good to see Taz getting back to his old self. The grin fell when he saw what appeared to be two walking kettles on either side of the officer.

"I have not a fucking notion," he said. "But it doesn't look good."

Carter dropped into one of two seats opposite them. "I've brought you something," he said. "They're bots. They're to provide access to the curriculum for you."

John exchanged a look with Taz, who didn't even try to keep his face straight. He found his own smile threatening and had to look away from his friend and back to Carter who was waiting, patiently, obviously expecting some kind of response.

"What, does it make tea in the morning?" asked John.

"A sauna: it'll give off steam and fill the room," said Taz, his voice shaking with laughter. John stifled a snort.

Carter didn't look amused. "These are your personal bots," he said, "and they cost a bloody fortune, so stop smirking."

John managed to pull his face straight, but he didn't dare glance at Taz.

"Do we need bots?" he asked.

"Yes. One day, we will get you out. When we do, you need some sort of education behind you." Carter leaned forward. "You're smart lads; there's going to be bugger all else to do wherever they send you." He paused, and went slightly red. "They might be good company."

That did it. John collapsed with laughter. Taz was already almost on the floor. John tried to speak, couldn't, and had to give it a moment. Finally, he squeezed out, "You don't think having a walking teapot for company might give us some trouble?"

He looked down at the bots. One seemed to be watching him. He frowned, and shifted away. It turned very slightly. The other waddled – it had legs, little dinky legs, like Stuart's Fisher-Price dog he'd had as a kid – to Taz, taking up position beside him. They were obviously crafted from the same sort of domestic appliance. John's – well, he thought it might be his, since it still seemed to be watching him – was slightly smaller, a tiny antenna where the nose might be on a real face. It had three arms, each seeming to have a different function, though he had no idea what. A circle of lights about two-thirds up looked like a hairline and flashed in what appeared to be a friendly fashion. He glanced at Taz's; it had a slower light pattern, making it seem ever so slightly grumpy.

Grumpy? He shook his head; he was mad, a bot couldn't be grumpy. Well, not one like this.

"If we don't want them?" he said. His bot's lights flashed, almost as if accusing him.

Carter shrugged. "I can't take them back, and they're programmed to you. Keep them – you might be glad of them. I do think you should do some courses, really I do." He made a face. "If you absolutely can't stand them, you can shove them in a cupboard somewhere."

Both bots swivelled to face the policeman. They had a range of metal panels across the rear of them, but none of the character of the front.

Carter put his hands up, as if in surrender. "I didn't mean it," he said. "Of course they won't stick you in a cupboard."

The bots swung back to their masters and seemed to be waiting. John glanced at Taz, who shrugged slightly.

" 'Course we won't," Taz muttered, and John found himself agreeing. He glared at the policeman. Bots? In a prison? What they needed was a set of master keys. Still... he glanced down; it was kind of cute. He'd have to find a name for it. He barely resisted the urge to pat the bot.

"Lads?"

John looked up at Carter's quiet voice. "What?"

Taz leaned forward, his hands clasped together, tight enough that his knuckles were white.

"The trial has been set."

John's stomach fell, right to the floor. He looked over at Taz, who had paled, and tried to find his voice to ask when, but it came out as a strangled choke instead.

"When?" asked Taz, keeping his voice steady. John nodded his thanks and looked back at the policeman.

"Soon; they're rushing it through." Carter looked at his hands, and then glanced up. "They have somewhere to send you. It's a new prison called Inish Carraig, run by the GC."

"Is it all right?" asked Taz. "I mean, if it's new, it can't be too bad, can it?"

Carter nodded. "I'm sure you're right, Taz."

John stared at the inspector, who met John's eyes, then Taz's, and looked away, a muscle in his cheek twitching. *Christ, he was lying.* John's stomach churned, loud in the empty room, and Taz didn't even take the piss out of him for it. Carter would only lie if it was bad news.

Bollocks; they were in trouble.

CHAPTER TEN

Josey looked through the window at the now-familiar view: a hill, lots of grass, and sheep that looked like chalkmarks on the board at school. During the past week or two – she'd lost count – there had been no signs of life. No tractors, or farmers tending sheep, no houses lit up to break the darkness at night. It seemed like there was no one left in the world other than her, Liz, and Gary's gang.

She tried to move her wrists, but hissed as the thick rope chafed her skin. Gary glanced over from the rocking chair, his eyes dark pools in the dim room, his mouth curled into a sneer. "Sit at peace."

She settled for watching the fire in the open hearth, glad of the heat. Her arm ached from where he'd twisted it earlier when she'd asked to go to the toilet. She'd never known, when John and Taz played mercy, how sore it could be. Just like she hadn't known how a slap over the ears could hurt, or a well-placed elbow in her stomach.

The flames flickered, dancing. It reminded her of Belfast when the Zelo had first come and the city had burst into flames. John said it was the bombs he remembered from the attack; for her it was the stench of fires, oily and thick in her throat, like tyres on bonfire night, only worse. This fire didn't smell like that, but caught in the back of her throat and gave her a cough that wouldn't go away. Liz had told her it was peat. All Josey knew was that it turned her stomach.

She glanced at Liz in the next seat and was glad to see she was asleep. Her wrists and ankles were tied, just like Josey's, and she looked much thinner than when they'd been taken.

She curled up and closed her own eyes. Sometimes, if the men didn't think she was listening, they got a little careless, and whilst she hadn't learned anything useful – she didn't actually know what she might find out – it seemed a good idea to try. And it took her mind off things.

"Carter, the turncoat, is running the lads." Ray, full of endless energy, his voice tight and hard. Demos had left the day before, sent back to Belfast to find the older McDowell. "He has that fucking bulldog Peters as their gatekeeper. They'll be looking for us."

"Let them look," said Gary. He stood and stretched, long and slow like a cat. His gaze strayed over Josey, taking his time, and she kept her eyes at a slit and her breathing steady. He glared across, making Josey's heart quicken. Last night, he'd taken her up to the bare, cold toilet, and told her to sit on the edge of the bath. He'd pulled a knife from his pocket, a flick-type like John carried, but sharper and longer bladed. He'd spent ages – it had felt like an hour – telling her how he always kept it sharp because he never knew when he might need it. He'd put the blade against her cheek, letting her feel its edge, and waited until she'd nodded, careful not to cut herself, and agreed it was a fantastic knife. He'd only stopped when Ray had banged the door to get in.

The front door banged open, and Demos came in: pale, like he was sick, with flitting eyes.

"What the fuck is wrong with you?" demanded Gary, getting up from his seat.

"Your da." Demos sank onto the ragged sofa, beside Ray. "He's dead."

"What are you on?" Gary shook his head. "He can't be dead."

"He is." Demos ran his hands through his hair. "There wasn't any doubt."

"Who did it?" demanded Gary. He didn't seem sad, but angry. "I'll make sure they fucking pay."

"No one knows." Demos held his hands up, as if defending himself from Gary. "Or at least, no one was saying. But –"

"But, what?"

Demos licked his lips. "Look... by the time the cops found your da, there'd been animals at his body, and the forensics were bollixed. I wondered about... well, you know, the job. The employers...." He lowered his voice. "The Barath'na, I mean."

Josey drew in a sharp breath. The Barath'na? They'd planted

54

the virus? They were supposed to be the peaceful aliens, the ones who helped negotiate the Zelo ceasefire on Earth.

"Bullshit. It'll have been one of the other gangs." Gary swore, and kicked a can sitting in front of the fire. It hit the wall next to Josey, and she ducked her head, making herself smaller, before he could decide she was an easy target to take his anger out on.

"Did anyone know you were in town?" he asked Demos.

"Of course they did." Demos gave a snort. "I didn't know until I asked around what had happened - all the old gang have scattered. No one's seen them since your da was killed."

Gary's eyes skittered from Demos, to Ray, to her, and back again, never settling, almost unhinged. There was a gleam in them, one that bore no resemblance to someone who'd just heard their da was dead. He almost looked pleased.

She pulled her ankles up onto the seat, scrunched as small as she could, and turned her head to the fire. It had died down, the embers shifting light and darkness, and the smell was sweet and fragrant now, settling her. She was getting used to it. That thought, more than any before, made the room blur around her; this was her life now and nothing, not the dancing fire, or Liz, or John, held any way to her freedom.

CHAPTER ELEVEN

ohn held the bar, his shoulders burning, and gritted his teeth. *Another four.* He tightened his grip, tensed his muscles, and pulled it down behind his neck. The repetition he'd known for the last couple of years, the concentration on building strength, kept his mind off what was going to happen next. For now, he could lose himself in the need to take a measured breath and count to five. Raise the bar, don't think. Three more. Steel yourself.

"John." Peters' voice cut through his concentration.

He pulled the bar down, following the same pattern. After he'd brought it up, he squeezed out, "What?"

"The inspector's here."

John nodded. "Can I finish the set?"

"Go ahead," said Peters, and John repeated the exercise. He finished the last but one, half wishing the sergeant *had* called a halt to it, and pulled once more, but when he let the bar up he was a little too quick and his shoulder gave a twinge of protest. He pushed his sweat-damp hair back and picked up his towel. It was nice to be back in the gym, even if Peters was always there too. The soldier had been good, though, giving John tips about his technique, and warning him off any equipment he didn't think John was ready for. John looked at Peters' muscled arms under his tight drill t-shirt, and it was impossible not to be jealous. One day, he'd be like that: too big to be knocked around or ignored. If he couldn't use his strength for rugby, he'd use it to look after himself. They couldn't take *that* away from him.

"Ready?" Taz was sitting on one of the exercise bikes, his brown eyes worried. "It's time to see Carter."

"Aye."

They followed Peters through the rec section and past two soldiers on the outer door, one of whom nudged the other and smirked. John clenched his fists. They were talking about him, he bet – the trial ahead, the possible Zelo revenge. He was sick of it; he couldn't even go for a piss without someone knowing who he was. He stopped in front of them, squaring up to the taller of the two. "Looking at something?"

The soldiers exchanged a glance, but didn't answer. Peters reached forward, opened the door to the main barracks, and pushed John through.

"Enough," the sergeant said. His voice was exasperated at best, pissed off at worst. "Stop playing the big lad."

"Get your fucking hands off me." John wrenched out of Peters' grasp. "I'll do you for brutality."

Peters growled under his breath. He led them to a small interview room, and John took the towel from his shoulders. He rubbed it through his hair and hunched forwards. It was cold, like the room hadn't been used recently, and his t-shirt was sweaty and damp. "Can I get a shower?"

"Later."

Peters left, and John glanced over at Taz. "He's a twat. If I get hypothermia, d'you reckon I should sue?"

"Aye, you could spend it on a break-out fund." Taz looked at the door. "He's all right, you know. You shouldn't wind him up."

"How else am I going to pass the time?" John rubbed his arms; it was brass monkeys in here. "You should do a bit of working out, you know. Wherever we're going, it mightn't do any harm for you to be able to look after yourself."

"If we're going to the Zelo, no amount of working out is going to help."

John's stomach turned over – they'd have to be told soon, surely, what was to happen to them. "True."

"Besides, if I lifted one of those weights, I'd end up squashed by it." Taz stuck his tongue out, miming being caught under one, finishing up with an exaggerated choking noise. Briefly, he looked like his old self.

"I'm serious about the gym," said John, laughing. "The doctors said it might make you feel better. Doing stuff."

"The doctors don't know shit. This isn't in my head. My bones *do* hurt. Like little shocks, right to the centre of them."

57

The door opened and Carter walked in, accompanied by a woman in a smart business suit. John's mouth went dry. She was hot. Tall, with big doe eyes. After a month of not seeing any woman other than the occasional soldier – and they were hard to tell apart from the male soldiers, frankly – he found himself looking at her stupidly. Taz had his mouth open too. He wasn't *that* sick, then.

"John, Taz, this is Ms Dean." Carter needed a shave and his eyes were bagged and tired. He looked about ten years older than when John had first met him. "She's a lawyer who specialises in youth cases. She's going to outline the case against you and talk about your options."

John stood, feeling self-conscious in his gym gear, and stretched out a hand. *This* was the promised counsel? Go, Carter.

"Hiya." His heart jumped when she took it and met his eyes. Taz didn't get up, and he nodded down at him. "This is Taz."

Taz's eyes widened, and John wanted to kick him, he looked so gormless. Then he realised he was still holding his hand out, and sat down. No point in both of them looking like idiots. Taz nodded, muttered hello, and the woman sat opposite.

"It's nice to meet you both," she said. "My name is Catherine Dean. You can call me Catherine, if you like. I'm here to talk about the trial, and how you intend to plead." She nodded to the door, and pointedly back at Carter. "You can leave us, Inspector."

The cop backed to the door. John exchanged a glance with Taz and got to his feet. "Wait a minute."

The counsel leaned forward and he could see down her top. God, she *was* fit.... He sat down at a safer angle.

"John, Taz... may I call you that?" she asked. "The inspector can't be with us when we talk. If you agree to me representing you, whatever we discuss is done privately."

John looked at the table, swallowing panic. Taz's leg jittered. Until Josey was standing in front of him, John couldn't tell anyone anything. That was why they'd taken her – to buy his silence. And only in holding that silence could he give Carter time to find her.

"We're guilty," he said, taking his time over each word.

"We took the virus onto the hill. We released it. We knew what it was, but we don't know where it came from. We were promised food by a bloke we vaguely knew, but don't have a name for, and we did it. On purpose. Knowing it would kill the Zelo."

"Lads –" Carter moved forward, his hands out. "Don't screw yourselves."

"Don't call us lads!" John stood and leant over the table, surprised that he was almost as tall as the policeman. "We're not going to be lads when they send us off Earth, are we?"

Taz's seat was pushed back and he got to his feet. John had never felt closer to anyone. It was the two of them against the world. Bugger that, against the galaxy. No one else knew how he felt, the fear that churned through him each night, only Taz.

"Let them throw the fucking book at us." Taz looked at the lawyer. "We don't need to meet you again unless something changes, and you know what change we mean. We plead guilty, whatever the charge is."

John didn't look at Taz. He didn't look at anything except his hands, fingers looped and tight, and he didn't try to tell himself it would be all right. He could keep it up with everyone else, but he was too damned tired to lie to himself anymore. He waited, shivering in the damp air, for Peters to come and take him back to his cell and leave him to wait another day, and another, until Carter came back and told him Josey was okay and this horror show could be sorted out. Either that, or she was dead, killed by John as surely as if he'd taken his own knife to her.

CHAPTER TWELVE

arter stood at the prow of the small private cruiser and took a deep breath; even on a day like this, with the winter sky so blue it nearly hurt to look at it, the boat trip had been rougher than his stomach liked.

He moved to the side, trying to stay downwind of Peters' cigarette smoke, and the two soldiers standing there walked away, pointed in their avoidance of him. He ignored them and looked across the glittering sea, molten silver despite the bright day, at the flotilla of boats jostling for position. Most were small, locally owned, and all were staying back from the GC boats lining the approach to Rathlin Island. Carter frowned at the water cannons mounted on them, and at the distant GC fighter planes, their dart-like forms nothing like any ships he'd seen from Earth, sharp and menacing against the sky.

"This is far enough," he said.

One of the soldiers held up a hand and indicated switching off. The engines stopped and the boat slowed, rocking from side to side with the waves. Footsteps approached from behind, making the boat rock even more. Christ, he wished it would stop that...

"I take it since we're not on a GC transport we're not here officially," said Peters.

"My superintendent knew we were coming," said Carter. "And she informed Colonel Downham. But the official boats were reserved for the GC."

Peters squinted at the GC boats. "Funny, they seem to be full of dogs..."

"Talking ones, too." Carter shrugged. "I wanted to see what the prison was like. I mean, we're filling half of it with our detainees from the riots, we should at least know where they're going."

"Right." Peters flicked his cigarette into the sea. "Well, it's a day out of barracks." He leaned his head back, rolling it until there was a crack from his spine, so loud it made Carter wince. "Who has the boys today?"

Carter stamped his feet. God it was cold. "They're with Catherine," he said.

"Getting anywhere, is she?"

Carter shrugged. "She won't talk about it. The lads say they haven't changed their minds."

"Can't blame them. If Sal was being held by that bastard, I wouldn't sing either."

Carter nodded. The island was bigger than he'd expected. From here he could see two of its three lighthouses, but the other buildings were gone, the small community shunted off to a new estate on the mainland. They'd complained, but the GC had quickly silenced them, like they did anyone who protested: what the Council wanted, it got, with a swift reminder that Earth was buggered without it. Around the island, a troop of construction-bots – he could never look at them without thinking how much like mini street cleaners they were – worked at smoothing the rocky surface.

A black line appeared in the sky behind the fighters, framed against the clouds. It got closer, became recognisable as a freighter, and Carter pointed. "There."

Peters turned, watching it approach. From its undercarriage, a clear structure was suspended, shimmering in the winter sun. A second, smaller ship appeared on the horizon.

The first ship came to a halt over the island, appearing to hang in the air. Its engines were deafening, making Carter pull his earplugs out of his pocket and stick them in. Peters didn't; according to the soldier, ever since a shell had exploded near him during his final tour in Afghanistan, loud noise never bothered him.

The clear structure – looking more than anything like a giant box with cut out doors and windows – was lowered, directed by the construction bots who hovered just above the island, lights flashing as they communicated with the ship. The structure settled into place, and the bots worked around the bottom of it, moulding it seamlessly to the ground. Once it was in place the bigger ship lifted off, letting the second take its place. Molten metal poured from the ship's belly in a steady stream, expanding through the walls, like mercury running over paper.

Peters gave a low whistle. "It's massive."

Carter nodded, and tried to guess how tall it was. At least seventy foot, he reckoned, and covering about half of the longer section of the island. He couldn't see a door in the side they were looking at, and if there were windows they were too small to pick out. He shivered; it looked like a tomb.

"They're calling it Inish Carraig," he shouted. "Fancy a stay there?"

Peters spat out to sea. "They can call it what they like. I'm using Rathlin." He folded his arms. "*I* don't get governed by what the aliens want."

Carter frowned, but Peters' face was bland. "It's going to be hellish," Carter said. "There's no rehabilitation, this is a street-cleaning exercise. It's part of the peacekeeping ethos, apparently."

"You're sure they'll be sent there?"

Carter nodded. "Taz turned sixteen three days ago; John does in a month." He nodded at the prison. "That's where they're going."

The filler ship pulled away and a new depositor appeared, this one carrying the roof. They watched it settle into place, making the structure recognisable as a building. Carter turned, ready to tell the crew to go, when a high whine split the sky.

Peters swore and covered his ears. "What the fuck!?"

The noise changed to an electronic voice, booming over the gathered boats.

"Do not approach GC lines. Repeat: do not approach GC lines."

One of the fighters came out of formation, streaking across to the island, focused on a single fishing boat which had drifted away from the flotilla.

"They need to get back," said Carter. The boat didn't stop. He stepped to the front of his ship, fists clenched, and watched as the crew of the fishing boat shouted something.

Peters cursed. "There's something wrong with the boat. It's not coming roun–" A line of light ripped across the sky, making the sergeant reel back. "Jesus!"

Carter brought a hand up to his eyes and turned his face away as an explosion ripped through the still air. It faded, replaced by shocked yells from the boats around him. He looked across to where the fishing ship had been: it was gone, only wooden debris floating in its place. His boat was lifted by the wash, sinking back down a moment later. "Christ almighty."

Peters moved back to the bow, and took a moment to review the scene. "A bit trigger-happy."

"Trigger-happy!" Carter ran his hand through his hair. "They did it in front of all of us..."

Peters nodded. "Aye." His face changed, becoming tighter; worried. "And they're the peacekeepers.... The GC boats are moving; we should go."

Carter nodded and signalled to the engine room. The boat started up, the skipper obviously eager to go. The other ships were pulling away, too. Carter watched the island vanish, his eyes scanning the water. He blinked and the beam of light was still imprinted on his eyes. It *had* happened. Should he report it? Maybe... but who to? It would only end up back with the GC. He took a last look at the dark cube of Inish Carraig – *Rathlin, Peters was right* – and turned, a feeling of not sea sickness, but fear, rising up from his stomach to choke him.

CHAPTER THIRTEEN

ights flashed. John had lost count of the news people ages ago, and it was even worse in the street leading to the courthouse. In the front seat, Carter looked straight ahead, his jaw clenched.

The car slowed. The lights were right up against the windows, their flashes brief sparks against the tinted glass. He'd dreamed of being in a car like this and having the press photograph him, but he'd wanted it to be for bringing home the World Cup. Taz stopped looking out the opposite window and met John's eyes. He looked as sick as John felt. The car pulled to a halt. It was time: the point of no return. More flashes popped, right up against his window.

Carter turned and raised an eyebrow. "Ready?"

John swallowed a rush of nerves. He didn't think he'd ever be ready for this. "What happens now?"

"We get up the steps as quickly as we can." Carter's mouth twisted as he unclipped his seatbelt. "Don't worry, half of them are here for me. What I do is tell myself they know nothing about the real me and dive in." He flashed a half-smile. "Ready to dive, lads?"

"Yes." It was Taz who answered first.

"Yeah." John could hear a tremor in his voice, and he tried to calm himself. He was going to be on telly – he needed to look like he wasn't scared shitless.

"Let's go." Carter tapped his window and all three doors burst open. John stepped out and a soldier flanked him. Taz came round the back of the car, escorted by a soldier. Carter had one either side of him – he hadn't been lying about expecting attention, then.

The media crews jostled forwards, pushing against the police lines. Questions filled the air, each drowned out by the next, and cameras flashed. John's escort moved forwards, keeping him close all the time. To the right, Carter dove into a forest of mikes and gave a terse series of no comments. The media flocked to the policeman, leaving John and Taz a clear run to the bottom of the courthouse steps. Briefly, John wondered if the officer had done it on purpose. If so, he'd been too smooth to catch.

On either side of a wide flight of steps, crowds of protestors were tightly corralled behind barriers lined with the Barath'na. It was the first time John had seen the second alien race up close, but he was pushed past so quickly he only had the sense of bared teeth and fur covering muscular bodies. Dogs, he thought - dogs on two legs. With long rifles and hard eyes.

One set of protestors shouted that he and Taz were Earth's saviours, not Deklon's to condemn. *Quite right; give that crowd a medal.* A woman leaned over the barrier and shouted, "They should be freed!" She looked like a nutso, her red hair - dyed, definitely, no one had that colour of hair - whipping as she yelled, and a placard thrust in the air, but John's breath still caught; he hadn't realised there was any support for him and Taz.

Shouts grew from the crowd on the other side of the steps and became a chant. It took John a moment to catch that they were asking for him and Taz to be expelled to Deklon. Hatred exuded from their glares and fist-punches, their chants that Earth had been risked by the actions of two cutting through the chill air. Taz's eyes went wide and scared. *Bastards.* John moved away from his escort. He'd tell them they knew *nothing* about him or Taz, just like Carter had said. The soldier, who knew him from the barracks, was quicker and grabbed his jacket. "Oh, no, you don't. Keep walking."

"Up the steps!" Carter reached them, trailed by the media. His face was set and determined, and John pulled himself straight. Deep breath. Dive in.

"Shit-lover!" The shout went up from someone in the human-rights camp. "It's the shit-lover!" The other side joined in, and their chants combined into a crescendo of hatred.

65

John climbed the steps, half-running. No one had told him it would be like this. The shouts followed him up the steps, getting louder by the minute. His breath was coming in gasps, quick and scared. The soldier accompanying Taz grabbed his elbow and half-hoisted him up.

Carter led the way to the now-open double doors, not looking left or right, even when one protester broke past the police line and almost reached him. The back of his hair was curling and damp. The protester was pushed back into the crowd, who surged forward. *Fuck, they'd break through.*

"Bless you, we're supporting you, John and Taz!" A man's voice carried over the other shouts. Should John acknowledge or ignore it?

The decision was made by the soldier pushing him forwards. "Keep going."

Something dark flashed across the edge of John's vision, and Taz ducked as an egg pelted past him and splattered on the ground.

"Missed!" he yelled.

Another egg flew. "You could have had Earth destroyed!" More shouts joined in, back to the pitched chanting. John ducked as another missile flew, inches from his head. His heart raced as he scrambled up the last steps. Carter had reached the doors. John was propelled forwards, half off his feet, followed by Taz, who stumbled and half-fell into the huge entrance hall. Carter closed the doors. The thud echoed and faded to silence.

"Jesus Christ." Taz's hands were shaking. "Wasn't there a back door?"

"It's just as bad," said Carter. "And the car would have been further away. Speed was the best option, we thought."

"All right?" Peters appeared from the shadows and gave each of them a short nod.

"Yeah," said Carter. He, too, looked shaky. "Nasty enough, though."

"Aye, they've been gathering all morning – I escorted Ms Dean in earlier." So, their defence attorney was waiting for them. That was good; even if Catherine wasn't able to get them off – and she hadn't sounded hopeful the last time they'd met – at least she'd be able to fight for terms for them. Peters glanced at John. "More exciting than the gym, eh?"

"Yeah." John had never been more pleased to see the big soldier. Next time they had to run the gauntlet, he was going to ask Peters to stay beside him.

Catching his breath, he looked around the entrance hall. The ornate ceiling was so high he had to bend his head back to take it in. All the doors off the foyer were dark wood, heavy he bet, and a staircase, running from the centre of the room, had banisters practically the width of his hand. The floor was a polished marble. It was much more formal than he'd expected. He pulled at his suit and ignored the butterflies holding a party in his stomach.

With the click-click of heels, Catherine approached. She wore a jacket and skirt and had her long hair pinned up. An adult stranger, not at all like the barrister who'd come to see them each week in soft jeans and tops cut a little low, so that she'd started to invade John's dreams. Well, the better dreams, the ones that didn't have Zelo trying to rip him apart.

She gave a composed smile. "Are you all right?"

Carter pushed his hair back and gave a grimace. "Nothing new for Belfast's most hated. And the lads handled it like troupers."

"Well done." Catherine took Carter to the side, and John heard her murmur, "Any update on Josey and Mrs Delaney?"

"No."

John pushed himself forwards. "The crowd out there. Some of them said we should be freed, not sent down, that it's for Earth to decide." He swallowed his nerves. If that happened, what would McDowell do? Call for him and Taz in exchange for his hostages? It was possible enough that John clutched the life-line offered. He touched Catherine's arm. "Is there a chance we might get off?"

She glanced at Carter, who gave a helpless-looking shrug.

"There is some popular support for you." She gave a soft smile, full of sympathy. "But the GC have the mandate for anything that reaches between the three races, and the Earth-committee have agreed to abide with the GC's judgement on you. It's your word they'll have to make a judgement on."

John's shoulders dropped. Without any of McDowell's gang still alive, there was no way to prove what he and Taz were saying was true. They'd presented their evidence in custody and it had been sent off-world to judge. He looked at Carter, and one look at the cop's eyes silenced him. Their sharp edge was gone now, replaced by a weariness that appeared to have shrunk the officer.

"Five minutes," said Catherine. "The courtroom is set up. It's quite formal. You and Taz will sit in the front row. It won't take long once we're in there."

John cleared his throat. "You still think they'll send us to the new prison? The one that has the weird name."

"Inish Carraig." Catherine looked sober. "They might. If so, it's very modern and safe, I'm told."

A pair of wooden doors opened in front of them, and a court official stepped through. Catherine nodded to John and Taz and pointed through the door.

"Right, lads, ready to face the music?" Carter smiled, but it looked more like a grimace.

God, no. John nodded, his head moving independently of any thought. Taz hunched into his formal jacket. He looked about twelve. They followed Catherine and Carter into a small courtroom and sat together in the front row. Apart from the four of them, the room held a handful of bored-looking soldiers, and three news-people hunched over tablets on their laps. The heavy door closed and Peters took a seat beside it. The soldier's mouth twisted in what looked like sympathy. Behind him, two of the Barath'na took a place at either side of the door. Christ, they were big. John exchanged a glance with Taz: they were in charge of peace on Earth? They looked about as friendly as McDowell on a bad day.

John faced forwards, away from the aliens. He wanted his parents here. Their absence was so strong it curled in him like a snake.

A humming noise started and a screen descended from the ceiling. A metallic voice came from speakers either side of the screen and announced the arrival of Justice Mackenzie. The screen came to life in a blizzard of white. John's muscles

68

bunched and tensed. They'd already made their mind up, the GC, halfway across the galaxy on the Barath'na homeworld. The screen cleared and the judge appeared, a human one, thankfully. His dull eyes scanned the courtroom, and John's stomach fell. There was going to be no miracle here today.

"The court is in session," said the court official.

Taz stopped fidgeting; John couldn't move.

"In the matter of John Dray and Terence Delaney," said the judge, "a verdict has been reached."

He paused, looking down at something, and the silence stretched. The muscles in John's shoulders tightened – *get on with it* – and he forced himself not to look at anything other than the screen. Peters coughed. *Come on.*

Finally, the judge looked up. "On multiple counts of xenocide, the defendants have been found guilty."

John's eyes closed. He'd known what would happen, of course he had, but still... he'd hoped. He wanted to put his head between his knees and not have to face it, but he opened his eyes and stared at the judge. Let no one say he'd been a coward.

"I sentence you to life imprisonment. You will be transferred to a GC-registered facility forthwith."

It was real. Lights flashed from the news people. Someone's hand was on John's back and he managed to straighten enough to see it was Taz. He took John's elbow, gripping it tight, so that when John clambered to his feet, heart pounding, it was with Taz's support. This wasn't fair, he wanted to say. They hadn't known what they were doing. He saw Carter, and his anger focused on the cop.

"You told me you'd help, the first time we met!" said John. He didn't care that the cameras were on him, or that his words weren't directed at the judge, where they should be. He needed to hurt someone real, not a screen.

Carter flinched and loosened his collar. "John..."

John wrenched his arm from Taz and stepped forward. "You said you'd find Josey – that you were getting close. You're a useless bast–"

"Calm down." Peters came down the steps. "I don't want them to take you out of here yelling the place down. Think of how that'll look on the news."

The news. Oh, god... the kids. John stared at Peters. "Stuart and Sophie - they won't see this, will they? Promise me they won't."

"They won't." Peters glanced at Carter, who gave a nod. "The people with them know what's happening today. They won't see any of this."

Taz left the row of seats and John followed. They didn't go back to the entrance hall, but down a narrow set of stairs at the side of the courtroom. He paused half-way down, wanting to go back and tell the judge he was sorry, that he hadn't meant to do any of this. Peters ushered him forward and the moment passed.

Besides, what did sorry matter? It wasn't going to make prison any easier. Something in John left him - the hope he'd carried through the invasion, his parents dying, this shitty mess - and it felt like he was shedding a skin to one beneath that couldn't be hurt. He put his head up. Nothing was real. He wasn't, the room wasn't, the cold cuffs being snapped on him definitely weren't.

He tried to pull his hands away, but a soldier held him firmly by the arms and led him out the back and into a transport, piloted by a huge Barath'na. Its back was turned from John, but he could see how its claws skittered across a control panel with precision. John stared at the claws, and how they tapered into thin nails, almost as thin as the blade Peters had taken off him.

A thunk on the seat next to him made him glance down to see Jimmy's lights flash in recognition, and he was surprised at how relieved he was to see the bot. Carter had taken it from him, a couple of days ago, putting in place some new ed-programmes, but he'd confirmed the bot would be coming into the prison with him. The transporter started with barely a sound, and pulled away from the courthouse into the new traffic lane designed for the alien vehicles. The normal lanes, carrying human cars, turned into a blur as it gathered speed, leaving Belfast behind them.

Within minutes they were into the countryside, and the life that John had led in the city was lost.

CHAPTER FOURTEEN

The car door opened, and Josey strained to see anything, but the blindfold was too tight. It wasn't good that she was being moved, she knew it in her bones.

A hand tapped her shoulder, just a little too hard, telling her who it was. She shifted along the seat until she got to the end, ducking her head as she climbed out, and listened while she waited. All was quiet. Even that told her some things: there were no cows or sheep, so this wasn't a farm; any birds had gone silent, so weren't used to the comings and goings of people. Either that, or it was night-time. A breeze touched her arms, and its coldness convinced her it was probably the latter.

Someone – Demos probably, it felt like his pudgy fingers – took one arm. "You're sure there'll be no appeal? We can't take this back if we need the women again."

A cold chill took Josey. This was it. She tried to keep her legs from shaking, but it was no use. She hated what had happened since Belfast; she'd cried herself to sleep every night, but she didn't want to die. Not like this, in the middle of nowhere with Gary McDowell and his thugs. She wanted to come up with words that might make them change their minds, but could think of nothing except to beg, and that hadn't helped the day Gary had taken her.

"There'll be no appeal. Da had plans for our two lads, plans that would keep them quiet forever. We don't need anything on them now." Gary took Josey's other arm, tightening his grip until she yelped. "Shut it or I'll kick your arse." She bit her lip and nodded. "Good girl. Right, three steps forward and then up two." He gave a short laugh. "Jaysus, you're shaking."

He held her as she walked forward, careful with her feet. She reached the top of the steps, and went into some sort of building – she could tell when the icy wind left her skin – and was guided forwards, steps echoing, until Gary's hand tightened again, stopping her.

He took off her blindfold. She was in a stable. Its ceiling was half-missing, letting her see it *was* dark outside. Apart from a few hay bales and a pail of water at her feet, emptiness stretched as far as she could see. It didn't smell of animals, just damp sawdust and mould. The only light came from a torch in Demos' hand, which he set on the floor, changing its setting so it lit up like a lantern, giving a small pool of light. There was nowhere to run to, and no one to help her. Her breath came in short gasps driven by fear, and the cold made her need the toilet. What if she wet herself, when they did it to her? Her eyes stung with tears.

Ray pushed Liz alongside and tugged off her blindfold. Liz looked around. "You can't leave us here." Her normally posh English voice sounded strangled and she had to break off to cough. She smothered it, and went on, "It's too cold for the child; she'll get ill."

She didn't know yet, and Josey didn't have the words to tell her. Gary's ever-present smile was on his face, harder than ever. She wished she could wipe it away forever. He stood in front of her, looking at her, as if working something out. Josey's shivers became shudders and she tried to tell herself it was the cold. Liz moved closer and put her arms around Josey; her wrists were red from the recently removed rope.

"Right, we need to get on with this," said Gary.

Demos clapped him on the shoulder and Gary laughed, the flat laugh Josey had come to hate. One day she was going to kill him, even if she had to come back from the grave to do it. Something must have shown in her face, because he reached out and grabbed her chin, squeezing so hard her jaw clenched against sharp pain.

"Take that look off your face," he said.

She struggled to nod and he let go. He left the stable, Demos following, but Ray took up position just at the edge of the light, his flicking eyes radiating pent-up energy, his gun cradled as if it was treasure. He nodded at one of the bales

73

and Josey was glad to sit; she didn't trust herself to stay standing. She shivered against the cold air and decided she hated Ray just as much as McDowell.

Liz looked ahead, her thin face composed, but Josey could see the shine of tears in her eyes and the tight line of her jaw. She *had* worked it out, then. They huddled together for warmth. Outside, a car door opened, and there was the sound of an engine. Josey strained her ears; it was driven to the other side of the stable, away from where they'd arrived, presumably out of sight of the road.

The door to the outside opened. An icy blast of wind made her teeth chatter. She tried to rub some heat into her arms, but it made no difference. Footsteps came closer. She strained against the darkness to see who it was, tense like the street cats back in Belfast. Demos stepped into the light and pulled Liz to her feet. "You first."

"No!" Josey lunged for Liz. Demos batted her away and yanked Liz against him. He turned, pushing the older woman towards the door. Josey tried to go after them, but Ray pushed her back onto the bale, so hard she nearly toppled off the back.

"Please!" she said. "She hasn't done anything."

"Shut up or I'll make you." He raised his hand as if to hit her, and she ducked her head. He nodded and backed away, still holding the gun.

How would they do it? Would it at least be quick? Tears streamed, warm against her cheeks. From outside, a low voice said something. Liz replied, her voice high and scared, the words indistinct. Josey put her head down, almost to her knees. *He wouldn't.* Gary was a thug, not a cold-blooded murderer. He was only a few years older than John; he couldn't have killed before. He'd back out when the act was in front of him.

The stable door slammed and she jumped. Steps echoed, crossing to her.

"Is he going to do it?"

"Aye." Demos stopped just at the edge of the light and waited, as if listening. "He says to keep an eye on this one, make sure she doesn't bolt."

Oh, dear God. The night stretched. An owl hooted somewhere in the distance. Ray's head cocked at an angle.

74

A single shot rang out. A bitten-off scream. Josey fell forward, slipping off the bale and knocking the water over. It spread across the concrete floor, dark like blood. A pair of hard hands pulled her to her feet, and she tried to say something – anything – but words wouldn't come.

The door to the outside opened. Gary was there, the look on his face like nothing she'd seen before – excited, high as if he'd taken drugs. He crooked a finger and beckoned her. She took a step back, but Ray blocked her.

"Now," said Gary.

Ray pushed her forwards and she stumbled. Gary's pistol shone in the lamp-light, deep black, deadlier than his knife. She stopped in front of him, and watched, almost numb, as he reached for her and tipped her face to him.

"I like you," he said, his voice low, intimate. "You've got guts, Josey Dray. I don't want to kill you, you know that."

"What do you want?" she husked.

"I want you to stay with me and do whatever I want." He wound his hand into her hair. "I had someone I thought would be right for me, but she didn't stay."

"What happened to her?"

He pulled her tight against her and put his mouth against her ear. "I hurt her. I hurt her bad."

She bit back a whimper. He held her firmly.

"Well," he said, "have we a deal? I get to keep you, you get to live."

Dumbly, she nodded her head. Live, to have another chance to run. Live to carry out her promise and kill him.

"Good girl," he said. He let her go. "Ray, Demos, take the second car and head back to the safe house. Make contact with the employers and tell them the job's done." He jerked his head at Josey. "I'll do her on my own, and see you back there."

Ray nodded but Demos looked at Gary, his eyes sharp. "Wouldn't we be better staying together? You'll have the bodies to dump."

"Don't argue with me!" Gary's face twisted. "Do you think I can't do a wee girl on my own?"

"Right, right," said Ray. He half-shoved Demos through

the door. It banged after them, leaving her alone with Gary. *Cowards.* She kept her head down, not meeting his eyes, but he took her arm and gave it a savage twist.

"You look at me when we're together," he said. "I'm in charge. You need to be alert to whatever I might want. Understand?" He twisted again.

"Yes!" The word was wrenched from her. She looked at him through blurred tears. "I'll watch you. Sorry."

"Good girl. Come on." He led Josey outside, and she cast her eyes around, trying to tell where she was, but it was too dark. She sniffed the air, and it smelt high and piney, like a Christmas tree. She wasn't going to have another Christmas – sooner or later, he'd get sick of this new game, and she'd end up dead anyway. A sob threatened and she choked it back.

They emerged from the shadow of the stable into pale moonlight. She glanced at Gary's gun, held tight in his hand. This wasn't like in Carrick, when they'd needed her alive; no matter how fast she ran, she wouldn't get away. She tripped on a stone and he grabbed her collar, yanking her back. Her eyes widened at the sight of a car just ahead. In its open boot lay Liz, her eyes open, not blinking.

"Get into the car," he said.

She tried to pull away. She needed to get to Liz, to close her eyes, to say a prayer. She didn't know the proper Catholic ones but surely any prayer would do – Liz had never cared about that sort of thing.

"In the car." He gave her a sharp cuff on the back of her head. "Do what I tell you."

He wasn't going to keep her alive. He was going to play with her, hurt her – worse, he'd do worse – and then he'd get rid of her. She knew too much about him, overheard on long nights in the cottage. A small trickle of wet dripped down the inside of her thigh.

"Please," she said, hating how her voice was shaking. "Can't you let me go? I won't say anything, I swear."

"Last chance." He raised his pistol. "Get in the car or you'll join her."

She put her hand on the passenger door. More wetness

trickled, warm against her thigh. Maybe she'd be better off dead; it'd be clean and quick. Her eyes cast around, wondering if she could run, but the empty farm buildings were too far –

"Poacher?" The voice came from behind her, and a disk of light appeared, bobbing along the path and over into the tree line.

"Must be. It was definitely a shot," said a second voice. Both were male with a country twang, almost a brogue.

Run, move away! It didn't sound like a thought, more an order in a Belfast voice, like her da's. Josey backed away. Gary moved forward, quicker than she'd ever imagined he could.

"The car. Move," he said.

Move. The word cut through her shock, and Josey did what Da had told her to – he had, she was sure of it – and ducked out of Gary's reach. She ran across the yard into the shadows. He cursed. The beam of light rounded the far end of the barn. Gary slammed the boot of the car. The light bobbed in the direction of the sound.

"There he is!" yelled one of the voices. Gary pulled open the driver's door. "It is a poacher, Da!"

Footsteps ran across the yard as Gary started the car and swept it round in a circle. Josey ducked further into the shadows. She was shaking so hard, she worried the movement would give her away. The men ran past, chasing the car as it skidded out of the yard.

"Get round the front, Sean, see if we can catch the bastard!"

Their torchlight swung around the side of the building, casting Josey into dense darkness. She was shaking, and she put a knuckle in her mouth, trying to steady herself, but that didn't help. She slumped against the wall as her legs gave way. She looked up at the stars in the clear sky; she might have wet herself, she might be terrified, but someone, somewhere, had just given her half a chance. She squeezed her eyes shut, and whispered, "Thank you, God, for taking care of me." She thought for a moment. "Though could you maybe, just maybe, tell me where I should go? Because it's awful dark here, and I don't even know where here is. Please, God. Amen."

She pushed herself to her feet and looked around the farmyard. No answer. Well, no matter what, she couldn't stay here. Gary would be back, she was sure of that. He'd be back, and he'd be looking.

CHAPTER FIFTEEN

ohn stamped his feet on the dock. The wind was keen, direct from the arctic, and the rain had turned to stinging darts against his cheeks. Beside him, Taz hunched into his coat, Carter holding his arm as if to stop him bolting. The cop stared resolutely ahead, his face impossible to read.

A wash of water hit the pier, splashing John's boots. He moved back, glaring at the grey waves. He'd always been told the sea was blue; evidently his art teacher hadn't been to Ballycastle in winter. Here, the North Atlantic was like a moving stone.

A shout came from the boat moored in the harbour, and Carter gave an acknowledging salute. "Okay, lads, let's go."

John glared at him. If Carter called him a lad once more, he'd swing for him. He followed the officer up the ramp onto a police boat. Four soldiers flanked them, and Jimmy and Sammy brought up the rear, hovering instead of walking, either because he and Taz found it so obviously cooler – Fisher-Price legs vs jet propulsion, back of the net, jets – or it suited the terrain better. They looked enough like mini UFO's that there might be some kind of cool having them in the prison after all.

John paused at the door to the small cabin. The quayside was the last place he'd see before Inish Carraig. Northern Ireland hadn't been much of a place to grow up, what with the politicians going on about crap that didn't matter a damn, and the arguments about stupid flags flaring into riots, but it was his place.

One of the soldiers jerked his head at the cabin and John went in, dropping onto one of the benches that ran along the side. Through the rain-drizzled window, the prison was a dark shadow in the gloom, bigger than he'd expected – when he'd looked Rathlin up on Jimmy's ed-programme it had seemed little more than a rock.

He'd done more than just look at the island, he'd memorised it. After all, who knew when the doors might be left open...? He'd traced the hills and inlets, the rocks and landscape. It was bleaker than he'd imagined. And boring; its only claim to fame was some Scottish king who'd stayed in a cave and watched a spider spinning its web before going back to beat the shite out of the English. Christ, you'd think kings would have better things to do than watch spiders.

The boat rocked in its berth. A mix of diesel and brine, familiar from the last time he'd been on a ferry, turned his stomach, and he told himself it wasn't possible to feel sick until the boat cast off. *It wasn't.*

The boat cast off. Carter sat on the bench opposite, beside Taz, who lay, seemingly asleep, arms crossed over his chest, one leg on the floor for balance. Sammy crouched in the crook of his arm, just as dormant, making John smile; he bet a stranger would be able to pick out whose bot was whose, like dogs and their masters. He'd have to tell Taz that, it'd get a laugh.

The ship dipped, taking his stomach with it, and he had no hope of swallowing the bile this time. He stumbled to his feet. "Carter! Can I go up on deck?"

He must have looked as bad as he felt, because Carter gestured at the two soldiers flanking the cabin door. "It's okay, I'll go with him."

The cop struggled to push the metal door open against the wind. John slammed against it, his hand over his mouth, and dashed up the shallow stairs. The horizon moved with the rolling sea. The boat sank into a trough, slamming him into low railings.

"John!" shouted Carter. "Watch yourself!"

He grasped the rain-slick railing, his hands slipping and threatening to spill him, but Carter grabbed his collar and tugged him back. He pulled free, leaned over the churning sea, and threw up. There were carrots in it, he noticed; why did boak always have carrots in it? He dry-retched a couple of times, until the sickness eased and he moved onto one of the benches either side of the engine room.

80

Carter sat beside him, his own face blending against the white paint. "Feeling better?"

"Yeah." The prison rose from the sea, black as the basalt rocks along the Belfast coast. "We're nearly there."

"At least the crossing's short; it's about the only thing going for it." Carter stood. "If you're feeling better we should go back down."

John clasped his hands together. Would he ever find out what had happened to Josey, or if Stuart and Sophie were okay? Or would he be left to get old and die in a cell on his own?

"Carter - would you be our liaison officer?" he asked, surprising himself. "We were told we could have one."

The cop stared at Inish Carraig, his silence giving John his answer, and he hated himself for caring.

"I can't," he said at last. "I'm sorry."

"Sure, I understand." The words were spat. "It's just that you said you'd help, and I thought maybe you meant it. But it doesn't matter."

Carter looked as if he'd been slapped. "John, I'm sorry. I didn't want things to end up like this."

"So you keep saying. Look, could you send me word about the kids sometimes? Let me know if Josey turns up?"

The officer ran his hands through his hair. "Okay, I'll do that. But I can't come to visit - I don't even know where I'll be based after this." He gave John a half-smile. "But look, the prison mightn't be so bad."

Fucking liar. John went back into the small cabin and sat beside Taz, ignoring Carter when he stopped in front of him. Fuck him. John would find a way out of this mess himself. There had to be something he could do. He blinked at that thought; he'd been sure his hope had gone, but it was just squashed and tiny and tired. And useless, damn it. He wasn't getting out of this mess, not ever.

***

Josey rubbed her arms. She had no idea how long it was until morning, but she needed to get warm, and find some food.

The darkness stretched, unbroken in each direction, and she had no idea which way to go.

She couldn't stay here and freeze. She started walking, parallel to the road. The ground crackled as the frosted mud broke. It would be easier to walk along the road, but she daren't; Gary might find her. She probably shouldn't even be following it.

She angled across the field, feeling very exposed, and followed the hedgerow on the other side. Her feet sank at every step, not just on the crusted surface now, but ankle-deep. At the end of the field a stile sparkled in the frost, and she tried to speed up.

At last she reached it, but when she climbed the steps freezing air gusted past her. She couldn't go on, not in this cold, not without knowing where to go.

Keep going.... Whatever I do, keep going.

She climbed down and crossed the next field, stumbling more than walking. Still, there was only dark night and cold, and she found herself falling.

***

A hand touched Josey and she scrunched away from it, whimpering. He'd found her.

"Give me your coat..." Something warm was laid over her. "Foundered, she is..."

Her sneakers were taken off and someone rubbed her feet; they were so cold it was sore. She tried to tell them, but her jaw was clenched.

"Did she say something?"

"Maybe. Keep going, she needs warmed."

She shivered, not able to stop. "Sore..."

"She says it's hurting."

A hand touched her forehead, warm against her. "We'll have to carry her to the house."

Josey opened her eyes to a slit, and saw green grass and a blue sky at a crazy angle. She took in a face, worried, just above her. It wasn't Gary, or any of McDowell's gang. A yelp of relief escaped her.

"Shhhh, you're okay. Close your eyes, we'll get you warm." A hand pushed her hair back, soothing her. Her mum used to do that. She drifted back to her old house in Belfast and went into her room where her mum had the Plain White T's on the player, singing about Delilah and New York City. Josey tried to sing along, but she was too tired. Her eyes closed....

In the air, floating...
hands holding her, stopping her from falling,
letting her fly....
She jerked, tried to sit. "McDow-"
"You're all right."

Someone carried her, their loping gait lulling her, so that she was taken back to the depths. A door banged and there was another voice, this one a woman's.

"For the love of God!"

She didn't know the voice. No, hold on, Mrs Graeme from school talked like that. Why was she at Mrs Graeme's?

"Oh Jaysus, she's freezing. Get her up into your room, Sean. Paddy, heat a water bottle..."

Carried...

thump, thump, thump, jaw loosening...

Soft. A bed; covers; so warm.

"Shhhh, love, go to sleep." Such a soft voice. She hoped it was Mrs Graeme, then she'd be safe. "It's all right, pet, I'll be here. You're all right now, love."

"Get a doctor?" A man's voice.

"Where from?" The woman again. "By the time we get down to town and bring him back, she'll either be dead or better. No, we'll have to do our best... heat another bottle; the child needs warmed."

CHAPTER SIXTEEN

arter led the way along the short pier and stopped just outside the force field surrounding Inish Carraig, keeping a healthy distance. He frowned at its low hum – it melded into his mind, making him grit his teeth – and looked up at the prison. It wasn't just that the installation was made from the strange metal he was growing to hate more every day, it was that it was so cut off.

A buzz sounded and one section of the force field melted, the air turning from cloudy to clear. The cloudiness was, apparently, a safeguard so no one walked into it and sued the GC. Carter almost laughed; unless the cormorants could sue for broken beaks, he couldn't see much danger.

He stepped through, and the governor was waiting to greet them. It ambled forwards, its heavy body picking its way over the rocks. Its golden eyes fixed on Carter. As it neared, Carter could hear the alien's panting and the odd growl; Catherine was right, they were creepy. Creepier than the Zelo; at least they walked on two feet.

The Barath'na stopped in front of him, and here it had the edge over the Zelo: its smell was the heavy aroma of wet fur, familiar and not unpleasant. It extended a paw, Earth-fashion – they were a lot more diplomatic about things than the Zelo had been – and the paw was surprisingly elegant, as long as Carter's hands, the claws like fingers. They shook hands. Carter activated his translator unit, feeling it buzz against his throat. It was painless, but not pleasant. "Governor Distryn?"

"Inspector Carter."

The governor looked at John and Taz, both of whom seemed small beside the Barath'na. Taz's head was tilted back, taking in the high walls. He swallowed and his bobbing throat made him look every inch his age. John, on the other hand, stood straight and alert, as if he might bolt. Carefully, Carter moved nearer to him; he'd been the one who'd taken the decision not to cuff the lads, and he would look like a bloody idiot if he'd been wrong.

"Which is which?" asked the governor.

Carter fought not to smile. He was sure from what he knew of Distryn – or at least, what he'd checked before he'd come here – the Barath'na already knew.

"This one is Dray." John nodded, curtly, and Carter pointed at Taz. "That's Delaney. He needs regular medical reviews; whatever happened the night of the virus left him in a catatonic state for several days and the doctors want him checked periodically."

"They'll receive the attention they need," said the governor. The translated voice was flat, but the growls underlying the words sounded amused. The hair on the back of Carter's neck stood up, and he tried to tell himself it was Catherine's distaste for the aliens rubbing off.

John's eyes, steady as ever, met his and the lad shook his head. At his feet his bot hunched, its lights flashing slowly, like it was uncertain.

"They need to be kept safe from the other prisoners," Carter said.

"We have been apprised of the security situation," said the governor. Its eyes, like a wolf's, were impossible to read. "To confirm: no visitor allocation, no medical conditions beyond Delaney's, no additional notes." It smiled in a toothy fashion, and took a set of papers from its belt. "I need you to sign the handover document."

Carter took it, and glanced back at John, who was scanning the walls. Apart from the wind and waves, there was no noise. Carter looked up at the building. *Fourteen hundred.* That was the number of prisoners incarcerated to date. Carter strained his ears. There had to be some sort of noise; you couldn't have that many people and there be nothing. The screech of a seabird overhead made him jump, but otherwise it was silent.

"It's creepy," he heard Taz say. John mumbled something in return, too low for Carter to make out.

Carter clicked the pen and paused. Bizarrely, the image of Nugent flashed into his head. Two nights ago, he'd dreamt his former captain was still alive and had come to ask Carter why he'd left him behind. His head had been canted to the side, one hand covering the hideous wound in his stomach, and his voice had rasped its accusation...

Carter rubbed his hand across his chin. He bent down, holding the paper against his thigh, and added his name. Twice. He gave it back, and the governor read over it. The alien looked up.

"The visitor allocation has been changed."

"That's right," said Carter, and John glanced at him, sharply. "I'm their court-approved liaison - I just hadn't activated it yet. I'll be coming to see them on their allocated days. First Sunday in every month, isn't that right?" Carter raised his voice a little, making sure it carried. "So this Sunday is the first one."

The governor dropped back onto all fours. Even like that, it came close to Carter's chest height. John and Taz passed him and he stepped back. They followed the alien, and he wanted to reach out to them. A poem came to mind, one he'd learned at school about an officer who'd led his men, whom he thought of as his sons, to die. He took a deep breath, and clenched his fists. *Stop it.* He wasn't sending them to their death, no matter how much it felt like he was. *He wasn't.*

***

The sound of the boat backfiring as it started made John jump. Carter was leaving. He stopped for a moment and watched the boat pull out of the harbour.

"Holy shit." Taz's words were sharp, filled not with fear, but disbelief. "John..."

John turned. Barath'na had appeared from the prison and were running across the rocks to them. No, not running; swarming. From everywhere, in groups of at least a dozen, low to the rock, their grey fur making them blend in, so that it was like the rock itself was shifting. They came silently, closer and closer, some up to the height of his waist, some smaller, up to

86

his knees. At the back, a pack of larger aliens, easily the height of his chest, herded the others.

The governor gave a low snarl. Its fur flattened against its spine, revealing a hunched back. Broad muscles ran the length of its body, knotted and strong. Its tail swished from side to side, thick and sinuous, like a rat's. The swarms drew nearer, encircling John and Taz, so they crushed together. Taz trembled. The first group came close, their eyes glowing in the low afternoon light, their teeth sharp and deadly, their claws clicking on the rocks, coming closer all the time. They herded John and Taz forwards.

They reached the prison. Huge doors opened onto an entrance hall. As they went in, the cold air was replaced by a different chill, this one sterile and unwelcoming. They walked forwards together, their bots on either side, the whisper of moving bodies growing in the darkness, the soft clicks of claws echoing. The door closed with a bang.

CHAPTER SEVENTEEN

The hall stretched like a cavern, its metal walls unbroken by any windows. The ceiling, easily twenty feet above John, was black, too, and the lights studded across it didn't make much impact. He shivered and pulled his jacket around him. Taz tensed beside him.

"We'll be all right," John said, and his words echoed slightly. "They're not allowed to hurt us."

"You reckon?" Taz took a step forwards. "It's like a dungeon."

John nodded and counted his steps, trying to keep calm. Forty-three, each accompanied by the whispering bodies. The governor kept pace, its golden eyes knowing, its belly low to the ground. All pretence at being friendly had gone.

See what we really are, its eyes said, know what we can do, how many we are, how we move as one. John swallowed panic. He wouldn't be taking those forty-three steps again, no matter what Carter said, or the aliens would have behaved as they had with Carter, not this massing entity that seemed one and not many. The darkness loomed around him, sinister in its starkness.

They stopped at a line of six clear cubicles. Taz was led into the nearest one. John tried to follow, but Barath'na prevented him. He had to watch, helpless, as the door to the cubicle swung closed, stopping Sammy from entering after Taz.

"Your bot will be returned once security is complete," the governor said in its translated voice.

Security? John looked around the room, saw a couple of cameras and nothing else. He assumed in the main prison there would be more; Carter hadn't stopped going on about how high-tech it was, after all.

"Come." A Barath'na's claws encircled his wrist, propelling him forward. He tried to pull out of the grip, but it tightened, twisting his skin so he sucked in a yell. The edge of the claw was sharp enough to make him wince; it could slice if it wanted to. A noise came from Taz's cubicle, loud, like an alarm.

"What's going on?" John demanded, trying to free his arm, but he was pushed into the cubicle beside Taz's. The door closed behind him, muffling the alarm a little. "What is this place?!" His breathing was loud in the enclosed space, rattling with fear. Three of the walls were clear, the other the alien dark grey metal, and he pressed against the glass, trying to see Taz's cubicle, but couldn't.

<TAKE OFF YOUR SHIRT>

The order appeared to come from the cubicle itself, not through any speakers. John crossed his arms; the alien bastards could fuck off and die.

A whine screeched through the cubicle and he yelled, bringing his hands to his ears. It got worse, making his head thump and eyes water.

"Stop!" he yelled. His ears were going to burst. Spikes of pain hit his face, making him close his eyes. They got quicker and stronger, each a separate agony. He spun, trying to escape, but they followed him, coming from each side of the cubicle. They hit his hands when he brought them over his face. "Jesus! Stop!"

His t-shirt: that's what they'd said. *Quickly.* He let his jacket drop and trailed the t-shirt over his head. The needles and noise stopped. He fell against the side of the cubicle, drinking in the silence. The governor passed the glass opposite. It met his gaze, eyes sparkling with what looked like amusement. John balled his t-shirt up and threw it on the floor, glaring back. *Bastard.*

A shriek filled the air, one he knew. *Taz.* He snatched at the door of his cubicle, tugging, but it didn't give. The scream stopped, bitten off. The silence was worse.

"Taz?" he called. There was no answer except a droning noise behind him. He turned to see a clamp unfolding from the metal wall.

"What the fuck?!" The clamp grabbed his right arm, just above the elbow, tight, encircling. Sweat broke across his forehead. Another scream sounded from Taz, a pain-filled cry he knew from the night on the Cave Hill.

"Taz!" he yelled. "What's happening?"

Muffled words came back, but he couldn't make them out. He kicked the glass. Whatever was going on, he didn't want to be next. A second lever extended from the metal wall, its tip formed into a small blowtorch, its blue needle of flame angled at him. Suddenly, Taz's screams made sense. John fought the clamp holding him, but there was nowhere to go.

"Jesus!" yelled John. "Get that thing away from me."

The flame touched his shoulder. *Shit, it hurt.* He tried to free his arm, wrenching his elbow, but the burner pressed down.

"Get it off me!" he yelled. It kept going, sinking into his flesh. He scrunched his eyes closed. He wouldn't let the alien bastards see him cry. A burning smell filled the cubicle and made him gag. He bit his lips, holding his scream back, sure he'd give in at any moment and join Taz. A moment later the burner pulled away, leaving pain writhing through his muscles, snaking down to his wrist. He gritted his teeth against a groan. *Bastards.*

The cubicle stood in silence for a moment. There were Barath'na outside, all around the glass walls. He glared at them.

"No!" Taz's shout wasn't muffled this time. "Enough! Stop."

"Oh, Jesus." A clunking noise made John tense. *What now?* A new lever detached from the wall, holding something small and round. It extended to his shoulder and touched his wound, bringing the burning into sharp focus. Sweat bathed him, running down his torso, trickling onto his stomach muscles. The lever deposited something cold into the laser-burned hole, and this time there was no holding his scream back. It joined Taz's, rising and falling in sickening pain.

Another lever extended, and he cringed away. Taz had gone silent and that was worse than his screams; anything could have happened. He could be dead.

"Stop!" John shouted as the lever touched his arm. "I haven't done anything!"

Cool, blessed relief. A probe closed the wound, and when it finished the clamp released his arm. The probe moved to his elbow, taking away the pain. He put his head back. The levers sank into the wall and the metal reformed, smooth and unblemished.

Let it be over. He brought his shaking hands up and wiped his cheeks. *Open the cubicle, get me out of here.* Whatever was in the main prison had to be better than this. The governor padded past, sending a smug look. John watched it, throat tight with anger. *If I get the chance I'll take the alien bastard apart...*

At a beep, a screen above the door, like those on a train displaying the next station, came to life, a single red dot flashing on and off. *Now what?*

<PARTICIPANT ANGER LEVEL: HIGH: BASE READING CONFIRMED>

A chair extended and he didn't need to be told to sit; Christ only knew how they would force him to. The walls went opaque, changing to a soft green, which faded into blue. Music, dreamlike and soft, filled the cubicle. A smell like Ma's washing wafted over him. His shoulder stopped aching, a slight tingling the only sign of what had happened. He closed his eyes. He was knackered; he hadn't realised until now just how much.

A small beep woke him and he glanced at the screen: <PARTICIPANT ANGER LEVEL: LOW: RESTING BASE READING CONFIRMED>

Now, what the hell did that mean? The walls changed back to clear and the one in front of him slid open.

<SECURITY MEASURES COMPLETE. STEP FORWARD>

He walked into a second, annexed cubicle, and picked up the black trousers and an orange t-shirt, so bright it could have been taken off one of the stalls set up for the Twelfth of July parades. Did the aliens know he was a Prod? They knew everything else about him. He wondered if Taz's was green for good measure.

Taz? Where was *he?* He craned his neck, looking through the glass, and saw a flurry of movement a few feet away. Taz was surrounded by a swarm of Barath'na, his heels dug in, his face contorted in a scream.

Didn't they know Taz was sick? Hadn't the governor told them? John banged on the glass, frantic and loud, but the only response was a tingle in his shoulder.

"Let me out!" he shouted. He watched, helpless, as Taz was forced to the ground. Grey bodies ran over him. Claws

91

gripped his legs and arms, slithering over his skin as he tried to buck free. A hypodermic needle extended.

John banged on the glass, hoping to get Taz's attention. He had to stop fighting. His shoulder buzzed, worse this time, his flesh rippling around the implant. *I have to stop this.* The glass couldn't be unbreakable, he just had to fight harder. He shoved it with his good shoulder, trying to topple it, trying to do anything.... The needle plunged into Taz's arm.

John drew his foot back, bracing to roundhouse the cubicle. Dimly, he heard a metallic whine, but ignored it. His shoulder was burning. The screen over the door had changed to flashing red, reflecting off the glass, turning the cubicle into a crazy disco. A pin pricked his arm, and a needle retracted.

"No!" He pulled his leg back, but stopped as a rush of euphoria washed through him. His muscles relaxed and a smile broke across his face. He could see Taz being attended to, but it didn't matter. The red line became a single dot. He put his hand flat against the glass, woozy.

<CHANGE CLOTHES>

That's why he was here. He pulled off his trousers. The aliens were watching him, but he didn't care. He picked up the new pair and looked at them. *How did they go on again?* After a moment he figured it out and pulled them on, fumbling at the buttons. He lifted the t-shirt. The orange was a-maz-ing, like the sun in the evening. He'd never seen better, he was sure of it. He pulled it on and stood, swaying, watching as Taz stumbled to his feet.

The Barath'na backed away, their movements smooth, in tandem with each other. His friend was docile, his face blank and relaxed. John pulled on his boots; they, like everything else, fitted perfectly. He did the laces up easily enough; whatever they'd given him was wearing off as quickly as it had hit.

The door opened and he stepped out, shaking the last of the dizziness away. He waited, too freaked-out to take any initiative. Not if it led to more of the cubicle-treatment.

"John?" Taz's voice was slurred. "You okay?"

He shook his head. "Jesus..." He checked Taz up and down, and he looked as shaken as John felt. "What was that about?"

"Dunno." Taz sounded stunned.

Barath'na shepherded John to stand in front of a cargo door. The prison. He started to shake, with anger more than shock; they'd managed him, made him obey them. The one thing he'd said wouldn't happen to him, that he'd always resist, and he'd been forced to give in on the first day. *Some brave guy I am.*

The cargo door started to open. Whatever lay in Inish Carraig was ahead. John forced himself to stop shaking, to wait and face it. *God, give me strength.* His shoulder buzzed and he tensed. It buzzed again, insistent, and the doors opened fully.

"Step through."

He put his free hand on Taz's elbow, and they walked forwards into the prison, their bots in tow.

CHAPTER EIGHTEEN

Josey's stomach growled at the smell of chicken soup filling the room. She opened her eyes but the bright sunlight hurt, and when she turned her head it pounded in protest. A blond bloke of about eighteen sat beside the bed, flicking through a magazine, which he put down with a smile. "Well, well, you're awake." He went to the door and yelled, "Mam!"

There was the sound of someone on the stairs and an older woman – maybe about fifty – came in. She put her hand on Josey's forehead.

"Your temperature's better," she said, smiling. "You had us worried for a while." She fussed around, patting Josey's pillow into shape. "Do you want to try and sit up, love? See if you can take a wee drop of soup, or a bit of water? You must be awful hungry."

At the mention of the soup, Josey's stomach rumbled and she tried to say yes. It didn't work – her lips felt like they were glued together – so she nodded instead. The woman nudged the blond lad.

"Sean, go and get a bowl of soup for the child. And a bit of soft bread."

After he left, she helped Josey sit up and take a sip of water. The room swung alarmingly, making Josey sure she'd be sick, but it passed and she managed to croak, "Where am I?"

"Hush, we'll get to all that. Sean and his Da found you in one of the paddocks. Lucky they did, too, another wee while and you'd have frozen. Do you have a name, pet?"

"Jos–" She stopped herself and coughed. She had no idea where she was, or if the woman could be trusted. In Belfast, half the city were on the take, looking after themselves and not others. "I can't remember."

The woman didn't appear to notice anything out of

place. Josey looked around; the room was nice and airy. It was painted blue, and looked like it needed freshened, but there was no bomb damage. She blinked. *No bomb damage at all?* After Belfast, it seemed like a miracle.

"Please, where am I?"

"Just outside Coleraine, love." The woman sat on the end of the bed. "Now, tell me where you're from and we'll take you home. Your mum must be worried."

Sean came back, carrying a small tray holding a mug and some bread, which he set on the bed for her. He glanced at his ma, having evidently heard the end of the conversation, and waited.

Josey looked down, suddenly not hungry. She tried to think what to say. She couldn't tell them she was from Belfast; they'd send her back, and then Gary would find her. She bit her lip. If she waited until she was a bit stronger, she could leave. *And go where?* She ignored the thought; she'd think of something. The silence stretched as they waited for her answer, and finally she picked up the spoon, and half-shrugged.

"I don't remember," she said. "I can't remember anything about me."

Sean crossed his arms. "You don't remem–"

Josey's cheeks burned and tears welled up in her eyes. She shook her head, but couldn't speak past the tightness in her throat. If she'd learned nothing else from her year in Belfast, she knew to trust no one. To throw that away just because someone seemed kind was stupid. To allow anyone to know she was from Belfast and give them the chance to send her back wasn't a chance she could take. Silence was her only safety.

His mum stood up. "Ssh, now, she's upset. Let the child get something to eat and a wee bit of time to think, then she might tell us."

Sean went to say something else, but his mother's scowl stopped him. She shooed him from the room, following, but stopped at the door.

"The GC have lists of who lives where, and you're not registered for here. We need to get you back to where you are listed." A shadow of what looked like fear crossed her face.

"They check, see. Even out here in the country, they send Barath'na patrols."

She left and Josey watched the door and the empty hall beyond. Registration lists? She had no idea what that meant. Maybe they were clearing the ghettoes. Maybe everyone had been sent to the country, and made to work. And what did she mean by Barath'na patrols – the aliens hadn't come to Earth. The questions whirled, with no answers.

She took another mouthful of soup and started to feel full. And tired. She set the tray to the side and slid down the bed, pulling the covers over her. *Later.* She'd think about it all later. She drifted away, warm, half dreaming. Something shimmered at the edge of her memory, something about people John was with who couldn't be bribed. She needed to remember... sleep took her, and the memory left with it.

CHAPTER NINETEEN

ohn followed the governor into a second cavern of grey walls and floor. This one stretched the length of the annex, unbroken and empty, except for one end of the room, set up as a dining area. Its regimented tables and servery counter at least hinted at others' presence.

Their footsteps echoed: his and Taz's booted and dull, the governor's nails sharper and quicker. Scurrying sounds from behind indicated the remaining Barath'na were following, and he barely resisted the urge to look back. A hissing noise made him tense: the Barath'na horde streamed across the floor to staircases that led to upper levels. They flowed up the stairs, some low to the floor, some loping like wolves, all fast and with a single purpose. Their tails thudded off the stairs, heavy and slow compared to the rest of their movement. Something in the way the tails moved, like entities apart from their owners, turned his stomach.

A clang in the distance made John jump. His shoulder gave a sharp bolt of pain, and he stumbled forwards. He'd never felt so spaced out. Even in Belfast, where he'd been scared half the time and petrified the rest, he'd come to know what to expect. Here, surrounded by creatures he didn't understand, in an environment that felt more alien than anywhere on Earth should be, he hadn't a clue. The governor sent a knowing look his way. *Bastard.* John straightened and tried to force his fear away but it lay deep in his belly, gnawing and cold.

They climbed one of the metal staircases to a corridor lined in black doorways, one of four forming a square overlooking the main room. The staircase led to more corridors above, it seemed.

The Barath'na swarm spread through the corridors, two guarding the top of each staircase, the others patrolling, their clicking claws setting his teeth on edge. The prison was otherwise silent, no voices, no televisions, nothing to say how many people were held, or where they were. One of the doorways fizzed as John passed. He put his hand out and touched the black entranceway. A stinging sensation made him jerk his hand away. Some sort of force field? He followed, cradling his arm, until they reached two open-doored cells, near the end of the row. The governor jerked its head at Taz. "Enter."

Just Taz: they were going to be separated. John choked fear. He'd go mental on his own; he needed Taz to talk to, to listen to, hell, just to argue with. And if Taz woke in the night screaming, who was going to tell him to shut up and go back to sleep? He couldn't let the governor separate them.

"No," said John. His voice was croaked and weak, and he hated himself for it. "We ... we'd like to share a cell."

"Enter." The governor's voice took on a different edge, a warning tone. Six Barath'na approached on all fours, their bellies almost touching the ground. They got to within a couple of feet and pulled onto their hind legs, releasing weapons strapped over their chests. As they continued to approach, their mobility seemed unaffected; their stance was balanced, almost graceful. He backed away. His shoulder gave a stab of pain, down to his elbow, and he cried out. He didn't know what to do – fight or run. Damn it, he needed to know how things worked. He met Taz's eyes, trapped, and opened his hands in a plea for advice.

"All right!" Taz stepped into the cell and raised his arms. "I'm in. No problem." He looked at John. "It'll be all right. At least your snoring won't keep me awake." Sammy followed and cowered by his right foot, and the governor gave a satisfied nod.

The force field came up, slowly, cutting off the sight of Taz's feet and knees, then his stomach and chest. It rose up his face, erasing his fuck-you-if-you-think-you-can-get-to-me smile. At the last moment he gave a wink. The force field closed; Taz was gone.

The governor indicated the next cell, and John walked past, striving for coolness. "Yeah, yeah, I got it."

The force field rose before him, filling the doorway, and

he tried to smile but it felt like a grimace. Taz was the master of smiling through crap, not John. The governor's eyes were focused on him, meltingly dangerous. Sweat broke between his shoulders. The force field sealed, and only then did John take a shuddering breath. He sank onto the edge of the small bunk. Jimmy gave a soft beep, worried and careful, and John managed to smile – it would seem he wasn't the only one freaked out. He picked the bot up, enjoying the solidness of its body, and stretched out on the bed.

He zoned out. The throbbing in his arm died away. Dimly, he was aware of the light in the cell fading but he didn't move. He was too tired or shocked or fucked off to care. Besides, it wasn't like he was pressed for time.

Eventually, hunger made him sit up. They had to feed him sometime, right? A small, slitted window showed the sky darkening towards night, a single line of orange against black the last reminder of the day. One section of the wall showed a line of green, steady and unwavering: another of the screens he'd seen in the cubicle. He got up and put his hands out and the lights came on, dazzling him. He hissed and covered his eyes.

He grew used to the light. A small desk stood against the opposite wall. On it was a sandwich, a banana and a glass of milk, like he was fourteen again and had a lunch packed by his ma. He was hungry enough not to care, and ate the sandwich in a couple of bites. He lifted the banana, went to peel it, but stopped, his instincts from Belfast still in place. How did he know when he'd get fed again? Best to be prepared for the worst. Besides, some hunger in his belly would keep his wits about him.

He started to tour the tiny cell. A chest of drawers was quickly checked out – a couple of changes of clothes, the same as he had on. The single door along one wall slid open to a small bathroom. Alien bogs: he had to see this. Sadly, the toilet was disappointingly normal, but when he touched the metal seat it was soft and dough-like, not at all as solid as it appeared. At least his butt wouldn't get cold.

He went back into the cell. The walls were of the alien dull silver metal, much like the toilet. And the cubicle with its hidden levers and blow-torches. He touched one of the walls and his finger sank to the end of his nail, the hard metal changing form into something solid but pliable.

"Jesus!" He pulled his finger out and looked at it. It was unmarked. Tentatively, he put his palm against the wall and the metal shaped around it, reforming under his touch. It made him feel queasy, for no reason other than walls should stay solid, not hide things within their surface or suck his hand in. He touched it again, and the metal gave until he released his hand. The wall sprang back, slowly filling in the shape of his hand and returning to its solid state of hardened plasticine. Urgh. Metal shouldn't *do* that. He looked at the tiled floor and gave an experimental bounce; it was reassuringly hard.

He turned, slowly, taking in the walls, all of the same metal, the desk, the bunk, and nothing else. No telly. No game console. Nothing to distract him from the ever-present hum of the force field and the fact he was a prisoner. He'd have thumped his head off the wall, except the thought of metal filling his nose and throat made him shudder. He bet *that* thought would come back in the wee small hours and he'd wake sinking into the wall, choking, drowning. That, or the Barath'na creeping across the rock, their eyes watchful.

He sat on the bed and Jimmy propulsed itself up beside him. Its central antenna rose, as if waiting.

"So," said John, mostly to break the silence. "Your island map was pretty off-beam."

The bot flashed once, but didn't drop its antenna. John frowned. He was able to read Jimmy pretty well now; the bot didn't think it *had* been wrong.

"All right, then, bring it up again."

Jimmy gave a soft beep and his light-antenna projected an image onto the wall. John got up, ready to trace his finger along it like he had last night, follow the hills and the path along the top of the island that linked two lighthouses, and ask Jimmy which part of the map matched where they were.

He touched the wall, tracing the square, featureless map. As he moved his hand, a block raised from the centre of the projection, forming under him. He snatched his hand away and squinted at the wall. He touched it, and the metal shaped under him again. He traced the raised section, feeling the stark lines replacing the map Jimmy had shown him last night.

It was the prison, he realised. He ran his finger along its edge. It fitted snugly into the cuboid projection of the island. He reached the first corner and saw a single tower standing to the prison's right. He touched it. The metal responded, rising out of the wall a good couple of inches into a facsimile of a lighthouse. *Bloody hell.* He looked at Jimmy. "Are you doing this?"

An affirmative beep. John shook his head, trying to take it in. Carter had said the bots were GC approved, and the metal was of alien creation – maybe Jimmy could interact with the alien habitat. John let go of the lighthouse and it sank back down. He traced the prison's shape again. This was nothing like the map Jimmy had shown yesterday.

He stared at the bot. It flashed its light. The bot had changed the map based on what it had seen? Or had it learned the new information from the prison itself? He had no idea, but somehow the bot knew that Rathlin had been replaced with Inish Carraig. John leaned closer and ran his hand over the map, focusing on the building itself. It changed, became three-dimensional, showing the structure.

"Can you show inside?" he asked. "Call it a design project?"

The map changed, zooming in on the detail. He felt his way around the prison. The entrance hall he'd come through – the one holding the cubicles from hell – was marked, and then the darkened main chamber. At one end of the chamber was the canteen, at the other a small, enclosed room. When John touched it, ridges formed under his fingers, line after line of them. A library, he decided.

He got Jimmy to go up through the prison, and traced the floor he was on, and the one above, which followed the same layout. Beyond that level, Jimmy didn't project information.

He counted the cells across the first and second floors. Twenty-five down each side, one hundred per floor: two hundred. Catherine had said there were six hundred prisoners. He looked around, confirming the cell wasn't a double used as a single. Fear curled, cramping his stomach.

The lights went off. He waved his arms, but they stayed off. It was creepy with the room closed off from the rest of the prison, silent and dark. His shoulder twinged and he put his hand over the implant, rubbing it. He stared into the dark; something was very, very wrong in Inish Carraig.

CHAPTER TWENTY

eters pointed his cue at the top pocket. "Yellow."
Carter shook his head. "No way is that going in; you can't even see it."

The sergeant shrugged and leaned over the cue, a cigarette held in his back hand as he lined the shot up. Carter's nose twitched; he'd liked the smoking ban, and the sooner the GC put it back in place, the better. He frowned at that thought. The smoking ban was a local matter, nothing to do with the GC. So why the hell had he thought of them? Anyway, there were more pressing matters than smoking in the barracks' rec-room: hospitals, schools, completing the citizen registration.

His frown deepened; the registrations must be almost complete. His own parents had been visited last week, their farm estate checked over and house searched for weapons. Dad's .22 rifle had been confiscated even though it was legally held and stored in accordance with regulations. Quite what they thought his elderly father was going to do with it other than shoot foxes...

There was a dull click and Peters straightened up, smiling. The ball rolled up the table, sinking into the pocket, and Carter shook his head in disgust; why he'd agreed to play the Alex Higgins of the Royal Irish, he had no idea. In fact, he shouldn't even be here, he should be down at the station, filing a report about the prison. "Good shot," he said.

Peters leaned down and looked at the table, squinting to assess if a red was pottable. "The boys," he said, drawing on his cigarette. "How bad did the prison seem?"

Carter paused for a moment, trying to find the words. This was why he'd come here straight from Rathlin; Peters was the only other who'd known the lads and gave any kind of a shit that they were gone.

103

"Grim." He made a face. "Like something out of a nightmare. It comes out of the fog - and you know up there, it's either sunny, or you can't see your own hand through the rain - and looms over you. And the governor..."

He perched on the end of the snooker table, leaned his head against his cue, gripping it tighter than he needed to, and waited while Peters lined up his next shot. Behind Peters an old black-and-white television showed some sort of talk-show, its sound low and muffled.

"What about him?" asked Peters.

"Him? We only have their word for that. I mean, how do you sex them?"

Peters grinned. "How do you ever sex a dog?"

Carter frowned at that. "So far none of them have taken a piss in front of me."

"Not like that. Teats." Peters pulled the cue back, shot, and the red dropped. "Look closely, next time. You can't see it easily under the fur, and not at all when they're wearing their ammo coats, but the females have teats." He pointed at the black with his cue. "Middle pocket."

"Can I concede?"

"No, just sit there and take your medicine."

Peters whistled as he prepared to take the shot, this time with the cigarette dangling from his lips. That, decided Carter, was just showing off.

"So," the sergeant went on, his words tight around the cigarette, "what are you going to do?"

"I'm not sure yet."

The cue kicked off the white, the sound like a dull crack, and Peters swore.

"Stand aside," said Carter. He leaned down, aimed, and the cue ball went into the middle pocket. Gracefully, though, with no hesitation.

Peters smacked his shoulder, just a shade too hard. "You know, normally I'd tell someone to keep practising and they'd get better. You, though..."

Carter straightened up. "Thanks for that." He lowered his voice. "I'm thinking that I'll go up on Sunday, and talk to the lads in private; find out a bit more about what goes on in there." He set the cue up against the wall, not giving up, exactly, more accepting he wouldn't get another chance to return to the table. "It felt wrong, leaving them. The governor took the boys, and they vanished into the entranceway, like they were being absorbed by it. Does that make any sense?"

"A bit, yeah."

Carter glanced at the sergeant. Peters, for all his faults – the yellow sailed in, and the cue ball fell perfectly for the green – was one of the most astute people he knew.

"What's your take on things?" he asked.

Peters sank the green and turned around, leaning against the table. He took his time – another thing Carter liked about him – and then said, "Honestly? It makes me uncomfortable. The whole set up, not just the prison. Most of my orders come on GC letterheads these days. I can't deny they've been very efficient, they've done everything they said they would. But..." He looked up at the ceiling, and then slowly, as if every word was being dragged out of him, said, "At least the Zelo were working with us, if that makes sense? Not just telling us what to do."

Carter nodded, trying to keep his face impassive. For Peters to say that things might be worse under the GC, well –

Things were worse. "Yeah, it makes sense."

He waited while Peters potted the brown, and racked up the points. 87-3. *Damn.* Peters sunk the blue and pink in quick succession, and Carter lifted the black, putting it in the hole nearest him. 105-3; better than last time, anyway.

"What the fuck's happening now?" Peters strode to the television set and turned the sound up. The chat show had been replaced by a head-and-shoulders shot of a grim-faced newsreader.

"Please wait for an announcement by Vorgleen Vicoar, head of the GC peacekeeping force on Earth."

"With a name like that, he's not from down the road," said Peters.

Carter smiled, sobering at a small rustle of static. A new voice – obviously from a translator unit – filled the room, and the face of a Barath'na appeared on the screen.

"This is an announcement on behalf of the president of

the Galactic Council. Investigations into the origin of the virus have uncovered new evidence. This evidence, which is robust and fully auditable, proves that the virus' compound structure was Earthen in origin."

Carter and Peters exchanged a look. Peters shook his head.

"The Earth authorities have been relieved of their planetary duties, and a GC-appointed governance has been put in place. All Earth military personnel are required to report to their GC representative." The screen went blank.

"Fuck," said Peters. His voice sounded stunned.

"Jesus," managed Carter.

"What do we do?"

"What they say: report in."

Peters' hand moved to his shotgun. He shook his head. "No way. Work for the aliens? You might be prepared to, I'm not."

"Phil, you have a family. If you don't do what they say, you'll end up reported or on a list. One you won't want to be on."

The sergeant was still staring at the screen, as if hoping a new announcement might come.

"Look, all it'll do is change the command structure; you'll still be doing the same job. They need the military."

He didn't even know if it was true, but the sergeant turned and faced Carter. "I don't have to like it."

"No." Carter lifted his jacket, and pulled it on, ignoring the low feeling of fear in his stomach. "No one has to like it."

CHAPTER TWENTY-ONE

The kitchen stool rocked as Josey climbed onto it and pulled Sean's t-shirt over her knees; it was so big his ma, Paula, had knotted it at the bottom. The trousers she wore were his long shorts, tied tight, and they looked weird, but she didn't care. It was good to be up, even if she did feel shivery.

"Another five minutes until it's all systems go," said Paula. She was chopping onions and garlic and the smell made Josey's eyes water a bit, but she didn't care. It reminded her of being with her own ma. She used to do her homework when Ma made the tea – and when Da made it, too, but that usually involved the smoke alarm and a lot of swear words. The familiarity of it pulled at something deep inside her, something she'd buried. Sean's ma didn't wear nail varnish, where her own ma had loved a deep red colour and had spent time every night fixing her nails. And their perfume wasn't the same, nor was Paula thin and fashionable, but a bit chubby in her jeans and sloppy jumper. Josey wanted Ma so much that tears started to brim.

"You okay, love?" asked Paula.

"It's the onions." Josey wiped her eyes with the back of her hand. It might be the onions, for all she knew.

The kitchen light pinged on, one of the old-fashioned fluorescent tubes. It took a few moments to come on fully, and it hummed when it did. Paula turned the oven on and put a pot on the ring, glugging oil into it, her hands working fast, moving from task to task. She went to the door and leaned out.

"Sean! Tell your dad the power's on." She smiled at Josey. "We get two hours in the afternoon and one in the evening. Next week we're going up to six hours a day when they repair the power station. It was taken out during the invasion."

She cooked while she talked, throwing onions into the pot and putting a chicken, already prepared, into the oven. Josey's mouth watered at the sight of it. A whole chicken. Sean had bartered it for some milk with another farm down the road. That was how they'd got through the invasion, he'd said. There might not have been bombs, but there'd been shortages, and it had been rough enough. He'd said the last as if challenging her, but she'd kept her mouth shut. She wasn't being tricked into saying who she was, even if she could tell him some things about surviving the invasion that would kick a few shortages into touch. Like bin-hoking, or taking your little brother and sister scavenging when Liz wasn't around to help, jumping at every shadow.

Paula glanced up from the pot. Whatever she was making smelled good. "Will your school miss you?"

"School?" It felt like a foreign word.

Paula frowned. "You aren't going to school?"

"Yeah," said Josey, " 'course I am." The lie was obvious, even to her own ears. "We're on half-term." She paused, knowing she shouldn't say anything else, but she had to know. "Do you have schools round here? I'd heard they'd had to close in places like Belfast." She hoped it sounded nonchalant; she didn't think it had.

"I heard *life* stopped in parts of Belfast," said Paula. Josey held her breath – *don't give anything away* – and Paula went on, "The kids here use the primary school in the village. All the bigger kids go there, too, although they're planning to get the secondary schools open, now we've petrol and can take them into Coleraine." She put a pot of potatoes on to boil and said, all casual-like, "Was it very bad in Belfast, love?"

It was out. Josey paused, caught in headlights. Lie or tell the truth? Her shoulders slumped; it was obvious Paula knew. She nodded, and this time, when Paula handed her a bit of kitchen roll, she couldn't blame the onions.

"I can't talk about it," she said, truthfully. If she said either of the kids' names, she'd break down. Or John's. She ducked her head. Here, in the quiet kitchen, surrounded by familiar smells, the enormity of the invasion hit her. Her family, her life, her parents: everything was gone, and she'd done nothing wrong. Liz had been shot and dumped in the boot of a car. Her own parents' bodies had been taken away and she didn't know where they'd been buried, or even if they had been. She lifted her head. Tears were streaming now, and she gulped out, "Why did the Zelo come?"

"They came because they wanted our planet," Paula said. She kept her voice matter-of-fact, giving no false sympathy, and Josey was glad. She didn't want sympathy, she just wanted things to be right.

"But it was ours," Josey said.

"They wanted hatching grounds. That's why they attacked the cities, and not here. But they cut our power, and stopped our fuel and food. Maybe they thought it would be a cheaper way to kill us. Starvation gets everyone in the end." She popped up on the stool next to Josey's, and lifted a blonde strand from Josey's face. "We'll get your hair cut tomorrow. Then I'll be able to see you properly. Can you tell me your name yet?"

Josey shook her head. She trusted Paula, a bit, but... she'd trusted John to come home, and she'd trusted Liz to be the adult and know what to do. She rocked back, away from Paula. The only person she could trust was herself.

Paula sighed and got up. "Anyway, the new aliens – the Barath'na – they're putting things back together. Mrs McKay, she broke her leg last summer and we set it as best we could, but she was still limping. Her family took her to the new hospital in Derry a couple of weeks ago, and her leg was fixed. She said it didn't hurt, that it only took a few hours, and now she's walking better than before she broke it. The doctors are scanning people for illnesses, using some of the Barath'na technology, picking up early diagnoses and treating them. We're due ours in a couple of weeks."

"So we have alien doctors?" asked Josey.

"No, love. Do you think I'd want their great paws all over me?" Paula shuddered. "I mean, they seem very nice and all that, but – you know.... There are limits. The medical staff are humans, it's just the technology that's new. It's part of the Barath'na approach: to make us better equipped, more knowledgeable." She gave a wicked grin. "Lord knows how we'll be milking the cows in a year. Sonic pumps?"

She talked on and on, about the new housing estates being built, and schools. It sounded good. Josey wondered if all this would have reached them in Belfast, and she supposed it might have done. Eventually, after the rest of the world had been sorted. She swung her legs, thinking. The Barath'na were aliens, too, but they didn't need hatcheries. They had no reason to help. "Paula?"

"Yes, love?"

"Why are the Barath'na here?"

Paula wiped the surfaces. "I suppose because the GC said they had to be."

"But why? The GC said they had to keep Earth safe and help to rebuild." Sean had told her that. He'd also described all their spaceships. She'd dozed off eventually – he was as bad as John about rugby. "But they don't have to give us all the stuff you're describing. They don't need to knock down our houses to build new ones. Only the bombed places need that."

Paula stopped wiping. She looked older than Josey had noticed before. She wrung out her cloth, not meeting Josey's eyes, and it took a moment before Josey realised she wasn't going to answer. In fact, Josey didn't think she had an answer.

CHAPTER TWENTY-TWO

The morning sun cut through distant, pink-tinged clouds scudding in the wind: sailors' warning, a storm was coming. John touched the cell's window. He wanted to break the glass and feel the freshness of the wind.

Fuck it, there was no hope, stuck in here. He turned, tripped on something, and hurtled forwards, arms spinning for balance. "God, Jimmy, watch where you're sitting!" A bolt of pain shot from his shoulder in tandem with his racing heart and he clamped his hand over his shoulder, holding it tight like that might stop the pain, and scowled. He hated this place.

A line of pain – clear, precise, driven along his nerves – reached his wrist. He bit back a yell and tightened his hand over the implant. Bloody hell, it hurt.

The line in the display over the door changed from green to amber, and another bolt shot from his shoulder, making cold realisation dawn. The *implant* was the high-tech monitoring Carter had gone on and on about? He took a deep breath, calming himself, and the line went back to green. *Bastards.* He couldn't even be pissed off in private. It turned back to amber and his muscles spasmed against fresh pain. He glared at the line, but found himself taking deep breaths to keep it from hurting until the green light returned.

The force field's buzz ended and the field fell as it had come up: slowly, draining the inky darkness covering the doorway. Relief flooded him at the thought of getting out of the cell. Without company, it had been the loneliest night he'd spent, worse than any in Belfast. The field came fully down to reveal the corridor beyond and the grey metal walls of the prison, a match for those of his cell.

"Stay, Jimmy," he said. It had been made clear by Carter that the bot must be kept in his cell or it would have to go, and he couldn't lose Jimmy. It was the only thing that was

111

actually his. He had none of the sports glory his teachers had been sure lay ahead for him: no house bought for his parents; no red Ferrari; not even sex and heaven with Katy Perry. Just a cell in a prison he'd put himself in, and the bot.

Jimmy sank to the floor, and John stepped into the corridor. It was crowded with blokes bunched together, smelling of soap and sweat. He put his elbows out, fighting for space, panicking a little as he tried to slow and check Taz's cell but was pulled along by those around him.

John ducked through a gap between two men, both taller and older than him, and reached the landing of the metal staircase. He pushed through to the corner and held the metal railing. Only now he had space did he notice his arm throbbing, the implant spasming against his muscle. He took a deep breath and waited until it eased.

Three other staircases, one from each side of the room, fed into the main room below. He craned his neck back; the staircase led beyond the mens' tier to the womens', the two lines converging in a conflux of bodies. Further up, a third floor had another series of cells, most with darkened entrances. No prisoners came down from it.

A final staircase stood against the back wall of the prison, stretching to a force field door on the top, fourth, tier. Two Barath'na, both armed, stood in front of the door, their eyes sweeping over the crowd below. At the bottom of the steps a swarm kept watch, risen on their haunches, their sharp eyes flicking between the streams of prisoners. One of them caught John watching, and drew its lips back in a slashed, bared warning. John looked away, down to the dining area below, but couldn't stop himself glancing back at the alien. It was still watching him, its eyes menacing, its teeth sharp.

"John!" Taz was making his way down the final flight of stairs.

John pushed his way through, ducking under arms and ignoring curses cast his way. He caught Taz's arm. "How you doing?"

"Like shit. I didn't sleep." Taz was shaking a little, and his face was pale. "I woke from a nightmare with my shoulder and arm on fire."

"It's the implant," said John. "Mine's been doing the same."

"Yeah, the shoulder is, but not the rest of the pain." Taz looked unutterably sad. "Even my bones hurt."

"Maybe yesterday set you back. It set me back about three years." John bit his lip, feeling more helpless than ever. If Taz wasn't well, who should he get help from? He thought of the aliens guarding the door to the fourth floor and tried to imagine going up to them and demanding help. His blood chilled at the very idea. He glanced at Taz; it hadn't come to that yet. Maybe after Taz had breakfast, he'd feel better.

He followed the crowd to the food counter and took the chance to look around the room now it was lit up. At one end was a library; at the other a door led to the outside, letting a tiny bit of wind shift the air. He wanted to stand on his tiptoes, to be taller than everyone else, and get a proper gulp of it. A giant screen, filled with green and amber lines, dominated one of the two longest walls. Below it, closed, stood the door he'd been brought through yesterday, the one that led to the entrance hall from hell.

This was it? Didn't prisons have TVs and computer games? Rec-rooms? His da used to complain about that when he was reading the paper. John could hear his voice, even now – "Supposed to be a punishment, not a holiday...."

The queue shuffled forwards. A conveyor belt moved, just ahead, carrying bowls on it. The prisoners took one each and moved to the seating area, where they ate in near-silence, their bodies hunched over tables as if protecting themselves. John frowned. He didn't know much about prisons, but he'd seen plenty of films – this room should be noisy, full of angry nut-cases. And these were people who'd survived the invasion, people who knew how to look after themselves. They weren't meek and quiet; he'd learned over the last year that being meek didn't keep you alive.

He lifted one of the bowls, identified the contents as some kind of porridge, and took it to a free table. The only noises were the scrape of spoons and the odd low, murmured voice. Taz slid onto a seat opposite.

"Here goes nothing," said John. "I wonder if the aliens cook

113

as well as they freak me out." He took a mouthful. It was worse than any of the bin-hoked shite he'd been living on in Belfast. He prodded it with his spoon. "Is it just me, or is this vile?"

Taz tried it. "It's vile." He put his spoon down, took a look around and gave a short laugh. "I might have bloody known."

"What?"

"Two tables back. Mad Neeta."

John spluttered his porridge. "From the Crescent?"

"The very one."

John looked over Taz's shoulder and saw Neeta, seated in a crowd of girls. Last time he'd seen her had been when their school was evacuated, but he'd heard plenty about her, and the gang of kids she'd led, during the war. She was at the head of the table, he noted, and he smiled. She would be. His smile fell away as he looked closer and saw how her eyes were bleak. She was much thinner than he remembered her, too.

Thin or not, there was no mistaking the shower of dark hair and the set of her shoulders: Mad Neeta, indeed, the one girl at school his ma hadn't just warned him not to go near, but had promised a belting for if he did. Chain-smoking at nine round the back of the school, shoplifting at eleven, Neeta had progressed to joyriding around the time John had been picked out for rugby trials. Her family had tried everything – grounding her, even home-schooling her for several months – but whatever the other girls in her class did, Neeta Sastry went one better, as if being the baddest girl in class was better than being the only non-white Belfast native.

"Not a bit of wonder," said John. "She was a one-woman crime shop." Neeta's dark eyes widened in recognition and John ducked his head. "Shit. She saw me."

"Well, you can't exactly hide." Taz pushed his seat back, managing to hide his stiffness pretty well. Neeta was already on her way to them.

"Well, well." Her harsh Belfast voice, honed by smoking, carried over the whole dining area. Prisoners watched, making John want to squirm away from their attention. She put her hands on her hips, and stuck one out an angle. John felt a twinge of envy – it was impossible to fake a swagger like that, you had to be born to it. He knew, he'd been trying to for the last year. She lifted her chin and her eyes were devilish. "If it isn't Taz Delaney and John Dray, the heroes of the war."

Taz shook his head, whether in admiration or in disgust it was impossible to tell. Everyone in the room looked at them, making John shift in his seat. Half the prisoners were here because of their part in the riots he and Taz had caused.

John straightened his shoulders. To hell with it; the one thing Belfast had taught him was to face trouble, not wait for it to come to you.

"Hey, Neeta," he said, putting every bit of fake don't-give-a-damn he had into his voice. "I see they finally put you where you belong."

A slow grin spread over her face, and John smiled back. He'd always liked Neeta - she'd never cared what anyone thought of her, not even her family, who'd dearly wanted a well-behaved daughter to attend temple and do what she was told.

"Only the best end up here," she said. "It's such a palace, y'know?"

An inmate, a long-haired lad wearing nerdy glasses, let out a loud curse. Neeta turned away, her forearm muscles tensing, ready.

"Oh, bollocks," she said. "They're on the move."

John looked past her, towards the library. Barath'na swarmed down the stairs from the fourth floor and ran towards the dining end. He had no idea how many; a dozen, maybe more, all moving quickly, their movements fluid.

"What are they doing?" asked John.

"Who knows? Whatever they want, it won't be good." She pulled out the chair next to his and sat on it. "Keep your head down and hope they want someone else for entertainment today."

Taz gave a quick nod and followed her lead, and so did John. Neeta had always known her shit. He willed himself to passivity, and looked down at his bowl of porridge, congealed and sticky. His stomach rebelled at the sight of it.

The whisper of moving bodies was close now, the aliens' claws a staccato pattern. The urge to look was overwhelming and he did, through his eyelashes.

The swarm had reached the first tables, ignoring the prisoners they passed, all of whom stayed still, like statues. John gulped but didn't move, fighting the feeling they were closing on his table, telling himself he was wrong, that they were looking for someone else. Sweat trickled down his back as more Barath'na joined the swarm, all strong and muscular, all single-focused.

Taz: the aliens were intent on him, their eyes beating onto him, but he was turned away from them, unknowing. John watched, frightened to shout in case he was wrong and brought their attention, terrified he was right. The first, feet away, pulled onto its hind legs and reached for Taz, its clawed forelimbs flexing in and out.

"Taz!" John jumped to his feet, ignoring the jolt of pain in his arm. "Move!"

Taz looked over his shoulder and let out a yell. He managed to duck and the swiping claw missed. Another Barath'na joined the first, more catching up all the time, and its claw snagged Taz's t-shirt. He was dragged backwards, into the mass of grey bodies. He thrashed, trying to break free, but the claws were holding him, pulling him down.

John launched himself across the table. "Leave him alone!"

Barath'na homed in on him. He threw off the first claw that fell on his shoulder, but more grabbed him, insanely strong. A needle came at him and he kicked out, knocking it from the alien's claw. It fell to the floor and shattered. More claws grabbed him, tightening, tightening, their sharp tips digging into his bare arms. A trickle of blood tracked its way to his wrist.

He bucked, trying to throw them off. The display wall showed his line, red and speeding up. He ignored the pain from his implant, focused on nothing other than fighting the alien bastards and stopping them hurting Taz. He dug his heels in, straining every muscle he'd built in the gym. They were all around him now, twisting between his legs, holding his arms tight to his sides, silent in their attack.

"Bastards!" he yelled.

The Barath'na shoved him against the wall, the group

working as one, and the wall gave way under him, moulding beneath him, shifting so he sank in.

No. His nightmare of the previous night, of being held and choked by the wall, came racing back. He tried to push forwards, but the metal came around him, encasing his legs and shoulder, covering his arms so that they were forced to his sides. Around his pelvis, his chest, right up to his throat the metal moved like a creature, solid but alive. He imagined it coming up to his face, filling his mouth, him swallowing it into his stomach, choking it into his lungs. He tried to shake his head, to refuse, but he couldn't.

"Stop," he croaked, hating himself for it, but desperate to get out.

The Barath'na had drawn back, watching him. One licked the fur on its arm, grooming itself as he drowned. Another, the one from the door earlier, he would swear it, watched him without blinking.

The metal stopped spreading. He could feel it just below his lips, at the crease of his eyes, around his ears, muffling the noise of the other prisoners being led away. Neeta passed him, dragging her feet. Her eyes met his, hard but not without sympathy, and she gave a small shake of her head. No help from that quarter, then.

His shoulder sent bolt after bolt to his wrist. His line was still going crazy. He dragged in a shallow breath, sure the metal would be too heavy on his chest to let him, and then another, gasping. The room started to spin; he was going to faint, and then the metal would cover him, and there'd be no way out.

The Barath'na stepped back as one. They were going to leave him here.

"No," he said, but it was barely a whisper. The aliens left the dining area. Two escorted Taz up the stairs. He looked over his shoulder at John, but his face was passive and still, his eyes confused, all their fight gone. Another Barath'na joined them, coming from the third floor of black doorways and silence. John saw the flash of metal in its hand before the group disappeared into Taz's cell. The door darkened behind them.

The room went quiet. John gasped air down his constrained throat. Black dots appeared in his vision, spreading like ink spots in water.

<SUBJECT RESTRAINT COMPLETE>

He waited, expecting the wall to release him, but it didn't. His line stayed amber. He started to breathe a little easier; if the metal was going to cover him, surely it would have by now. He could smell it, a dull, rotting stench. He tried to flex his fingers, but there wasn't enough give.

"Let me out!" he shouted. It echoed in the empty room. Above, the Barath'na guarding the door to the fourth floor watched impassively. "Come on, let me out!"

The room remained silent. Taz's door stayed black and closed. What was happening up there? He wriggled to get free but the restraints didn't loosen, and he found himself standing, tired, and staring at the metal walls of the room.

Thoughts came at him, each worse than the last. They were going to do something to Taz. Neeta had been scared – and he'd never known her scared, ever – of what the Barath'na were doing. Sweat trickled, slick against the metal. He had to get out of here, up to the first floor, and stop them. He strained against the metal, but it didn't give.

He couldn't help Taz. He couldn't help *anyone*, not Josey, or the kids, or even himself. He hadn't been able to stop his parents dying. He was a useless mate, just like he'd been a useless son. He stared at Taz's door; if will alone could have stopped what was happening, it would have opened. Instead, it stayed black and dead and terrifying.

CHAPTER TWENTY-THREE

omeone cleared their throat. "We need to tell the GC." The voice – an older man's – was clipped. "Paula, love, I know you don't want to, but someone was down at the McCrackens' barn the other night, and we found her not far from it."

"There was a woman's body discovered today," said a younger voice. Sean, she presumed. His voice dropped to a whisper. "Tom Davies found her in a ditch. He said she'd been shot. The Galactics have been there all morning."

"How do you know?" asked his mum. "You were supposed to be working at the bottom fencing."

"I saw the transport arrive."

"You went to see the transport, you mean," said Paula.

"It doesn't matter." Sean's voice carried an edge of guilt. "The Davies' place has been shut down – no one is allowed in and out. The Barath'na were starting to go around the doors, checking registrations."

"The Davies are only five miles away," said the older man. He sounded worried. "It'll not take them long to work their way here."

Josey kept her eyes shut, the practice with Gary and his lot paying off. What would the GC do if they found her here? Would Gary have told the Barath'na that she knew they were behind the virus? The aliens had killed McDowell's gang, they weren't going to care about her.

"She's someone's wee girl; they'll be worried about her," said Paula.

"She won't tell us who she is," said the older man.

"Maybe she doesn't remember."

"She was cold, Ma; she wasn't hit on the head."

"Paula, we *have* to tell them." The voices had moved away, towards the hall. "We've nothing to hide. But if they find her here, that won't be good. For us or her."

"We don't know that! They're peacekeepers, here to look after us," said the woman. "We can't call anyway, not with the phones still down. You'd have to go into Coleraine, and we don't have the petrol to spare for that."

There was a pause, and then Sean spoke up. "I could walk. If I take the railway tracks, it's not far."

Josey's ears perked up. A railway line. If she went that way, off the main roads, she could make it away from here. Find her way back to Belfast and see if she could find Sergeant Peters. She couldn't remember the other name – had only remembered Peters' after ages of thinking about it – but was sure of his. She'd go to him and she'd be safe, and no one would know Paula had hidden her, so everyone here would be safe too. It was the only solution.

The door to the bedroom closed and she waited for the footsteps to carry on down the corridor. She swung her legs out of bed. The room swam for a moment but it wasn't as bad as yesterday, and she waited for it to pass. When it did she tiptoed to the wardrobe and pushed the doors open: tops, trousers... finally, a coat.

A couple of minutes later she looked at herself in the mirror and had to force back a giggle. As well as the shorts and t-shirt, the coat she'd pulled on drowned her. She remembered Stuart using Da's as a blanket.... Her lip quivered at the memory of him curled up, thumb in his mouth, and she had to force herself not to think about it.

Food? That was a problem; she didn't want to go downstairs. She glanced at the bedside table, saw the lunch Paula had left earlier, and picked up the bread, squashing it into her pocket. She took the cup of soup and, even though it was cold, drank it; that would keep her going. She had a look in the drawers of the little unit and was rewarded with a bar of chocolate. Finally she drank all of the glass of water, not knowing how to carry it with her.

Last thing, then: shoes. She looked at Sean's sturdy boots lined up along the bottom of the wardrobe and wanted them so badly it made her tummy feel funny, but they'd never fit. Instead, she pulled on her mud-caked sneakers. When she'd got them, she'd been dead pleased; they'd had glitter sides and lit up when she walked. Ma had said they were twice as expensive as normal trainers, and she'd better wear them enough to get their money's worth. Now the lights were long gone, the glitter obliterated by months of trekking the streets of Belfast, and the soles had started to come away from the uppers.

She stood, listening. The upstairs was quiet. Had Sean already gone? She crossed to the window and looked out, as if expecting the miracle of a railway line running through the farm, and saw a double gate in the distance, like the one where the girl in the news had crossed listening to her iPod and got hit by a train. Josey wished she had an iPod.

She lifted the window frame and squirmed out. Below was a flat roof, part of an extension. The drop was no further than theirs had been in Belfast. But if she jumped and there was anyone in the kitchen... she looked to the side, saw the drainpipe, and decided that was much more sensible. She edged towards it, glad of all the times she'd scurried across the estate, into empty houses whatever way possible, and half-jumped, half-stepped onto it. From there, she slipped down, using the sneakers' rubber soles to slow her. No wonder her shoes were ruined. She landed with a jar that went through her ankles right up to her knees, and stopped, listening. Nothing.

She took a last glance at the house and its little kitchen, not wanting to go. She'd felt safe there. It was hard to take the first step, easier to take the next. This wasn't her place. She ran across the farmyard, keeping to the shadows, and reached the double gates, but they were only a farm gate.

She bit her lip. Which way? In the distance, a small footbridge took her attention and she smiled, setting off for it. Finding her way back: no trouble, no trouble at all. Not for Josey Dray, who'd managed to get away from Gary, who was smart enough to know who she needed to ask for, and who'd climbed down a drainpipe. She strode, confident, and even found herself singing. She saw the glint of the track ahead and ran to it. This time, not like in Carrick, she made it down the embankment without a hand stopping her. She paused. Right or left? Each had to go somewhere. Left, she decided; John was left-handed. It was as good as anything. She started to walk.

CHAPTER TWENTY-FOUR

John had no idea how long he stood. Most of the morning, anyway, long enough that all he wanted was to curl on his bunk and lick his wounds. His eyes drooped and the wall around him loosened. He hadn't been imagining it, then; when he was fighting it, the wall held him tighter.

He tried to think pleasant thoughts. Blue skies, sand... a day out with his parents and siblings... picking raspberries from the allotments and eating so many he puked pink juice. His line stayed stubbornly amber. He wasn't made for calm. He never had been – his da used to say he was only quiet when he was asleep.

The sea, the quiet sound of the sea.

Amber. *Fuck.* Breathe in, out, in, out, in, out. Amber. *Change, you bastard.*

No good. *Woodland. Birdsong. Breathe.* He closed his eyes, let the time go by. Easy, easy, easy...

Footsteps. He jerked awake, and in front of him stood Neeta. Her eyes were a glinting black, hard to read. Others streamed in from the yard, jostling for their place in the queue. Some looked over at him – a few smirked, one or two gave smiles that may have been sympathy. Neeta crossed her arms. "You spiked. You need to learn not to spike, or they target you quicker." She gave a lazy smile. "You need to let it all wash over you and get someone else targeted that day."

"Anything else you want to tell me?" he asked. "*Before I do it, this time.*"

"Ain't no joke. I've been here five weeks, I've learned."

"What are you in for?"

She puffed out her chest. She wasn't a bad looking girl, never had been, but now she had a caged way about her, a wariness that was new. It suited her.

"They found out I led the York Street runners."

"Your gang were good," he said. She gave a hard smile. She already knew, he guessed. He shifted in his restraints; they were definitely loosening a bit. "You know, I'm kind of busy now. Catch up later?"

"Why? You're going nowhere." She leaned forward. "We'd have taken you into the Yorkers if you hadn't been with McDowell. You did good work, keeping your family together, bringing in food. Not many made it through on their own. I was watching you."

The last line, so sassy and proud, pronounced him as a Someone, if Mad Neeta had noticed. A part of John surged, enjoying the faint praise, and wanted more.

"I just did what I was told," he said, modest-like.

"Yeah, and then you did for the Zelo. That's what we needed: someone to show Earth wasn't weak."

"I – I..." He should tell her he'd been a dupe, but she was looking at him like he was something special. He couldn't lose the feeling it gave him. "Well, like you say, someone had to."

"Aye, well, it'll be a mixed blessing in here," she said. "There's some that think you brought the Barath'na instead, and no one here is a fan of the bastards. We know the shit that's going down here."

He raised an eyebrow. She was likely to be behind the shit. "Want to share?"

She shook her head and stepped back. "If you get your line onto green, they'll let you out. If not, they'll come and force lunch down you." She made a quote shape in the air. "Health must be maintained for all prisoners. No hunger strikes allowed here."

"They can't keep me here forever," he said. "I have my liaison cop coming tomorrow and I doubt they'll want him seeing me like this."

Neeta's eyes brightened. "You have a cop coming? Why?"

Because he has a guilt complex as big as a house. "He ran our case. It was high-profile, and the GC were all over it. He agreed to be our liaison officer."

She licked her lips. She was pretty rattled, he realised, nowhere near as together as she looked.

"We have to talk." Her voice was husky. "I'll arrange it." She leaned in, real close. "Stay alert." Her voice was a whisper against the exposed part of his cheek.

"What for?" he croaked. He needed her to back away and give him some space. This close, she dominated his thoughts, his body, so he couldn't think.

"Life, death and aliens," she said. She put a finger on his lips. It was warm, alive. He wanted to kiss it, but she pulled away, tutting. She knew, damn her. "No more. Not inside." A bell sounded. "Chow time. Good luck."

John watched her go, trying to make sense of the conversation. She joined the queue of prisoners. Ahead of her, Taz waited, his fuck-you smile absent, and John's relief at seeing him was quickly doused by his vacant stare and pale face. It wasn't fair. He'd been getting better over the past few weeks; the decent food in the barracks and regular visits from doctors had helped.

John drew in a breath. Beyond the canteen area the room was dimly lit and cast into shadows. The devil hides in darkness, his da used to say. What was hidden in the corners of Inish Carraig?

With a quiet sucking the wall gave way, spilling him to his knees. He didn't move for a moment, but waited for his legs to stop shaking. When they did, he got to his feet. He had to learn the steps of the dance of survival in here, just as he'd done in Belfast. Then he'd know what was happening here and deal with it. It was what he'd always done, after all.

***

It was well into the afternoon and the trees were casting the tracks into dim light. The line hadn't been used since the Zelo had invaded – none of them had. About an hour ago she'd come across one of the old trains, sitting empty like a ghost. She'd been tempted to try to break a window and spend the night there, but it had creeped her out to see the silent carriages. She'd wondered if the passengers had got home, or if they had died inside it, and hadn't been able to bring herself to climb on and see. Now, she regretted the decision.

She'd have to stop soon. She'd tripped twice already, and the last thing she needed was a broken ankle.

Six miles, that's what Sean had said, and she must have walked that far already. Maybe she should have gone right. She tried to think of her limited geography, but all she knew was Coleraine was near Portrush. The summer scheme had gone to Portrush last year, and she and Sandra from down the street had shrieked when the roller coaster got to the very top. Taz, in the row behind, had tapped her shoulder and shouted, "I know the fella working the brakes. Christ, you wouldn't let him drive your car."

John had laughed, the roller coaster had dropped and all of them - even the boys - had shrieked even louder. She'd been sure they'd overshoot and die. After, she and Sandra had got off, clinging to each other, and went to the stand to get candy-floss.

Josey had to stop and wipe her eyes; Sandra had died on the first day of the invasion, trying to get home when school closed. About a week later, her mum had gone into the Waterworks and filled her coat pockets with stones. She'd climbed through one of the gaps in the railings and waded into the big pond. When Josey's da and one of the other neighbours found her, swans were swimming around her body. Like they were looking after her, Da said. A week later, John had come home, really upset. All the swans had gone, except a few dead ones floating in the water after a Zelo bomb –

The sole of her shoe caught under one of the sleepers and Josey went flying forwards. She put her hands out and managed to catch her fall, skidding on the stones between the tracks. She sat up and brought her hands to her face. They were dark from the dirt. A moment later she felt a trickle running down her wrist and watched, fascinated in a weird way, as the blood ran down, separating into rivulets. Maybe she'd get blood poisoning and die. Or she might freeze to death. Or starve. And she was thirsty too.

She sat like that, she didn't know how long, until something darted across the tracks ahead of her. A rat, it must be. She screamed and got to her feet, and then stood quietly.

Her heart was beating too fast – she hated rats, filthy things – and her mouth was dry. She glanced to the side and the thick undergrowth. If she tried to sleep up there, the rats could be anywhere, but if she was here they'd run all over her. They'd run all over no matter where she was... she looked up, into the tree line, and wondered if it was possible to make a hammock out of the coat.

She took another moment, comparing the embankment and the railway line. She'd be better off the tracks, rats or not; she was too exposed.

Decided, she climbed the slope, into the undergrowth, and found a tree trunk that had some bare grass at its base. She leaned against the trunk; the undergrowth in front would hide her, and it felt high enough to be safe. She made sure Sean's coat went beneath her bum. A year ago she wouldn't have known heat was lost quicker to the ground than the air. It was amazing what an alien invasion could teach a person. She huddled into the coat.

She was so tired; she needed to sleep. She closed her eyes and dreamt of giant spiders coming down and eating the rats. Somehow, the spiders seemed cute, their little eyes twinkling at her, and she climbed on one, letting it carry her to its web in the trees, far away, where she couldn't be found.

***

John sank onto his bed. He hadn't believed he'd be glad to see the drab cell again when he'd left it that morning, but he was. He stared out the window at the darkening evening sky.

Taz hadn't spoken to him over dinner, just looked on, his eyes glazed, and ate docilely when a Barath'na fed him. His right arm had needle marks tracking from his wrist to his elbow, and when his t-shirt had ridden up there'd been a gauze plaster, a big one, on his abdomen. John had pointed at it and asked what it was for but the Barath'na had ordered him to quiet, in the electronic voice underlain by growls that set John's teeth on edge.

A reassuring thump on the bed announced the arrival of Jimmy. The bot waddled along the covers until it was right up beside John. They sat in silence. John found himself reaching down to pat the bot.

"This is a bloody mess of a place." The bot's antenna focused on him. "I'd give anything to know what lay beneath what I'm seeing. There's so much not right."

Jimmy gave a quiet beep, and projected a map onto the wall. John shook his head. "Not tonight, mate. I'm knackered."

Jimmy gave another beep, insistent, and the projection flashed twice. Puzzled, John got up and went over to it – it was the same map of the prison from the night before, the same stark line of relief.

"You showed me this last night," he said.

Another beep: exasperated. John put his hand on the wall, waiting as it became less solid. He should be used to it by now but when it began to move under him it was flowing, like mercury in the science class. He let out a yell and took his hand away.

"Jimmy, stop it," he said. "That's creepy." The bot flashed, but the projection didn't come down. The bot wanted John to touch it. He lifted his hand again. "All right, all right, this had better be good."

He laid his palm on the wall, gritting his teeth, and the metal moved again, seething under him, shifting the way the Barath'na had last night over the rocks. He forced himself to track the movements as the map showed a series of tunnels and corridors, each filled with the seething bodies.

He'd asked to know what was under the prison. He took in the contours of tunnels, and tried to count the swarms filling them, but there was no way to keep up. Was this for real? *Were* there more Barath'na underneath?

"Oh, Jesus-fucking-H-Christ," John muttered. "They're everywhere."

127

CHAPTER TWENTY-FIVE

Another day, another bowl of porridge over and done with. John glanced up at the first floor. Taz wasn't in the dining area and his force field was still up. John's stomach knotted, all the worse for not having anything concrete to worry about, just what-ifs and maybes.

A girl elbowed him, her tired blonde hair pulled into a rubber band.

"Come with me," she said. John frowned, not sure he should, but the prisoner tutted. "Stay chilled, keep your line down, and they won't ask questions. Stay beside me, we're on yard-time. Lady Neeta herself wants to see you."

John followed her through the double doors to a small yard guarded by three Barath'na guards. He fought the urge to look down, imagining what lay beneath the prison, seething and shifting, growing in number all the time.

Neeta was already in the yard. She gave a sharp nod, but her eyes were wary and she made no attempt to come over to him. John took the hint and walked to the opposite side of the yard, if he could call it that: it was little more than a platform surrounded by low railings and - he stretched out his hand, jerking it back at the now-familiar crackle - yes, force fields behind the rails. No chance of hurtling over, then. Damn.

Across the yard a group of four men had gathered. They glanced over at him from time to time, once with a sneer and a mumbled comment. The skin on the back of his neck tightened and his implant gave a fizz. He turned his attention to the land on the horizon, but watched them from the corner of his eye.

The air smelt of salt and seaweed and a sweet smell from the north, promising snow. In Belfast, he'd have struggled to keep the house warm. At least Stuart and Sophie were safe and might make it to a better year beyond. He thought back to Gary McDowell and his promise that John wouldn't need to worry about the winter, and his mouth twisted. One way or another, it was true - here, there were more pressing things to worry about than a cold snap. On balance, he'd have preferred heating to be the issue.

The sound of footsteps behind him made him rise onto the balls of his feet. He spun and relaxed: it was Neeta.

"Keep your line down," she said. "Out here, the only monitors are the lines, but the bastards move quickly if they're raised. Inside, they hear everything. Understand?"

"Yeah." He tried to be casual, but his heart was quickening. "You wanted to talk to me."

"Your friend isn't doing good."

"How do you know? He wasn't at breakfast this morning."

"Exactly."

He managed to keep his panic down, but it was crawling in his guts. "What's wrong with him?"

"Maybe nothing. Some prisoners don't last long; the Barath'na are quick to sort the weak from the strong." She gave a short laugh. "Although even the healthy ones don't last long." Her voice dropped. "I've never seen them target anyone so quickly before, though."

He paused, half of him wanting to stay in this moment of ignorance, the rest needing to know what lay ahead. "What happens when you're targeted?"

"When, not if - you never were stupid, John." She jerked her head back at the prison. "Did you notice the third floor in the prison?"

"The private one?"

"Yeah." She raised her eyebrows. "You've been paying attention, haven't you?"

He took the praise, but didn't tell her about Jimmy and his magic wall. Just because she said there was no monitoring didn't mean it was true, and he was damned if he was going to get caught out by her carelessness. "So, what about the third floor?"

"It's a medical wing." She looked towards the guards and then back. "Nobody who has ever gone there has come back."

He had to lean in to hear her. "The Barath'na are doing something secret."

She crossed her arms, closing herself off from him, the way she used to in class when the whispers of Paki, or jibes about dirty skin, started up. He used to feel sorry for her; now he wished he'd been brave enough to tell his classmates to shut up.

"I don't get any visitors," she said. "Even if my family had survived the war, they'd have disowned me for running a gang, no matter how bad things were."

"Why did you do it? What did you get from running a crew of kids?"

She frowned. "I don't have time for history." But she stopped, swallowed, and then said, her voice proud, "No one else took any notice of the kids. They were going to be alien fodder if someone didn't look out for them. And I wasn't doing so good on my own – I needed a gang to make me harder to bring down."

It made sense, in a way. Belfast had been harsh; it had only been McDowell's food payments and clothing for the kids that had kept John going as long as he did. "But you were brought down anyway?"

"Yeah. Just before you did the job on the Zelo, I got caught nicking food from one of the banks." She shrugged, and made a throw-away gesture. "But that's history. What you need to know is that I don't get visitors. No one does. Most of us don't have family anymore, and those that do, don't have families in the position to get passes into a GC-secured prison. That sort of thing takes people to fight for you." Her eyes narrowed. "I bet you had a solicitor in court."

He thought of Catherine and how hard she'd worked for him and Taz even though they wouldn't help her. "Yeah."

"I got pulled in front of a juvenile judge on the Monday and sentenced on the Tuesday," she said. "Kicked my heels in a cop-cell until they transferred me up here. That's what happened to most of us." She gave a savage smile. "Your cop is the only official visitor I've heard of."

"So?"

"So, you have to tell him that two thirds of the prisoners sent down aren't here anymore."

130

It tallied with his own count. The confirmation only made things worse. He had to bite his lips from asking what lay ahead. There was no way he'd keep his line down if he let his fears take hold.

"What about the Barath'na?" Information, hard facts, that was what he could deal with. "What do you know of them?" He kept his voice steady and managed not to look down at the island-nest below. "How many are there?"

She shrugged. "Hard to tell. Plenty; they patrol all the time."

Should he tell her what Jimmy had shown him? But how would he make it sound like it was even possible? 'I have a kettle-bot in my room who showed me the Barath'na overrunning the prison. There are more of them below it, and I think they might be planning to take over Earth.' He shook his head; she'd never believe him. Hell, he barely believed it.

"So, will you do it?" she asked, her voice edged, not quite pleading. He doubted if she knew how to. "Tell the cop if he makes it tomorrow?"

John started. "What do you mean, if he makes it?"

She leaned her head back and swallowed, hard. "I know the pattern. A month, maybe a little more, and then it's the third floor for you. Quicker if you're like your mate and already sick. I'll be in the next selection. And you?" She met his eyes. "They don't like troublemakers. As soon as the Barath'na work out a way to get your policeman off-side – and they will – they'll take you, too. I'd be surprised if he even makes it tomorrow."

"Of course he'll be here." He took her arm, pulling her closer. "Inish Carraig is an audited facility. There could be – hell, there *must* be – other reasons for the prisoners being taken. What if they're just moved to another part of the prison?"

She raised an eyebrow. "Hundreds of them? I've seen it, John."

She looked so sincere. He let go of her arm and stepped back. Could it be true? What Jimmy was showing him, what Neeta was saying, Catherine's numbers.

"It starts like electric shocks," Neeta whispered. She must know she had him, because her voice had become harder, more factual. "I heard Orla, one of my runners, screaming when her force field came down, and that's what she said,

131

that she was being shocked." She leaned in, close enough that he could smell fresh soap, and a hint of musk below. "The Barath'na laughed. Said it was getting quicker every time, that they were nearly ready to increase the trial."

"Trial?"

"I don't know what happens up there." Her voice shook a little. "I just know no one comes back, and that when they came into the prison they were as healthy as you and me." She crossed her arms. "I heard Orla; it happened. You can believe me, or you can hide your head in the sand, but it's true, and I need you to tell your cop."

Electric shocks. He remembered Taz a lifetime ago, on the Cave Hill, yelling that he was being shocked. The thought settled, taking shape. Taz, who'd taken the alien virus and never fully recovered, Taz who was covered in needle marks and a gauze bandage, like Ma's after the biopsy of her mole. He knew the virus could hurt humans – how hard would it be to make it *kill* humans?

"What is it?" asked Neeta. "You've gone pale."

"Nothing." If the Barath'na *were* listening and knew he'd made the connection, he'd be on the third floor before he could blink, let alone see Carter. They'd kill him like a bug, helpless to tell what he knew. Like they'd killed his da and ma: falling, with a quick cry. His shoulder buzzed and his line went amber. "You should go."

She glanced at the screen, but didn't move. "Will you help?"

Her question hung in the clear, sweet air. The Barath'na watched him, their eyes cruel, their vicious teeth exposed. Whatever they were, they weren't the good guys they claimed to be. He thought of Taz's sickness, of Josey, taken by McDowell's odious son. It wasn't fair, any of it.

What would the lad before the war do? The lad who'd never stuck up for Neeta? He'd have been too scared to do anything. Slowly, he drew in a breath. That was before Belfast, when he'd learned that to survive you had to be brave. When he'd learned that what mattered was sticking together. Slowly, he nodded. "I'll try."

"Thanks." She smiled and it made something deep in

him move. She was the most alive thing in this place. Her eyes glittered and he thought she might be reading his thoughts, but she only gave another of her tight nods and walked away.

The virus being given to prisoners. *Why?* The mainland was just a stretch of water away, the rest of the planet beyond it. A planet that sustained life, a gift so rare an alien race had searched the galaxy for it.

Two alien races. Realisation hit him. The Zelo couldn't breed on Earth or their own planet now. They were wiped out. He'd done that. Not knowing wasn't an excuse; he'd known his actions were criminal. His head throbbed along with his shoulder, and he wished he could tell the Zelo he was sorry.

The Barath'na wanted living space, like the Nazis and their lebensraum: three planets for a single race. No GC, no rules, no other nations, just Barath'nas, expanding, taking Earth and inheriting Deklon from the dead Zelo.

He watched the grey shapes on the rocks below until he started to see the pattern in their movements, how they paraded in front of the prison, up and down, always safeguarding the harbour, keeping close to it. He watched long enough for his shoulder to stop aching and the chill to reach his bones. Long enough to think over every option, to come up with a million ways of telling Carter what was happening. None of them was clever enough. Once he told the cop, he'd die. Maybe he deserved it.

"All right, Dray?" He spun and saw the three men who'd been watching him earlier approaching. **One angled in such a way as to block the Barath'na's view of the corner.**

John folded his arms. Damn it, he'd been careless. "What do you want?"

They were all bigger than him. Their t-shirts were tight over their chests, showing their build. The words brick and shithouse came to mind. A tattoo stood out on the leader's bicep, and he recognized the red hand of Ulster and the letters U.D.A. below. McDowell must have decided to shut him up for good. His muscles bunched, ready; his blood started pumping, loud in his ears. He pushed away from the railings. He'd bloody known this would happen, that

McDowell would shut him up. "You can't touch me. The Barath'na will have you."

"You reckon?" The first bloke launched himself at John, his line changing from green to flashing red in an instant, and landed a solid punch on John's cheekbone. "They'll have to be quick."

John pulled his fist back. "Guards!" he yelled. His arms were grabbed and pinned by his side. The first man brought his knee up, doubling John, sending sick pain through him. He pulled John upright by his hair, his fist back for another punch. The Barath'na started towards them, but were blocked by four prisoners appearing from the other side of the yard.

Another punch snapped John's head back. A flash of steel – not a knife, but something metal and sharp – caught the sunlight and a line of pain blossomed across John's neck. Warm blood trickled down. He tried to pull away. The arms held him. He kicked out in desperation and the blade dug deeper –

The man reeled back, shouting, blood pouring from his arm, turning the tattoo bloody, as if the Red Hand itself was bleeding. The others let John go and he doubled up on the ground. Something flashed past him, quick and mobile, and he saw it was Jimmy, hovering, aiming a thin laser beam at John's attackers. *What was the bot doing here?* Blood trickled down John's neck and he wiped it away; there seemed a lot.

The first man came again, pulling his foot back to kick. John tried to roll out of the way of the heavy boots. Jimmy moved, so that he was between John and the attacker. The little bot extended a pincer and seized the attacker's leg, toppling him. Another laser beam sliced across the attacker's right leg. The bloke yelled, clutching his leg.

The Barath'na reached the group, pulling his attackers away. John had managed to get onto his hands and knees when a soft mist hit his face, coming from the direction of the prison and filling the air. It smelt of peaches. He closed his eyes, but couldn't stop himself inhaling.

Peace came, the same peace as on the first day in the cubicle. He opened his eyes. Had the sea always been that colour of turquoise? This was the best place to be in the world. Without a doubt. He was lifted to his feet but didn't care. He heard a whirring, saw Jimmy retract his arms, and giggled. *Giggle?* He'd never giggled in his life. He tried to touch Jimmy, but the bot was further away than he should be.

"Nice bot," John said, and he could tell his voice was slurred. Say what you liked about the aliens, they had some seriously good shit. "Good bot. I'll have to thank ol' Uncle Henry." *What?* The stuff must be potent. He laughed and wiggled his fingers. Lovely, lovely fingers. He bet he could do magic with them....

His vision went dark, and he let everything go.

CHAPTER TWENTY-SIX

osey paused and looked both ways up and down the track. Yesterday, she'd followed the tracks to her left but now she didn't know which way she'd been facing when she'd chosen it. She bit her lip, looked up into the sky and tried to remember where the sun had been. Finally, she gave a nod. "Righto, can't just stand here. Left it is."

She unbuttoned her heavy coat and trailed it along the tracks behind her. The morning air was losing its chill and it wouldn't take long for her to get warm, especially if she kept up the pace. She hopped and skipped along the tracks, hurrying as much as she could. She'd already wasted precious moments feeding a robin that had looked as hungry as her. She'd scrabbled in her pocket where the bread had been and pulled out a few crumbs, sprinkling them for the bird.

Her hand had hooked on something at the bottom of the pocket, something small and cold. When she'd pulled it out, it had taken her a minute to recognise it as a St. Christopher's medal – Jordan at school used to have one, she said it brought her luck – and she'd clutched it in her hand, figuring she needed any luck she could get.

That had been ages ago. She lifted her head and looked down the tracks, hoping to see a station. Ahead stood another abandoned train. She walked up to it, keeping to the side of the tracks, and then stopped. Why would there be two trains abandoned so close together?

"No," she groaned, and looked the other way. Then back again, but there was no mistaking the train. It *was* the same one as yesterday. She'd spent an hour at least, maybe more, walking the wrong way.

She turned to face the other direction, but a bramble caught her ankle and she lurched forwards. Her yell was loud in the still morning air, startling birds and sending them squawking into the sky.

"Josey!" The shout came from down the track. Sweat broke across her palms. She needed somewhere to hide. The old train loomed, daring her to approach it. She ran to the driver's carriage and pulled herself onto the little step, but the door was locked. She looked along the length of the train and saw that one of the doors about halfway along was open. That must have been how they got the passengers off. *If* they got off. Visions of skeletons swarmed up in her mind: some holding tickets; all grinning at her –

"Josey!" The voice was muffled, impossible to make out, but whoever it was knew her. *Gary.* She jumped down, darted along the train, and climbed into the open carriage.

What now? A little mew of panic escaped and she stuffed her hand into her mouth, biting down until she could feel teeth on her knuckles.

The train shifted; someone else was in the carriage. She glanced out from the row of seats she was in. Whoever it was stood framed in the doorway. They were tall, definitely a bloke, and dark haired. It had to be Gary.

Go the other way, she willed. He looked both ways. *Please, go the other way.* He started towards her, taking his time, checking every seat as he did. She remembered his whispered voice in her ear, telling her she'd have to do what he wanted; the cold, dead eyes of Liz. He'd done that – shot a disabled woman in a stable yard in cold blood.

She pulled back into the shadows, clutching the medal to her, not sure what to do. Maybe if she ran she could get past him. The steps came closer and she held her breath. If she moved now, he'd find her for sure. She gripped the medal so tightly it hurt.

"There you are." He bent down, leaving her no way past. "Ma was worried."

"Sean?" It wasn't Gary – he hadn't found her. She realised she was shaking, and fought to stop it.

"Who else? I told Ma you'd maybe gone down to the tracks, if you heard us talking. Come on out, I brought some food."

Food. "You came for me?"

"Aye." He stood and reached a hand down. She took it and let him pull her up. He didn't sound angry. "You gave us a fright, walking off on your own. Anything could have happened to you."

"You were going to call the GC."

"We were going to talk to you about it when you woke up," he said. "Let's go outside – it's rank in here." They sat on the step, feet dangling. He reached into his coat and pulled out a small container. "Here. Sandwiches. They're only jam, but they'll do."

Jam sandwiches? It sounded like heaven. She set the medal beside her, and took one. "Thanks."

"You're welcome." He glanced down at the little medallion. "Where'd you find that?"

"In your coat."

"Don't tell Ma, I'm supposed to wear it all the time." He took a bite of his sandwich. "You can keep the medal, if you want. I reckon you need it more."

She nodded. The sandwich tasted really good. For a while they sat eating in the sunshine.

"So, why did you run?" he asked. "We were only going to see if the GC could find your parents. They must be worried about you."

She swallowed the last bite of sandwich, and it seemed to stick in her throat. "Ma and Da died in the war."

"I'm sorry," he said, and looked uncomfortable, his eyes not quite meeting hers. "So you do remember, then?"

She nodded. "I'm from Belfast, and I lived with my brothers and sister. And then..." She looked down at the stones beside the tracks, and they were indistinct through her tears. She wanted to tell someone and let them take charge. Without stopping any longer, she opened her mouth and the whole story came out. The only thing she didn't tell him was that the Barath'na had released the virus. It was bad enough that she knew, and was in danger. She wasn't going to put him at the same risk. Sean listened, not interrupting, until she'd finished. She glanced at him and ducked her head; she'd said too much.

"Jaysus, what a bastard." He squinted into the sky. "So,

what do we do with you, Josey? I don't think you should go back to Belfast, not until you're safe. If your man Gary is as determined as you say he is - and he must be a desperate man, losing you - he'll be watching. I think you're right. You need to find this Peters. I'll take you into Coleraine, and then see about how to get you back to Belfast. You can't walk - it's fifty miles - and I can't take you back to our house. The place is crawling with Barath'na. But if we get into town, I might be able to arrange something at the depot. Some of the farmers have started supplying the city again."

He jumped down. He reminded her a bit of Taz, the way he was always cheerful. "If we set off now, we'll be in Coleraine in a couple of hours." He held his hand out, smiling and handsome in his black sweater.

He set off down the track, and she struggled to keep up with his longer strides. They didn't talk, and she fell into a rhythm: a step onto a track, a jump to the next, another step. Some time later she glanced up and saw a house to the right of her, and then another. A small estate. Josey blinked, sure it would vanish, but it didn't.

"Keep your head down while we get across town," said Sean. "You can hardly walk down the road without needing a permit." He pursed his lips. "They say it's to allocate resources, but I don't like it. We used to track cattle movements the way they track us." He flicked her ear, gently. "Next thing you know, we'll be wearing tags."

He set off and she half-walked, half-ran beside him. She found herself looking all around, on edge in the familiar way from Belfast, when every step had been a danger, every movement a chance for discovery. They reached an empty train station. To the right stood a building, metallic, but gleaming oddly, like it had rainbows painted onto grey. There was a gate across the entrance, closed and unwelcoming.

"The barracks," said Sean. "Careful, now. Don't look worried and they shouldn't stop us."

A huge animal - too like a rat for her liking - guarded the gate. She pulled on Sean's arm. "What is that?"

He frowned. "You have been out of it, haven't you?

That's a Barath'na. Don't worry, they don't bite." His face darkened. "Or so they tell us."

The guard's attention moved onto her. She froze in the middle of the street and, even as she did it, knew it was the wrong thing, that it made her look guilty. The alien brought its gun around to point at her.

"Shit." Sean pulled his documents from his pockets and walked up to the alien. "We're needed at the depot," he said in a cheerful voice.

The alien barely looked at his documents, but focused on Josey. Its eyes narrowed, knowing.

"Yours?" it asked. She shook her head. She glanced behind her, but there was nowhere to go, just a wide, empty street.

"Into the station," said the alien, and there was no friendliness in its eyes or voice. Her legs went rubbery, and it was only Sean's arm that kept her on her feet as the Barath'na lifted the barrier and watched her walk into the station.

CHAPTER TWENTY-SEVEN

eters tapped a rhythm on the arm of the chair next to Carter, over and over again, setting his teeth on edge. He'd ask the big soldier to stop but Peters was tense, his jaw tight, and it wasn't worth the aggro. Carter got up, stretched, and shivered in the chill air. The Belfast army HQ hadn't been upgraded – read for that demolished and replaced – and two of the small windows running along the top of the waiting area were glassless.

Posters filled the noticeboards: Join the army and see the world; first aid arrangements; a fantasy football league listing clubs that hadn't played in a year, all achingly familiar. Many of the football players must be dead. It didn't matter how fancy your house was, or how high your gates were, the Zelo had bombed wherever they liked.

The biggest board, highlighted with coloured pins, showed a list of new housing developments and a reminder that Earth-citizens should be mixed in the estates so ghettoes didn't re-form; in Belfast it always came down to who lived where with whom. Carter fought the urge to laugh. He'd give it a few months before old issues resurfaced and people forgot how they'd pulled together in the city's defence.

The last noticeboard held a copy of the Intergalactic Charter binding Earth to the Zelo and Barath'na. The terms were in perpetuity for space-faring activity, but enforceable on the planet only as long as the peace-keeping forces were in place. He didn't need to read it; he'd taken a copy home weeks ago and memorised its references to an Earth being managed back to health, not given space to breathe.

"Sit down, you're making me nervous," said Peters. He tapped his cigarette packet against his thigh, and glanced at the smoke alarm. "Reckon that still works?"

"Probably not." Carter sat and picked at a piece of frayed

upholstery, pulling it along the seam of the chair. On the whole he preferred dilapidation to the sterile conformity of the new alien buildings, all soft metal and seamless walls. "But it would be our luck that we'd start an evacuation and have to explain it."

Peters put his packet into his top pocket. "Any idea what the colonel wants us for?"

"The boys, I suppose." Sharp fear accompanied the words, quickly smothered. John and Taz had only been in the prison a couple of days – nothing could have gone wrong yet.

"I knew that, Einstein." Peters gave a half-smile. "I don't remember working with you on anything else."

"I just got told to report here." Carter glanced at Downham's door opposite and ignored the niggling unease. "I don't fancy another run-in with your colonel, though. Still, he's not in charge of me –"

Superintendent O'Brien's voice rang up the corridor. *Shit.* He exchanged a nervous look with Peters.

"Well, one of us has done something they're interested in," said the sergeant. "I'm pretty sure it's not me."

Carter didn't reply. If both the colonel and the superintendent were here, this was serious, probably GC serious. He thought of the bots with their kettle bodies and little legs, and the last meeting he'd had with the designer. The niggle intensified to an itch. The colonel swept up to them, and Peters stood, saluting. Downham stopped and glared at Carter, who got to his feet but didn't salute. O'Brien joined the colonel.

"Ma'am," Carter said. O'Brien gave a curt nod, but her blue eyes were harder than he'd ever known. He swallowed his nerves and nodded at Downham. "Sir."

The colonel's face was tight and angry. "Carter, you first. Peters, wait here."

Carter followed O'Brien into the office and faced Downham's desk, noting how tidy it was. A computer, a couple of photos – his wife and kids, presumably, all golden-haired and white-toothed – a pad and pen. *Anal-retentive, obviously.* The door slammed so hard his teeth practically rattled in his head. Not good. Not good at all.

Downham stopped and looked out of the window, making Carter wait. At last he turned. "Who had responsibility for the bots? You or Peters?"

Crap. O'Brien was glaring at him. Carter faced her, meeting her eyes. "I did."

"Peters?"

"He recommended the designer, that's all. And the designer is fully approved." Carter remembered the designer's desperation, how he'd been torn between the bribe and the need for the GC's business. "If something has happened with the bots, it's entirely down to me."

A trickle of sweat ran down his back; the bots *couldn't* have been activated. But, if they had gone off – why? They were programmed only to act if there was a threat to the boys' lives. The trickle was joined by another. "Ma'am, may I ask –"

"Do you understand the term 'police state'?" O'Brien's voice was high, barely constrained. Carter dropped his gaze and looked at his shoes.

"Look at me, Carter."

He raised his eyes. She wasn't just angry, but disappointed too. He liked O'Brien; she'd done a good job during the invasion, determined to uphold some kind of law in the city. He hated disappointing her.

"Did you have anything to do with a security function within the bots?" she asked.

There was no point lying; the designer would have to tell them what had happened, and the trouble would only get worse.

"Yes, ma'am," he said. "I arranged it before the boys went to the prison."

O'Brien leaned back in her chair, and Carter waited for Downham to leave. When he didn't, Carter looked between the two senior officers. "Ma'am? Sir?"

"The colonel and I are taking a joint approach to this matter. It will have to be taken to the GC."

It wasn't a surprise, but he still had to draw in a breath. "Yes, ma'am."

"Explain why you did it."

Carter took a moment, trying not to wilt under their

combined scorn, until he said, "It didn't feel safe, sending the boys somewhere I knew so little about. I was worried." Perhaps honesty would count for something.

"You're a damn fool who knows nothing about what you are dealing with." Downham slammed his hand on the desk.

"Sir, I..."

"Be quiet." Downham's face was red, his mouth a thin line of anger. He looked nothing like the controlled soldier who'd pulled a rag-tag army out of the remnants of the British forces and the paramilitaries purported not to exist anymore. That army had held Belfast for weeks. It had been his resistance that had given time for the first alliance with the Zelo to be forged, the city unsurrendered. Without him, Belfast would have been unsalvageable.

"Sir, ma'am," Carter managed. "May I ask how the programme was found? Was it activated? Because if so –"

"Enough!" thundered Downham.

The superintendent picked up a pen and began to write on a notepad. "The bots will be taken from the prison tonight and decommissioned once their data has been appraised. After that, you'll have a chance to put your side of things to the GC."

Carter's chest tightened. "I'm being disciplined by the aliens? Why not our own people?"

"You're facing a serious accusation," said O'Brien. Her eyes, at least, showed some sympathy. And frustration; her already stretched force were going to struggle to cover his workload. She handed him a chit carrying his orders. "Your line of command was from the GC. You had an obligation to carry out their work with your detainees correctly."

"Ma'am, I understand that." Carter forced his shoulders a little straighter. "But –"

"The GC *will* be leading the investigation, Carter. That's not negotiable."

He shook his head, shocked at the hold the GC evidently had on O'Brien. Downham, too.

"Ma'am, if the bots went off, there was a threat to the boys. Did you ask the Barath'na why the bots had to

144

intervene?" O'Brien started to say something, but he went on, "Ma'am, we don't *know* anything about that place –"

"Quiet."

Carter fell silent at the colonel's order and stared straight ahead. The smell of burning, he decided, was his bridges going up behind him.

"You are facing a tribunal over your direct disobeyal of a GC-ordered action." The colonel nodded to the door. "Get your office cleared out – you're suspended."

"Ma'am?" Carter looked at her. This was her call, not Downham's, surely.

She looked at the colonel, who crossed his arms. He was the one with the direct line from the GC, remembered Carter, and he didn't like that line being confused.

O'Brien gave a soft sigh. "You heard the colonel."

"And you might want to warn your designer to expect an audit of his facilities," said Downham.

Oh, hell, the designer wouldn't get any work if the GC struck him off. Carter remembered his threadbare suit, his shoes shone so often they were practically in holes.

"I requested the chip," he said, the words falling out in the haste to explain before Downham physically threw him out. "And I signed off the documents, it's not his fault."

"Enough." Downham returned to the window, his tone a clear dismissal.

"Ma'am..." He spread his hands. "It's not fair to blame the designer when I gave him his orders."

"It's for the GC to decide." She pointed at the door. "Ask Peters to come in on your way out."

Carter paused, wanting to argue further. He closed his mouth; it was only going to lead to more trouble. "Yes, ma'am." He nodded over at Downham. "Sir."

He walked out, closing the door after him, and leaned against it for a moment. He could be fired over this, and if he was, it wouldn't even be decided by his own top brass, but by the GC.

"Well, any idea what it's about?" Peters' voice cut through his shock.

"The bots." His chest gave a small spasm of stress,

tightening. "I had extra programme chips put in, ones the designer had decommissioned from a security bot. The security function went off."

Peters whistled. "You stupid bugger."

"So I've been told. Pointedly. But when we saw the prison being put up and how remote it was... I was worried. The boys were bound to be a target." Carter pushed himself off the door. "You're in the clear. I told them it was down to me."

"Where are you going?" Peters looked at his watch. "You're supposed to be at Inish."

Carter shook his head. "I'm to clear my office."

"You mean..."

"Yeah." His breathing was coming easier; there was nothing he could do now, anyway. "The boys will have to manage without me." He jerked his head at the closed office door. "They want you."

He left and walked down the corridor to the main door, ignoring those he passed. He wasn't able to face anyone. The police had been his life. He'd been in the force since he'd left university, had fought alongside the army and the hoods through the whole Zelo invasion. He'd taken the promotion he hadn't wanted and worked with the aliens when everyone else refused to, because a cop did what was right and made the best of things. Now what was he going to do? Go back to his father's estate and breed pheasants? He'd go mad in a week.

He got into his requisitioned car. It'd have to be handed in, too, he supposed. He joined the right lane to go to the station, driving automatically. The road was a new one, replacing the bombed, pot-holed one of a few weeks ago, carrying two lanes for ordinary traffic and one for the alien transporters to zip along, so fast they blurred.

He stopped at traffic lights, and looked at the city laid out in front of him. The Barath'na weren't wasting time: they'd been told to rebuild Earth, and that was exactly what they were doing. Except... the buildings on each side of the road, and the housing estate in the distance, were constructed of the same alien metal as the prison.

It didn't feel like Belfast anymore. In fact, it looked more like the pictures he'd seen of Tahro than any place on Earth: replace the light sky with a darker one, add some red to the ground and riddle it through with the traditional underground tunneling of the Barath'nas' ancient cities, and they could be interchangeable.

The lights changed to green, but he paused, foot on the accelerator. The boys would never know why he hadn't come; they would think he'd run out on them like everyone else. He remembered John pleading with him on the boat, how much it had cost the boy to ask him to come, the wariness in his eyes as he waited for the rebuff, the relief when Carter changed his mind. And Taz, hunched in pain, smiling even when there was bugger all to smile about.

Carter yanked the wheel to the left. *Fuck it, he was screwed anyway.* Ignoring a honk of protest, he swung into the lane leading out of Belfast and up the coast to Inish Carraig. His shoulders relaxed. Nothing was resting on him anymore. No job; no responsibilities. Just time to take his own decisions and not care whether they were the right ones. He wound the window down and started to whistle.

CHAPTER TWENTY-EIGHT

wo Barath'na came for John sometime after the tranquilliser had worn off, their clicking claws announcing their approach. They were unarmed, but it made no difference; their claws alone could finish the job on his neck.

"Come," one said. Its translator unit was low, so the word was barely discernible over the growl of its native language.

John left his room and walked before them down the quiet corridor. He itched to look back and see how close they were, but wouldn't give them the satisfaction. The clicks kept pace and he tensed, expecting a claw on his shoulder at any moment. Had they picked up his conversation with Neeta? He reached the stairs and waited, ready to be told to start climbing to the third floor. What would he do? Run, he supposed, for what it was worth – they'd be onto him in moments. He thought of Taz, thrashing in a writhing mess of grey, his yells muffled by the aliens' bodies, and it was all he could do not to rise onto the balls of his feet and take flight.

"Where am I going?" he asked. Somehow, his voice had stayed steady, and he managed not to look up the stairs.

"Your visitor allocation has arrived."

He gasped relief. Carter *had* come. He'd been sure Neeta had been right, that the cop would either have been convinced to move on with his life, or been forced to. But, no, there was an opportunity, a chance. Hope grew inside him, growing from the tiny kernel he'd managed to hold onto, guarded and bare.

He went down the stairs and reached the main hall. A door beside the library, one that had always been closed, stood open. Beyond, a corridor stretched. A Barath'na glared at John and bared its teeth. John held his ground, his body so tense it felt like it could break. He'd faced the Zelo for a year, through patrol after patrol; he wasn't about to back down to this lot.

148

The alien jerked its head at the door. "You may go through."

He went into the corridor, his footsteps ringing on the metal floor as he walked. He was going to have to let Carter know what was happening. Except he didn't know exactly what was happening, he only had half-guesses from a source who'd say anything to save her skin and a bot that might already have been scrapped. He might be risking himself to tell Carter something that meant nothing.

He stopped at a door guarded by another alien. It swung open to reveal Carter, sitting at a desk in the sparse interview room. The cop looked awful, in need of a shave, his eyes dark-ringed. Apparently, John wasn't the only one having a bad day. The door closed with a soft click.

He took a step forward and a camera in the right-hand corner of the room moved to track him. A red light blinked on. *Fuck*. Watching and listening. He glanced at his shoulder. And monitoring. Slowly, he pulled out the seat opposite the cop, and sank onto it. He had no hope of getting information across.

Carter's eyes widened. "Jesus. What happened to you?"

John ran his hand along the cut on his neck and felt rough stitches. He couldn't remember being stitched. In fact, he couldn't remember anything between knowing the sea was very, very blue and coming round in his room. He shrugged. "McDowell wanted to keep me quiet for good." He tried to smile, but his swollen lip throbbed.

Carter's hands, looped around each other, tightened. "I'll put a complaint in. This place is supposed to be secure."

John thought of the force fields and the blinking lines of control. "It is," he said. "Most of them won't dare to have a go at me, not unless they want to face restraints." He brightened a little. "Anyway, you'll never guess what came to the rescue –"

"The bot. I know." Carter sounded smug. "I arranged its security function."

"*You* arranged it?" John rubbed his neck, along the scar. "Why?"

The cop's smugness fell away. "I think you demonstrate why." He looked down at his hands. "Anyway, I'm glad it was worth it. I'm being suspended. In fact, I shouldn't be here." He frowned. "Where's Taz?"

John's hands started to sweat. Neeta was right; Carter *was* being taken out of the equation. What if she was right about everything else? The camera focused on him; he had to do something now, if he was going to at all. He leaned forward; time to find out how smart Carter really was.

"Taz is sick." He kept his voice normal, but the urge to whisper was strong. "He's had a relapse, back to how he was in Belfast." He tapped the desk, giving slight emphasis.

Carter's eyes creased into a slight frown. John watched him, intent. *Please, Carter, work it out.*

"The kids..." John's voice cracked. "I don't want them to get sick, and I'm worried it might spread. I need someone to make sure they don't catch it."

He rubbed his face with his hands, feeling the swollen lip and eye. He'd die in this prison if he didn't get the word out. He was sure of it. Carter's eyes narrowed; he hadn't got there yet, he needed more.

John inhaled. "Tell Catherine she can't count for shit, as well. She's four hundred over." He drummed four fingers on the desk. "You know what I mean?"

"Yes." Carter was deathly serious. Pale and stunned. He gave a sombre nod. "Yes, I get it."

John put his head back. Should he tell Carter about Jimmy's projection, and the teeming swarms of Barath'na tunneling under the prison? A discreet buzzer sounded, making the decision for him: the meeting was over. Time to let Carter get some sort of investigation underway and then everything would be exposed.

Carter returned to the organised cop John knew well. "I'll do what I can. Hang in there."

John scraped his chair back. He tried to smile, but was empty of anything but relief. He'd done it. "Taz – I'm worried."

"I know. Tell him I'll be in touch as soon as I can."

The door opened and a single Barath'na came in. Its fur was fluffed up, hiding the corded muscles that ran alongside the alien's spine. John got to his feet before it reached him, and Carter stood, too, meeting his eyes, and gave a nod. John let himself be marched back to the main room.

150

Let me not be taken to the third floor. He stumbled. *Let me live.* He hadn't realised how precious life was and how much he wanted to keep it before today; he'd only thought he had.

The Barath'na turned right at the top of the first set of stairs. He was being taken back to his cell. He stumbled forwards, relief making him dizzy, until he reached his cell.

The force field came up and then, only then, did John let himself sink to the bed and curl up. He ached everywhere. He missed Jimmy. Briefly, he wondered what they *had* done with the bot - a cupboard, like Carter had mentioned at the beginning? Or something even worse? A bot-dismantlement plant? He hoped not; Jimmy deserved better than that.

He rolled onto his back and stared at the ceiling. It was up to Carter now; all he could do was be ready.

***

Carter left the prison and maintained a steady walk down the pier. He'd been sure the Barath'na would have refused him access, but his suspension obviously hadn't filtered into the system yet. Now, he half-wished it had.

He replayed the conversation with John, making sure he had it right. Taz was ill, and John thought others had the same illness. Taz's illness had been caused by the alien virus. The doctors in Belfast had confirmed it, without offering a cure other than time and hoping it would clear his system. Evidently it hadn't.

Four hundred prisoners. John had to be wrong. Carter paused, listening to the silent air, and glanced at the prison that held its own secrets. It had felt like a dead place.

And if John was right? He was the one on the inside, and he'd been serious, more than Carter had ever known him. If so, if the virus got out of the prison....

Carter's throat tightened, remembering the adult Zelo, the night of the virus' release, its last laboured breaths as it handed over its dead, silvered baby. So human, seeking help for its child.

He imagined his parents on their country estate. They'd survived the war with some amount of grace, using the Aga for

151

heat and cooking, chopping trees for fuel, providing supplies to the village attached to the estate. The aliens weren't after pheasants, his father had said, they wanted the cities, where rebellion grew daily. 'Your mother and I will keep our heads down and see the war out,' he'd said, and he'd been right. While Carter had battled in Belfast, when he'd bartered to get kids like John out of the estates to some sort of safety, his parents had managed. But this... he looked into the clear sky. This attack would be invisible. It would steal people in their sleep, crawl into their cars and houses, wrap them in deadly air.

He stopped walking. *If* John was right, the Barath'na must have been behind the first virus. There'd be war between the Barath'na and Zelo. Would Earth side with the Zelo or the Barath'na? Earth-based groups had released the virus; they were as culpable as its creators. But they were to be the next victims. Galactic war, with Earth as the weakest partner. Fear crept up his throat and choked him.

His phone rang. He fumbled it out of his pocket, glad of the distraction. "Carter."

"You went to prison, didn't you?" Peters' voice carried an edge of laughter, a knowledge of Carter that he barely held himself.

"Yes."

"Good. There's a wee girl up in Coleraine, with the Barath'na. She's about fourteen, and she's on her own. She asked for me by name, said she'd heard about me."

Josey. Carter's eyes closed. He hadn't got her killed. *Yet.*

"I thought you could pick her up," said Peters, "since you're closer."

"Have you told anyone else?"

Peters' voice dropped to a low rumble. "I decided I'd wait until we heard what she had to say. I figured you might want to deal with it before you hand in your badge. See things through to the end, y'know?"

Carter gripped the phone tighter. He needed support, he couldn't bring this down on his own. Especially not on suspension. He stared at the horizon, thinking about Peters. Peters who kept his own counsel but was no one's fool. Peters, who wanted Josey Dray safe before he made any official move, and who knew how important it was for Carter to finish things. *Trust, or be damned.* Carter took a deep breath. "Get Catherine, if you can. The kid needs to make a statement. And, Peters... I need to talk to you."

"About?"

"I can't say over the phone." He reached the boat and stepped in. "But it's life and death. Will you support a stupid bugger who needs help?"

"Is it kosher, what you plan?"

Trust went both ways. "Not entirely. It will be with more proof. But it's important."

There was a pause, and the sound of a lighter flicking on. "Aye." The relief made Carter lightheaded. "I'll be with Catherine when you get back, and maybe then you can make some sense. If you do, I'll hear you out."

Carter ended the call. He leaned on the railing as the boat cast off. A dart of movement close to the harbour made him squint, but whatever it had been was gone. A rat, he supposed. If so, it had been a bloody big one. The boat left the harbour and the swell slapped up to meet it. He closed his eyes, not looking at the horizon, and gave a half-smile. Josey was alive, that was half the load off his shoulders. Now he just had to deal with the other half.

***

Gary slammed the door of the car. Another day out of the house, not answering Ray's question about where he was going and why, and no sign of Josey. He'd run out of roads to drive down and fields to check for her body. Wherever she was, he wasn't going to find her. Panic swelled in him, making him pause on the driveway, not sure he could face going back into the dingy house.

Calm down. It was his da's voice he was imagining, and the hard blow that came with it. *If you don't learn to get control of yourself, lad, it'll be the killing of you.* A kick on the back of the knee had crumpled Gary to the floor, making his da's point unforgettable. He went up to the door of the house, but paused on the doorstep. Evening had fallen into night and it was quiet. Too quiet – no rustling in the bushes of the night animals, just a silence so deep it could be touched. He scanned the darkness, but there was nothing there except his own fear. He relaxed and turned to let himself in, but stopped at a soft click behind him.

Gary spun on his heel. Barath'na were emerging from the bushes, low to the ground, snarling. A lot of them: ten, twenty, more. He took a step back.

"Ray! Demos!" he shouted. The aliens approached, moving as one. He held his hands out, and they were shaking. "What do you want?" His crotch was wet. He bit back a sob. His da would have kicked him from here to Belfast for pissing himself like a kid.

"What is it?" Demos said, behind him. Then: "Oh, shit..."

Gary backed away until he reached Demos' fat belly. There was a lull as he faced the aliens. They waited, teeth bared, until, as one, they surged forwards, and then there was nothing other than teeth and tearing claws, and screams cutting the night.

CHAPTER TWENTY-NINE

The sound of feet made Josey sit up. She hoped it was Sean. She'd been separated from him when she'd been brought into the station. Since then, she'd had the chance to have a shower and, most importantly, proper food. She hadn't realised how hungry she was until they'd set it in front of her, and even though it wasn't that nice – some sort of chicken stew – she'd eaten it all. And then a lady doctor had come in and checked her over, proclaiming her a little weak, but all right otherwise.

After that, they'd taken her to a room and a Barath'na and a human soldier had asked her questions. She'd held firm, though, and told them she'd talk to Sergeant Peters, that he knew her from Belfast, and no one else. In the end they'd forced her to give them a name and she'd told them she was Niamh Doherty, and that she'd run away after her mum had died. She'd had no way of knowing if they knew who she really was. Surely, the only way to would be Gary telling them? They'd stopped asking after that and then came in and told her Peters was on his way. That's when they'd taken her into this room and even though she was pretty sure it was a cell, it felt okay – safe even – and she'd been able to sleep for a while.

A man in a police uniform came in. "Hi," he said, "I came to get you."

"Sergeant Peters?" she asked.

He shook his head.

"I'm not talking to anyone else," she said.

He nodded at the seat beside the bed. "May I?"

She crossed her arms. A woman soldier took up position in the doorway and Josey recognised her from the interview room earlier.

The policeman sat down anyway. "My name is Henry

Carter," he told her. She gasped; he was the one that worked with Peters. "Sergeant Peters asked me to come and get you, Niamh, as I was in the area and he's still in Belfast." He paused, glanced at the soldier, and then gave a half-smile. "You know, you really look like your brother."

"You know Jo-"

He shook his head, ever so slightly. "Yes."

Her heart jumped and she almost blurted out their names, and then remembered his caution. "The kids?" she asked.

Carter nodded. "They're fine."

They weren't dead. The room swam under tears: she had been so sure they were dead. Gary had been so matter of fact, and Ray had never said anything to contradict her belief that he'd killed them. Her world tilted, like she was on the roller-coaster, and then came back, just a little, to where it should be. She had to swallow against the tears and when she looked up Carter was watching her, his eyes full of sympathy. No, not quite – understanding, that's what was in his eyes. He knew about her, about the kids, what they'd been through.

"Look," he said, "what we need to do is get you discharged, and up to Belfast." He said it like it was urgent, and his words came back to her – Peters had asked him to come because he was closer.

"Okay."

"I want you to talk to a friend of mine called Catherine. She's a lawyer."

A lawyer? She'd known she'd be drawn into John's trouble. She made her eyes big and round, the way that used to get her out of bother with Da. "Am I in trouble?"

He smiled and shook his head. "No. We'll get you to Belfast and have you registered." He nodded to the soldier on the door. "Corporal, can we get her discharged into my care?"

The corporal paused and Carter stood up, smoothly taking Josey's elbow and getting her to her feet. He guided her to the door, and if the corporal thought about stopping him, he moved too quickly for her. They were out the door and going down the corridor before Josey was fully aware of where he was taking her. He stopped at a reception desk and smiled

156

pleasantly, as if he had all the time in the world, and yet Josey could feel how tight his hand was on her arm.

"Okay," he said to the corporal, "where do I sign for a discharge to my care?"

The woman hesitated. "I'm not sure... we're supposed to detain anyone who isn't registered." She clutched a piece of paper in her hand. "The Barath'na won't like it."

"All the better then, no?" Carter smiled broadly, and took the paper from her. "Got a pen?" He took the one offered. "Brilliant, thanks. You're very efficient up here." He half-whistled through his teeth. "We *are* detaining her. You saw my pass – I'm taking her back to Belfast. People are supposed to be registered in their home town, you know that." He handed the paper back to the corporal, who looked at it, still doubtful.

"I think I need to check this before you leave."

"No problem." But it was a problem – Josey could feel it in the way he tensed. He managed to keep his smile, though, and say, "Have you met Sergeant Peters from the Eleventh? Big man, smokes like it's going to be banned at any moment."

The corporal smiled properly for the first time. "Phil Peters?"

"That's the one."

"I was on a training course with him," she said. "First aid; he almost destroyed the dummy with his compressions."

"That'd be him. You should see him doing it for real; the medics groan in advance." Carter nodded at the phone on the counter. "Look, if you need to, give him a ring, he'll confirm who I am – we've been working together for a couple of months. It was him who asked me to come and pick up..." Josey waited, heart thumping. He'd forgotten the name. "...Niamh. He's been looking for her since she went missing – he's a friend of her uncle."

The corporal put the discharge request into a file and snapped it closed. "No, that's fine, Inspector." She nodded to Josey. "Take care, Niamh. Make sure you get on the register. It's not safe to be wandering around if you're not." Her eyes darkened and she looked out the main doors at the Barath'na guarding the entrance.

157

Josey nodded and Carter pulled her arm. "Come on," he said, through what sounded like gritted teeth. "As the actress said to the bishop, let's get the flo-" He looked at her and reddened a little. "Never mind. Let's go."

They crossed the car park, and she had to fight the sense of eyes watching her, knowing that she was lying.

"Aren't you going to say goodbye?" said a voice.

She spun and saw Sean, leaning against the station wall.

"Wait," she said to Carter. "He helped me. Can I say goodbye?"

"Be quick."

Josey ran over to Sean and hugged him. His top was rough against her cheek, but when he hugged her back his embrace was strong. Her stomach went a little funny. She stepped away, embarrassed, and ducked her head.

"I'm going back to Belfast," she said. "I think it's going to be okay; Carter knows about Joh- ...about everything."

Carter approached and held out his hand. "Inspector Carter. Thanks for all the help you gave."

"I'm Sean." He pushed off the wall. "I better get back. Ma will be worried. Look after yourself, Josey."

He made as if to go, but Carter put a hand on his arm, stopping him. He turned to Josey. "He knows who you are?"

Josey nodded. Carter leaned towards Sean. "Did you tell the GC her name?"

"No." Sean's eyes narrowed. "I thought it was better not to. I told them I didn't know, that I found her wandering along the railway line. I thought it would be better to let Josey decide what to tell them."

"Good lad." Carter pulled Sean away, and said something that Josey couldn't catch. She saw Sean write something down and nod, and then the officer opened the car and ushered her inside.

"What was that?" she asked. "What you gave him?"

Carter started the car. "My number. I told him to give me a shout if he needed anything."

His voice was casual, too casual, and panic caught in her throat. "They'll be all right, won't they? It will be safe, them knowing me?"

Carter nodded and moved the car forward. "Sure, it'll be

158

safe. I mean, the cops here don't know who you are, so why wouldn't it be?"

His face was tense, though, and when they drove under a street lamp his eyes looked shadowed with worry. Josey scrunched herself up in the seat and sent a quick prayer that Sean and his ma and da would be okay. The town fell behind as they reached the open road. She was going to have a wild lot to thank God for when all this was over.

***

The policeman had driven from Coleraine even faster than her da would have. He'd stayed to the country roads and when he'd reached bumps in the road, one after the other, he'd driven over them so quickly that by the last one the car was flying and her stomach had been left behind. When she'd looked over, he'd been smiling.

"Been years since I drove the Seven Sisters," he said. "My father used to go twice as fast as that – by the end I was nearly ready to jump out of the car, even if it was still moving." He'd lifted his phone from his pocket and it was a good one, one of the smart ones. "I want to ask you some questions, if that's okay, and record your answers. When we get to Belfast, there's someone else who'll need to do the same thing again. This is like a practice run."

"Do you want to ask about John?" She kept her eyes on the road ahead, trying to decide whether she should trust him. Gary and his gang definitely hadn't.

"Partly," he admitted. "But mostly I want to know what happened to you. Who you were with and what they told you." He stopped at the end of one of the country roads and then pulled out to the left. She had no idea where she was. If Belfast was anywhere close, there was no sign of the city. Nor could she see the sea. She crossed her arms over her body, and watched out the window for a moment. A sign came up at the end of the road, and she read it. Belfast, 30 miles. Her shoulders relaxed – he was taking her the right way, at least. He quirked an eyebrow at her. "Well? Will you tell me?"

"What do you want to know?"

159

"Tell me what happened the day they kidnapped you."

She had to trust someone, she couldn't keep it all to herself. She thought back to the day waiting in the house for John, knowing already that he wasn't coming back, and said, "I heard them coming into the house; they were breaking down the door..."

He was a good listener. He didn't interrupt, except once or twice to check something she'd said. When she told him about the Barath'na – she had to, someone had to know – he hissed through his teeth but didn't interrupt. By the time they reached the outskirts of Belfast it was getting dark, and she'd told him everything. Even about Gary's offer and how she'd felt. She finished and glanced at him. Was he annoyed at her? She chewed her lip. He looked angry.

"Josey..." His voice was croaky. He swallowed, and shook his head. "That's an incredible tale."

"You don't believe me?" This was what she'd been afraid of, that she'd get back and be told it was all lies.

"Oh, I believe you," he said, quickly. "I think you did well getting away."

He wasn't annoyed. She'd done the right thing. She had to bite back tears; she'd been so scared she'd mucked everything up. He turned the car into the entrance of a complex of buildings, all made of the rainbow metal, faceless and austere. He pulled up outside one of the buildings.

"I have a friend waiting here. Her name is Catherine, and she's a lawyer. She's trying to help John."

She got out of the car and followed him up the path, but when the door opened it wasn't a woman, but a soldier with red hair. A cigarette dangled from one side of his mouth.

"About time you got here," he said to Carter.

"Nice to see you too, Peters." But the cop smiled, taking any sting from his words.

Josey's eyes widened – this was the promised Peters. He wasn't as friendly as she'd expected. Carter ushered Josey in. He stopped on the doorstep and checked outside, but it was quiet, and then headed into the living room where a woman was waiting. She gave a smile and Josey melted with relief – she looked nice.

"They let her go?" Peters nodded at Josey. "No problem?"

Carter pointed to one of the armchairs. "Go on over and sit down, Josey. Catherine needs to chat to you." He turned to Peters. "I had to use your name. Does anyone in Ireland not know you?"

The big soldier shrugged. "You were lucky. The call went out about half an hour ago, identifying her."

"There didn't seem to be anyone looking – the roads were quiet. I came by Ballymena and across country, though."

"What about the two lads?" asked Peters. "You saw them?"

"Just John. I was coming from the prison when your call came through."

John really was in prison, then. Carter went over to the window and perched on the sill. His eyes flitted from looking outside, to her, to Peters, and back outside. "There's something going on in the prison. A sickness. He thinks it's related to the virus." He paused, and then said, in an even quieter voice, "He also said Taz is ill."

"Taz...?" Josey looked up at Catherine. "What's wrong with him?"

"He hasn't been very well," said the lawyer. Her face was worried, but she didn't have that look adults gave when they were lying. "But we thought he was getting better." She glanced up at Carter. "I can contact the GC and ask that he's checked."

"No. Definitely not. I need more information first."

"You certainly do." Peters folded his arms, his face skeptical. "How does the boy-wonder know this?"

"He's the one in there."

"So you don't know."

"We didn't get much of a chance to chat about it. A Barath'na at the door can be a bit off-putting." He jerked his head at Josey. "But it's not just John. McDowell confirmed to Josey the Barath'na were behind the virus."

"No wonder they've put in an all-units search for her." The soldier ran a hand over his chin. "If you start snooping where you shouldn't, you *will* lose your job. You're hanging on by your fingernails as it is."

Carter gave a snort that might have been a laugh. "I'm

fuc-" he glanced at Josey "- buggered anyway. They'll take my badge in the morning."

"I can ask around," said Peters. "I'm in the colonel's good books for not being the one who got his high-profile operation in the shit. Apparently the GC threatened to put a Barath'na in place of Downham. If you were one of his men, he'd have you demoted to toilet cleaning duties for a year."

"If I was one of his men, I'd be facing a military tribunal," said Carter. "And that's one of the reasons you can't be seen to be involved with this. That and the fact you have two kids. Phil... *if* John and Josey are right, it must go high up. Someone in authority must know about it." He paused, and he looked scared for the first time, his face pale and drawn. "If I don't find anything at the station, I might need you to get me into the barracks. After that, you leave me to it. I'll give you a shout in the morning, once I know what's happening. Until you hear from me, stay away from it."

Peters crossed his arms. "This could all be a load of shite, you know that, don't you?"

"Let's hope so. I'd rather look like an arsehole than be right." Carter's eyes flitted back to checking the street. "I need Catherine to take a formal statement from Josey. After you have the statement, get Josey hidden."

"What are you planning?"

Carter cracked his fingers. "I'm going to see if I can find anything to corroborate what John says. Faked audits, maybe? He says the prisoner numbers are out." He fished around in his pocket, and pulled out his phone. "Speaking of which, I need you to hold this. It's got Josey's testimony on it - I recorded it as we drove down. An insurance policy, if you like." He cleared his throat. "One other thing - if you don't hear back from me, get in contact with Bar-eltyr, in the Zelo command. Tell him, and only him, what I've told you. They have to know about the Barath'na."

Catherine got up and went over to the cop. "Be careful," she said. "Don't take chances."

"I'll try," he said. "But whatever is going on - and I really don't know - it stinks worse than a Zelo. I can't ignore it."

"I know." Her voice was small.

Carter gave Josey a tight smile, half-saluted Peters, who nodded back, and then pulled up the collar of his jacket. He left the room without looking back.

***

Sean leaned forward, taking in the interior of the Barath'na transporter. He hadn't wanted to take the lift, but they'd insisted on it. Slowly, he looked over the control panel. No joystick or wheel, just a flat panel of swipe controls.

The Barath'na pilot got in, running its paws across the control panel. The transporter rose to just above traffic level, hovered for a moment, and zipped off. It followed the main road from Coleraine, passing cars so quickly that if he'd blinked, he'd have missed them. The transporter was smooth, its engines purring. Even at this speed, the panel read-outs showed it was using barely a quarter of the power. This baby must be able to go at a serious speed. Sean wondered was it space-worthy, but a quick look round showed him no hand-holds for zero-G, no protective core or air supply. No, this was designed for Earth flight. He'd love one.

They veered away from the road. A direction finder blipped steady directions. Sean started to recognise where they were as they dropped lower. There were the train tracks; there Kenney's farm. They soared over his own house and landed, barely bumping, on the front lawn. The Barath'na pilot, smaller than many of the aliens but still the size of a sheepdog, focused on Sean. Sean fought not to shiver; the alien was worse close-up when you could see its teeth, white and pointed, and couldn't escape the sharpness in its watchful eyes.

"This is your residence, yes?"

Sean nodded and tried to find the door handle, eager to get away from the Barath'na. "Yeah. Thanks for the lift."

The Barath'na looked around, and Sean followed its gaze, taking in the curve of the pathway, the little wall surrounding Ma's vegetable patch and chicken coops; everything that made the house individual. It took its time and then met Sean's eyes, as he tried to tell himself being an alien didn't make it sinister.

The Barath'na leaned over, reaching for the door, and Sean could smell its breath, foul, like dead meat. The alien's eyes narrowed as it looked around the yard again. Fine mist, just starting to come down, was cut through by the transport's lights. It made everything look alien, like the Barath'na was the native and not Sean.

"You can go."

It opened Sean's door and cast its gaze around once more, taking everything in. Sean scrambled out, a low worry settling deep in his stomach. The ship lifted off, but his anxiety stayed, gnawing at his innards.

CHAPTER THIRTY

The afternoon stretched towards darkness. John tried lying on his bed and zoning out, but there was only so much of that he could take. Looking out the window, taking Zen-like deep breaths, proved only an excuse for scanning the skyline in the hope someone was coming to get him. Monitor line-watching wasn't any more engrossing. Pacing brought no relief. God, he missed Jimmy; even a good, old-fashioned maths-set would have distracted him.

The buzz of the force field coming down made him spin round, his line surging into deep amber, but it was only the cell-release for dinner time. Bugger, he needed to settle down – the Barath'na would watch him if he stayed so hyped. He stepped out of his room, ready to do battle with the food, and saw Taz's force field was still up. He tried not to look at the third tier, but did anyway. Had they already taken Taz? He glanced back at his own cell and the small window looking out on nothing but sea and sky. *Come on, Carter, we haven't got long.*

John followed the crowd to the dining room below. As he stood in the queue, he saw Taz's force field come down, and three Barath'na exited the room, sealing it behind them.

"You okay?" Neeta's voice interrupted his thoughts.

He nodded at Taz's room. "I'm worried."

"You're right to be." She scanned the tier, her eyes taking in the closed force field and the Barath'na walking away. "Any idea why they're so interested in your friend?"

"Maybe." He lowered his voice. "Do they take people before they're sick, or after?"

She paused. "Before. They get moved to the third floor. The first time, the prisoners didn't know what was happening. Last time, they did." She breathed, slow and steady, keeping her line down. "They fought hard."

165

"Did the Barath'na do anything to them? Separate them from the others? Anything?"

She shook her head. "We can't talk about this; they'll hear us."

"We've nothing to lose." He looked round at her. "I had my visit today. It might make things move faster. I need to know what happens. I need to know when they'll make a move."

His urgency must have reached her. She pointed to the third floor. "The force fields are down." His own fear was reflected in her eyes. "They're getting ready for the next lot." She swallowed. "And I'll be in it. You might be all right, since your cop is still visiting. It might even keep your friend out of the call-up."

A stone settled in his stomach. "No," he said. "I don't think that's going to make any difference. My cop is about to lose his badge." He leaned closer to her, and murmured, "Taz tasted the virus, the night we released it. It's already in his system. I think that's why they're keeping him apart. They must be testing him." His mouth was dry from fear. "Now that Carter's out of the equation, Taz will be joining your trip to the third floor, and they'll have a lot to learn from him. Stuff that'll bring them closer to whatever they plan to do."

He stared at Taz's door. It wasn't fair; Taz was a good guy, he hadn't done half the hateful things John had to survive. It should be John dying, and if Carter didn't come through, it would be. The Barath'na knew he'd been on the hill with Taz; they wouldn't keep a witness alive. Tonight, or tomorrow, or whenever the Barath'na took their next selection, he'd be in it, just as surely as Neeta and Taz, and then the shocks would be running through his body, too. He had to stop that thought right there. Carter would get here in time. He had to, there was nothing else for it....
John's shoulder buzzed and he glared at the implant. Christ, he was getting sick of that little Inish Carraig quirk.

It buzzed again. He didn't care, he realised. He didn't want to be forced to calm, or made to keep his line down and behave. He stepped out of the food line. What he wanted was to see Taz and know he was alive. He didn't know about Josey, or Liz, but he could find out about Taz. He stepped towards the Barath'na.

A hand fell on his shoulder. "John..." Neeta's voice held a warning.

He shrugged her away and walked towards the Barath'na guards, heart pounding.

"I'd like to see my friend. I'm worried about him." The dining area fell silent. "I want to see him."

One of the Barath'na approached to a foot or so away, its mouth curved into a grotesque imitation of a smile. "Taz Delaney is undergoing medical treatment and responding well."

"Then show me." John's voice was loud. "I'd like to see the governor and request to see Taz. I have that right, don't I? To see the governor." The implant twisted viciously in his muscle, and he had to bite down against a yell. "I want to request it."

"You cannot see the governor on behalf of another."

"Well, he can't make the request," said John.

Another pang, masked by his anger, and John grabbed the alien's forearm and twisted. Let it have some of the same medicine. Its hair was coarse under his hand, and when it tensed its muscles, they coiled under John's grip. It threw him off without difficulty, and then raised its head and let out a call, ululating and echoing off the prison's walls. There was nothing human in the call, nothing for the translator unit to repeat.

Barath'na exploded from everywhere, running down the stairs from the fourth floor, aiming for John. This had been a bad idea. He had no choice but to see it through. He took a step back and yelled, "I want to see the governor. Now!"

"John!" shouted Neeta. She dove at the first of the aliens, her sliding tackle taking it across the floor with her.

"No, Neeta!" The Barath'na were surrounding him, but he fought to reach her. The Barath'na she was holding righted itself and slammed her against the wall. She sank into the metal, and it drew her down, like a mother's embrace.

"Calm down!" John urged. "Close your eyes, be somewhere else, and bring your line down." Claws grabbed him but he fought them off. "A beach. Warm, with sand and some waves..."

"Screw that." She closed her eyes, and her chest rose and

fell steadily. The metal oozed back a little. "Out on the streets, knowing you're on top of your world," she murmured, and gave a smile. "Quick, moving in the shadows, the pump of your heart in the dead of night." She stepped forward, out of the metal. "Now you."

"Fuck it." He grinned. Turned and faced the Barath'na. Took a deep breath. "I. Want. To. See. The. Governor."

They took him in a seething mass of bodies, each stronger than him. Claws clutched him, dragging against his skin, and propelled him towards the wall. He fought them, wilder than wild, ready to rip them all apart.

The wall hit and he pushed himself into it – fuck them if they thought they had the right to control him. "Come on, you miserable fuckers, do your worst."

The metal came round him, tighter than before, so that each breath was an agony and panic. He laughed, breathless and heavy, and stood as the dining room emptied. The lights fell around him. Each time the metal loosened, he filled his lungs and yelled that he wanted to see the governor. When calmness threatened, he clenched his fists. Some things were worth fighting against, and he was buggered if he'd let the bastards pull him quietly from some darkened room. He'd fight them every step of the way; every single one.

CHAPTER THIRTY-ONE

ean stepped into the hall of his house. Nothing felt right. It was too quiet, the night too long; the house lay waiting, vulnerable.

"Is that you, Sean?" His ma's voice came from the kitchen, and it sounded shaky and old. Nothing like she usually was.

"Aye, Ma." He hung up his coat and went to close the door. His gaze drifted over the pathway and the lawn. The alien had done the same, its eyes taking in everything. He picked up his coat as his parents emerged from the kitchen.

"Where have you been?" asked his da.

Sean swallowed and pulled his coat on. "We have to go."

"Go?" said Ma. "Go where, Sean? We're registered to here, we're not allowed to go anywhere else."

"Anyway, why would we want to?" demanded his da. "There's the farm to see to, and they've upped the quota for milk, son."

Sean lifted his ma's coat down and held it out to her. "The girl, the one that was here... I think the GC are after her."

"She's not here anymore," said his ma. "Anyway, she was only a wee slip of a thing."

"I know," said Sean, "but they want her, and I was with her when she went to the GC." He gave a harsh laugh. "Hell, I was stupid enough to bring her in. And there was a cop, one from Belfast, who took her. He said I was to call if anyone asked after her."

He paused, remembering the cop's face, how worried he'd been, how there had been something behind his words. How he'd given a firm nod as if checking that Sean understood his hidden meaning. At the time, Sean hadn't, but now, remembering the Barath'na's knowing eyes, its close attention...

"One of the Barath'na gave me a lift back. It knows where

169

we live. And the girl, who she is, when they find out, they might not want anyone else to know-"

"She told you, then," said Da. "I knew she was lying."

"Aye, she's yer man John Dray's sister." He forced the coat into his ma's hands and pulled down his da's, ignoring their shocked looks. "The Barath'na... it... its eyes were..." He shrugged, not sure what to tell them. He just knew the bottom of his stomach felt like it had ants crawling across it, and that he had to get them away. "We need to go. I know it. And soon."

He opened the door and outside the night was still, the only sound a distant fox call, yowling through the night. The mist off the hills wreathed the yard, thickening all the time. It was so peaceful he was tempted to close the door, go into the living room and sit by the turf fire until he settled down.

He pulled the door wider. It wasn't peaceful, it was quiet. Too quiet.

"We have to go." He glanced up. He could hear something, a low thrum, not quite in the range of his hearing, more a sensation. It might have been his blood racing through his body, or the sound of a silence so deep it was impossible not to pay attention to it. "Please Ma, Da, trust me. We can't waste time." He jerked his head at the door. "They *know* where we are – we can't stay here. We *can't*."

Something in his voice must have got through to them, because Ma put her coat on and Da took down his cap and tugged it onto his head.

"Do we have petrol?" asked Sean.

"Aye; we got an extra allowance because of the milk agreement," said his da. Sean led his parents around the side of the house to the car. Da put the headlights on and Sean, in the back seat, tapped his shoulder. "Turn them off," he said. "And keep to the back roads."

His da nodded, and it was as if the quietness of the evening had infected him. The thrumming sensation had grown louder, becoming a noise separate from the night. His mother's shoulders hunched up, and he didn't think he was the only one hearing it anymore.

They drove to the bottom of the back driveway and out

170

onto the country road beyond. Da took a right towards Coleraine and then a left onto a narrow road. It ran under an avenue of trees, and Sean nodded at his good sense. He wound down his window and listened. The distant thrumming was unmistakable. They drove on, moonlight flashing between the trees, its light diffuse and dull. Sean leaned his head out of the window, listening even more carefully. A low drone replaced the thrum, a distinct noise, like engines. He looked behind and saw lights in the sky, back in the direction they came.

"Pull over," he said, "and stay under the trees."

The car cruised to a halt and his parents turned and looked out the back window. The drone increased and then there was a whump, carrying through the air.

The dark sky changed to a flickering orange.

"Mother of God," said Ma, "is that our house?"

Sean grimaced. "I think so."

"Jaysus," said Da.

The droning receded into the night. Sean looked forward, and his da's eyes met his in the mirror; he looked drawn and old, shocked.

"Where do we go?" asked Ma. "We're not supposed to be out after dark. We're supposed to be at home."

At home. Sean looked out the back window and saw that the sky was a steady orange now, deeper. The house must be well ablaze. The noise in the sky had vanished, as if it were never there, leaving only the memory of it.

He put his hand in his pocket, pulled out the slip of paper and read the policeman's number. He brought his mobile out, but there were no bars on it. There hadn't been for months, since the military had taken the networks off air and commandeered them for themselves. He only kept it charged and with him because it had his music collection on it, and he'd paid a fortune for that before the war. Was there still an iTunes store? Somewhere out there, did Apple even exist? Or was that gone, like the old Earth, replaced by an alien version? He shivered, and looked at the number again. He needed someone to help; there was no way they'd get across country on their own...

"Sean!"

He glanced up and realised his father had been calling him. "What?"

"Where do we go?"

"We need to go one of the towns, so that I can get some network coverage," he said. "Or a pay-phone. If we can't get that, we'll have to go to Belfast."

"Belfast?"

His da spoke of the city as if Sean had asked him to take a trip to Outer Mongolia, yet before the war they'd have been there a couple of times a year.

"Aye. We need to find Inspector Carter and tell him what happened."

His da nodded. His ma was quiet, her shoulders shaking with silent tears. The car moved forwards in the darkness, furtive and hunted, and Sean made himself look forwards, not back at the angry sky.

CHAPTER THIRTY-TWO

The cell's lights dimmed around Neeta, but she didn't move to bring them back on. Instead, she kept her hands on her knees, her control firmly in place. The trick was to not let fear into the chinks, because once it found a way in, it wormed to the centre of you. She'd learned that in Belfast, left in the house with Nani, no food, and no idea why her parents hadn't come back. Presumably, they were dead; nothing else made any sense.

Sitting in the darkness was like being back in the house, with Nani telling tales of India's Independence long into the nights. The stories had been about real people in the war – not just men, but women too. Women like Tara Rani Shrivastava, who'd marched for peace as her husband lay dying of gunshot wounds, and others who'd fought quietly, providing food and support behind the scenes. They'd talked and talked, her and Nani, and tried to ignore the hunger that dragged at their bellies and the constant fear of the shooting.

After three days, Nani had started to frighten Neeta. Her paper-thin skin had paled to near-grey and she'd started to wheeze. Fear for her had forced Neeta into the city for food, blankets, medicine, and she'd made it to the main road, through the changed city, all rubbled and dented. Zelo transporters flew overhead, scanning for anyone that moved, making Neeta keep to the shadows. She'd passed a half-bombed mural that marked the gable-end where the local shops had been, but when she'd rounded the corner all that was left was a crater, with nothing to scavenge – anything that had survived had long been picked over.

She'd gone home empty-handed and had sat with Nani through the rest of the night, holding her hand and brushing her hair from her too-hot forehead. After daylight had faded, she'd gone back into the city, using knowledge from her nightly joy-rides before the invasion, when she'd got out of the house no matter what her father had done to stop her, because she was smart on the streets, and quick.

She'd headed over to the Crescent to try their shops, but had come across a group of three kids going from house to house, taking anything useful and stashing it. They'd reached the end of the street, unnoticed by either of the two transports that had passed overhead, but were stopped by a group of the new-revolutionaries. She knew them, they were the same thugs who'd run the streets before the war.

Later, running for home with the little food she'd managed to find – some stale bread snitched from a bin, and a wizened apple – she tried to tell herself there was nothing she could do to stop that sort of thing happening. But it wasn't true. Tara Rani wouldn't have let something so unfair happen. Nani wouldn't agree, either: she'd been forced from her home, into a tent for weeks, because her father had refused to deny Gandhi's beliefs. That was the blood that ran through Neeta, blood that couldn't be doused by aliens or thugs who purported to be fighting for Earth's freedom.

The next night, she'd drawn the kids together and they'd cleaned out another street before they were stopped again. She agreed an exchange with the thugs: some food in exchange for her kids working as look-outs and decoys.

The next night, there were more kids waiting for her, and the next, and the next, until she'd had fifty under her protection. She trained them how to divert a patrol and hide before the Zelo could catch them; how to split up and lead the aliens on dashing runs through the estates they knew well and could lose them in.

When she'd told Nani, late on the last night when her paper skin had stretched to breaking, Nani had squeezed her hand, telling Neeta she'd done the right thing.

Well, tonight she'd do the right thing again. She stared into the inky blackness, listening to the force field's steady hum. The Barath'na would come for her soon; she'd seen it in the long look they'd given her as she'd climbed the stairs, in their knowing growl. But mostly she knew it in the pit of her stomach that had saved her so many times in Belfast, the voice of warning she always listened to, even when, like tonight, listening would make no difference.

She clasped her hands together. Let her carry her dignity to the end. She could be like her Nani, and so many in the war, unsung and unknown, but still brave. She'd seen others taken and heard their screams, their pleas. Some of the hardest blokes she'd known had broken. She would not. She watched the screen's steady green line of calm and reached deep into herself for the courage she'd always had and had never needed more than now.

CHAPTER THIRTY-THREE

<Diagnostics>
A small whirr echoed. A beep. Another whirr.
<Diagnostics>
A whirr. Two beeps.
<Diagnosed>

***

arter pushed open the front door of the police station, his heart thumping so hard it felt like it was going to rupture through his shirt, *Alien*-style. He stopped at the reception desk. "I have to clear my desk, shouldn't be more than half an hour."

"You need to sign in, Inspector." The duty sergeant put a slight emphasis on his rank – obviously his fall from grace was not a secret.

Carter lifted his chin. Damn, he'd hoped not to. "Of course."

The sergeant watched him sign, a slight sneer on his face; any false respect had gone out the window along with his badge. Carter shrugged; to hell with them. Maybe he'd get the chance to tell Sanderson what a creep he was.

He passed offices, mostly in darkness. He assumed the Barath'na plans for the virus weren't recorded anywhere on Earth, but the prison audits might be on a system somewhere. If he could throw up a discrepancy, he could take it to O'Brien.

He pushed open the door to the general office, the automatic lights flickering on. Fifteen minutes later, he straightened up from the filing cabinet's bottom drawer and kicked it into the cabinet in disgust. Nothing.

He went back to the corridor and looked both ways. O'Brien's computer? He cursed; he knew nothing about computer hacking and he daren't search under his own password. He screwed up his face, trying to remember what he knew of O'Brien to come up with possible passwords, but wasn't even sure of her husband's name, let alone her eighteen, or however many, kids.

He crossed to her office and slipped through the unlocked door. Her desk stood, a computer casting light across the old-fashioned desk, blinking its demand for a password. He pulled the drawer instead, until it gave way with a loud splintering sound. He took out a bundle of papers. The top sheaf were budget reports, but he smiled when he read the second: official audit figures.

The main light came on, blinding him.

"Looking for something, Carter?" Downham stood in the doorway, flanked by two heavily armed Barath'na.

Carter set the papers down and backed away, licking his dry lips. These Barath'na looked different; gone was their fluffed-up fur and slightly hang-dog manner. Their hair had flattened to reveal lean, toned bodies, and the look in their eyes was anything but apologetic. His chest tightened, making him wince.

"The name I'm to report to, sir," he tried. "I didn't know where else to look other than the super's office..."

"Give me the report." Downham closed the door and locked it. "Sit down," he commanded.

Carter shook his head. "I think I'd prefer to stand."

One of the Barath'na raised its weapon; it was like nothing Carter had seen before, built around a cylindrical chamber filled with liquid, a more traditional cartridge on each side. It was alien enough to tell him the Barath'na didn't care about fitting in anymore. Not good: things were happening too quickly.

"Sit down," said Downham.

The Barath'na jerked the gun and Carter sat in O'Brien's seat. The colonel dropped into one opposite. His eyes looked shadowed and tired. He sighed. "I want to talk about Josey Dray. What she knows and where she is."

Carter cocked his head to the side. "I have no idea. Where's Superintendent O'Brien? Isn't this her pitch?"

"The superintendent isn't fully conversant with facts."

The colonel gave a soft laugh. "In fact, you're more up to date than she is. Now, where is Josey Dray?"

"I told you. I have no idea."

"We'll see what we can do to focus your thoughts." Downham nodded to the Barath'na, who brought up his forelimb, showing clawed talons, their razored edges shining in the light. Carter's blood became ice.

"Is she with the lawyer?" asked Downham.

"No." His voice was a croak. "No." He managed to put some conviction into it the second time. He had to: he couldn't let these alien... *things* turn their attention to Catherine. The claw opened and closed, raking the air as it came close to his face. Carter flinched away. Sweat broke across his shoulders. "Downham, look, I really don't know anyth–"

"Peters, then? He didn't report in tonight."

"No." But his voice wasn't as strong, not looking at those claws.

"Well, we'll soon know for sure." Downham nodded at the Barath'na. "He's all yours. Do what it takes."

Carter shrank back at the first touch of the claw on his face.

***

"So, you can't positively identify Gary McDowell as the man who killed Liz?" said Catherine.

Josey winced at the word *killed*, but nodded; the barrister had explained that she needed to be very precise. Peters was leaning out of the window, smoking a cigarette and scanning the road outside. She was safe here, that was why Carter had brought her. She thought back to the night in the stable, taking her time so that she got it right.

"I heard the shot, and I saw her body. Demos and Ray were both with me..." She started to shake, remembering the crack of the shot. "It was Gary, definitely."

"But you didn't see him?"

"No...." Josey bit her lip. "But I saw her body – it was in the back of his car. And he was with me, so he knew about it, that's definite." The two adults exchanged a glance, and

178

Catherine shook her head a little. Josey's heart skipped a beat, thinking of Gary's hard eyes, his words to her, wanting to own her. "Will they arrest him if they find him? Is it enough?"

Peters flicked the cigarette out of the window. Josey had lost count of how many he'd had. He gave curt nod, and the counsel said, "Yes, it should be enough." She reached out her hand. "You're safe now, Josey, okay? He's not coming back for you."

Josey pulled her hand away, bringing it close to her chest and clasping her other hand over it. What did this woman know about safe? Liz had told her she was safe after her parents' death, and she hadn't been. Peters was practically lighting one cigarette off the other, the way Ray had done when he was in charge on his own. None of it felt safe. "And will John be freed? I mean, I heard them say McDowell - Gary's da, that is - set him up."

"I don't know," Catherine said. "It will have to go to the GC and they'll decide if there are grounds for an appeal. But I think if we can prove you were being held, and that my clients knew - which we can - there's a good chance they'll be freed."

Josey bit her lip. "But will the Barath'na agree? If they run the prison, couldn't they just refuse or something?"

"We can take it to the Zelo," said Peters. He flicked his cigarette out of the window and came over. "They form part of the Galactic Council; we just don't see them because of the virus. That's what Carter said to do. He reckoned they were easier to deal with than the Barath'na. I think if we get the evidence, we can bypass Earth and the Barath'na, and take it straight to the Zelo. After all, it's about the virus."

Catherine smiled over at Josey. "You're doing really well." She looked down at her notes. "So, he took you outside, and then what?"

"It was really dark, and -"

The sound of ringing made her jump. Peters pulled his phone out. The ringing kept going and he swore, patting down his pockets. He pulled out a different phone and answered in a low voice. "Who?" He glanced back at Josey. "Do you know a Sean?"

She nodded, remembering Carter giving him his number. "Is he all right?"

"He's fine." Peters lifted the phone again. "Where are you? Right. Don't go anywhere near the GC, stay off the main roads and find somewhere to hole up."

He closed the phone and Catherine raised her eyebrows. "What is it?"

Peters came over and crouched in front of Josey, and he looked serious. "He said that there was an accident - a fire - and they had to leave the house."

Josey's hand went to her mouth. A fire? She thought of the bright room, its blue walls and Sean's guitar propped against the wall. Of the kitchen's range, and flickering lights.

"The house?" And then his words really sunk in. "Paula?" she asked. "And Sean's da, are they okay?"

"Aye." Peters glanced up at Catherine. "But the boy thinks it was deliberate. More than that: he says it was the Barath'na."

"The Barath'na? How can it be the Barath'na?"

Peters shook his head. "I don't know. And he might be wrong... but the thing is, he knew who Josey was, and they knew she'd talked to him."

The silence held in the room. They'd tried to kill Sean, just because he knew her name. She hadn't told him everything, not like she'd told Catherine and Carter, all the names and the whispers. She pushed her hands against her tummy, pressing her skin until it was sore, and scrunched into her seat. It wasn't just Gary who wanted her now. She wasn't safe. Not at all.

"Henry!" Catherine said. "We have to warn him. If they're bold enough to do that, they won't be worried about him. Not anymore. He needs to be careful, Phil."

Peters held up the phone. "We can't reach him." He took his own phone from his pocket and punched a number. "I'm going to talk to Downham, and see about getting her somewhere safe. He needs to know about this - it goes way above my pay grade."

He walked out to the hall, and Catherine gave a weak smile. They sat in silence, listening to Peters' deep voice, not able to catch any of it. A few minutes later, he came back into the living room. "We're going. Now."

"Why?" Catherine stood up. "What's wrong?"

Josey watched between the two adults, nervous. Peters reached for her hand. He was gentle, not hurting her, but he pulled her to her feet.

"The colonel knows Carter had Josey. He says Carter told him she was with me and wanted to know where we are."

"So? That's what we wanted: to let the colonel know."

Peters paused just a moment too long. "Why didn't Carter tell him where we are? Or send a squad car." He rubbed his chin. "Downham was very insistent that I should bring her directly to him. When I asked to speak to Carter, he hung up."

Catherine's face changed, crumpling a little. "Phil, we can't leave him, we have to go and get him..."

"Not until this little one is safe." Peters marched Josey to the front door and opened it. He pointed at the car. "Over you go, love." Catherine followed, protesting, and he cut across her. "Catherine, they know you worked with Carter. They'll come here. They might try my place first, but th-"

"Sal and the boys?" asked Catherine.

He shook his head. "They're at Sal's mum. I didn't want them in the middle of any more riots. I think I aged ten years last time, worrying about them." He unlocked the car, its lights giving a flash.

"Peters, we can't leave Henry," said Catherine. Both she and Josey climbed in. "We could drive past the station and pick him up. It would take seconds..."

Peters started the car. A soft click echoed as the central locking activated, and he pulled out and down the road. The rain was heavier than earlier, running in streaks down the windows, and the mist was thick enough to obscure the houses. It felt like they were driving through an empty world.

"Catherine," he said. "I'm sorry. It's too late to warn Carter."

They drove out of the small estate and into the darkness.

CHAPTER THIRTY-FOUR

ohn jerked as his restraints gave a little, and glanced up to see his line had moved to a soft amber. Bollocks, he'd almost fallen asleep.... He forced his hands into fists and dug his nails into his palms, waking himself fully. It was dark in the empty dining hall. He opened his mouth to shout but his lips were dry, and the scab from earlier tore away. His yell changed to a hiss of pain. He forced his mouth open and croaked, "Come down here, you bastards. I have a request."

Nothing except blackness, the tightness holding him up, the numb cold of his fingers and toes. He blinked tiredness from his eyes and spent a satisfying few minutes imagining what he would do to the governor if he got his hands on him. His line deepened to red, the restraints tightened and he half-smiled; he could wait them out. He had fuck all else to do.

"I want," he yelled, and it came out only a little stronger. He tried again. This time it carried. "I want to see the governor!"

Nothing. His eyes started to close and he tried to work out how long he'd been standing here. Hours, anyway, and he'd already been knackered after the fight. He stood, half-dreaming of flying over Inish Carraig like a bird, looking down at himself pinioned, the soft clicking of a Barath'na the only noise in the dark room...

His eyes shot open. The clicking noise didn't go away, but came closer, claws scraping on the hard dining hall floor. John looked up at the tiers of cells: they were all closed, keeping their own secrets. Neeta and Taz were up there, waiting for the same click of claws. Fear pierced him, and the wall tightened. A sudden light made him blink and try to turn his head.

"The wall is linked to our control room," the governor said, coming closer. "It changes shape. Today a prison, tomorrow, who knows? A ship, a transporter, a body-harvester. An ark? We control its shape and movements." The

182

alien stepped into the pool of light around John. "The restraining programme has parameters for safety built in." Its muscles bunched under the thick fur, as if ready to pounce. John swallowed, determined not to show his fear, but the breath he took was ragged.

"Those parameters include ensuring breathing orifices remain clear."

The metal at the edge of John's eyes moved. He blinked. The idea of it flowing over his eyes and blinding him...

"Apparently you've shown considerable determination in wanting to see me," said the governor.

Now the metal was drawing closer to his mouth. He tried to shake his head, as if that would dislodge it, but was held too firmly.

"I'm worried about my friend," he said. "He isn't well."

"Your friend is ill. Shock, psychosomatic, from whatever happened in Belfast. You are related to that incident; it isn't in his best interest to interact with you."

"He was getting better." It wasn't his imagination, the metal was oozing over skin that had previously been clear, a slow flow that threatened to push him into panic. He tried, on reflex, to bring his hand up to wipe his face, but it couldn't move. He licked his lips and imagined he could taste sharp metal. "Please, the metal. Don't..."

"Unfortunately, he took a considerable turn for the worse earlier." The governor's voice cut John's off. It gave a pointed gaze at the third floor. "He is being moved to the medical wing tonight."

Fear surged through John. "You can't – I'll report it."

"To who? Your police ally has had his visit. He won't be back." The governor snarled and leapt forward. Its teeth were inches away from John's face. Saliva dripped the length of sharp canines. "I've heard he's already been taken care of."

John's stomach sank. "What will happen to me?"

"I think you'll find that you're about to encounter a regrettable malfunction of our security systems, Mr Dray."

The governor turned away. The metal oozed, touching John's lips and spreading under his nose.

"You can't do this!" John shouted. It echoed around the

room. He stuck his tongue out, trying to reach the metal, as if he could lick it away, but the steady flow kept going. He closed his eyes as the metal touched his lids. He couldn't let it cover his eyes, he'd go mad. He stood, barely breathing. No one he cared about would know what had happened, how he'd tried to get the word out of the prison and tried to save Earth from the Zelo's fate. How he'd done the right thing at the end.

***

"Who has her? We know she left Coleraine with you."

Carter opened his right eye - the one he could - at Downham's voice. At least they hadn't worked out where Peters was. Either that, or the sergeant had remained one step ahead. He was smart enough to.

Downham crouched in front of him. The door of the office remained closed; if anyone had heard Carter's yells, they hadn't interrupted. The openness of the attack chilled Carter. One of the Barath'na moved forward and he flinched away, but it extended its claw and set it against his unmarked cheek.

"You don't understand," said Downham. "We need to stop this now, before it goes further, and brings more people in. I mean, that poor family in Coleraine....who knows what fabrication the child told them?"

Oh, God, I should have told that lad to run and keep running. Carter tried to get up, but the claw dug into him. He sank back.

"She told them nothing, she ran before she had a chance," he said, his words exhausted and drawn out. "It's in her testimony. You don't need to hurt the family."

"So you *can* speak," said Downham. "Tell us what we want to know. I don't want to hurt you. Hell, you're a police officer, a good one..."

He looked like he meant it. Carter's heart jumped with hope. "I don't kn-"

A claw raked down his cheek, making him shout out at the sharp pain. Blood tracked to the side of his mouth and tasted of salty iron.

"Where is the testimony?" Downham asked, his voice tight, almost desperate.

Why did it matter? He looked at Downham, saw the sweat beading his forehead, and it clicked. "Knew McDowell well, did you, Downham?"

The Barath'na tugged the gash on his cheek, pulling the skin back. Carter yelled and tried to move his head, but the alien held him. It moved its claw to just under his eye.

"Don't," said Carter. "I really can't hel-"

The claw moved closer, so that it sat right at the very corner of his eye, where he could see the shadowed length of it.

"The testimony," said Downham. "Where is it?"

"Safe." This was only going to end one way; they'd never let him go. He opened his mouth and found he could squeeze out the words. "You're not getting it, so go fuck yourself."

The colonel looked up at the Barath'na, nodded, and the claw raked down Carter's cheek. Carter screamed and writhed, trying to get away.

"We won't stop until you tell us. Best to make it easier on yourself." Downham nodded at the Barath'na by the door. "If you don't talk, I'll get someone to fetch her kid brother and sister. That should encourage her to come in."

"Don't." Carter's voice rose. "What the hell happened to you, Colonel? Using kids? You fought to keep the kids saf-"

Sweat broke across his chest as the Barath'na ripped his claw along Carter's shirt, tearing it down the middle. Carefully, Downham pushed the material back and neatened the edges.

"I knew you were anal, you bastard," muttered Carter. His teeth were chattering, and he doubted the colonel could understand him.

The colonel laid his hand on Carter's knee, stopping it from shaking. "We'll work from the top down, until you manage to remember exactly what Josey Dray knows."

Carter moaned as the Barath'na reached for him, and closed his eyes. Dear God, let this be over quickly.

CHAPTER THIRTY-FIVE

eters' fingers drummed on the steering wheel, and Josey realised he didn't know what to do. She bit her lip. If he didn't know how to help, and he'd been the one Gary was worried about, who did?

"What about O'Brien?" Catherine asked. "Can she be trusted?"

Peters glanced in the mirror. "I don't know. She was standing with the colonel earlier. I don't think we can take the chance."

They turned to the left and street lights passed, quick blurs in the night. Catherine glanced at Josey and managed a smile. "You okay?"

"What will happen?" asked Josey. "Will I still be able to see the kids?"

Catherine sat up straighter. She ran a hand through her hair. "The kids. Peters, if Downham wants to bring Josey in..."

Peters' eyes met hers in the mirror. "Shit."

"Do you know where they are?"

He shook his head. "Carter set it up with Downham." Peters tugged a cigarette from his top pocket and punched the lighter into the dashboard.

Josey looked between the two adults. Her stomach felt like it had dropped from the car. She grabbed Catherine's arm. "You have to stop him."

"Let me think," said Peters.

"You should pull over," said Catherine, but he shook his head, keeping the car moving, and Josey understood why; it felt like if they stopped, it would be the end of everything.

Peters tossed Carter's phone back to Catherine, and lit the cigarette. He took a long drag. "Start going through his mail; see if you can find anything to tell me where Sophie and Stuart are."

Catherine started to search. She looked up after a few minutes, her eyes frantic. "There isn't anything."

186

Josey let out a small yelp, one she didn't mean to. She leaned over, scanning the phone.

"Keep looking," said Peters. "Carter dropped the kids off. He'll have a record of it somewhere. He's the messiest person I've ever worked with; he won't have wiped it. He *won't*."

He wound down his window and flicked the cigarette out, so that it flew away in the wind, sparking. The rain made big splotches on the glass, and he put the wipers on full. On another night, in the warm car, their thrum-thrum would have been comforting; tonight, it seemed to mark every minute that passed. Catherine went back to the phone's menu. "Emails, websites, maps, games, an app for the Guardian," she muttered.

Josey pointed at the phone. "My da used to save the last map he used."

Catherine opened the app. "Yes!" She reached the phone forwards. "Peters."

He took the phone, balancing it on the steering wheel, and tried to read it. The car swerved. He pulled over. "Date's right. The kids were moved about a week after the Galactics arrived. The area looks okay, too – Carter went past his parents' place on the way home. He brought me a brace of pheasants from the estate." He spun the car in a tight circle. "Let's go get them, shall we?"

Josey's head spun, dizzy. Stuart and Sophie. She was going to see them. She squeezed her eyes closed. It was going to be all right. It *had* to be all right. Please God, let it be all right. She sent the prayer with all her might.

***

"Stop." Downham's quiet voice cut through the pain. The alien took its claw off Carter's chest, pulling at the latest tear, more for fun than anything more serious, it seemed. Carter bit down against a scream and dipped his head, exhausted, but Downham pulled it back up by the hair. "Tell me about the boys' bots."

Carter blinked; *the bots?* Downham already knew about the bots. He tried to speak, but his lips were swollen and thick. He licked them and mumbled, "Wha' about them?"

Downham pushed his head further back, sending a spike of dull pain down Carter's spine. "What were they designed to do?"

He didn't answer. Someone – or something – lashed out, catching him square on the balls. Carter screamed, loud and long.

"Their security function: what was it?" Downham demanded.

Carter gulped air. The pain raced through him, and he needed to double over or throw up. The colonel held his head back and he could do neither. "I dunno," he gasped. "Just ... act'vate if the boys in danger."

"Keep going."

"Tha's it." Christ, it hurt. "I didn't think they would work."

Downham let go and Carter's head fell forward. He panted against the pain. Dimly, he heard the colonel telling the Barath'na to go out and get the transport ready, they'd go up to the prison and see what it meant for themselves. The Barath'na left and Downham turned to Carter.

"Wha's gonna happen..." Carter licked his lips.

"You can join McDowell and his gang."

This was it. He'd never get the truth out, and Peters had no chance, not buried in Downham's command. The Zelo's dead baby, the image of the virus creeping over his parents' estate, cut through the pain. He managed to lift his head.

"Why?" he rasped. "Wha' do you get from the Barath'na? You're not immune?"

"What are you talking about, Carter?"

"The virus." Downham bleared in front of him, coming and going. "They're gonna release it. On Earth. Do the same to us as ... Zelo."

Downham swore and reeled back. "You're wrong." He started to pace, coming and going from Carter's vision. "The Barath'na assisted us in removing the Zelotyr."

"It's them." Carter tried to follow Downham, but was too tired. His eyes drooped. "The Barath'na did it. The boys – there's proof in the prison, I think."

Downham shook his head. "You're wrong." He sneered. "You'd say anything to get out of this mess."

"Think about it," said Carter. "Did you see a Barath'na

188

show itself, no' all cute before? Did you see them handling their own weapons? Or their fur all matted?"

Downham's face twisted, as if in denial.

"They're showin' ... true colours." Carter coughed and the pain nearly doubled him. It took a moment to be able to speak again. "They don' care anymore. They know they have us." He lifted his head, met Downham's eyes. "We're prey."

Downham shook his head. "No, we're partners. Earth released the virus – the Barath'na got share of the planet."

He crouched in front of Carter and peered close at him. Carter watched him, woozy, taking in the words with a sense of almost-relief. If he was being told this, the end was near. His breath raked in and out, but there was something else he had to say, something important. He licked his lips, wincing at the sharp line of pain. "The boys. Not fair. Set up."

"The boys are lucky they're not already dead; McDowell was told to release the virus and ensure it couldn't be traced back to the military. Whatever means he used was to be destroyed."

"Killed," said Carter. It was pedantic, and useless, and not worth saying, but important. "Not destroyed."

The colonel waved a hand.

"But..." Carter gasped. "Zelo were at peace with us." Tiredness seeped through him, heightening his misunderstanding. "They'd stopped killing."

"*After* they'd wiped our people out." The colonel stopped, looking out the window. The lights of a transport swept across the blinds, and he pulled one of the slats to the side. "They didn't need to fight anymore, we were beaten. But without access to space-technology we had no hope of withstanding another war if they reneged on their deal. We couldn't leave Earth open to that. The GC would have to send the Barath'na in once the planet was closed off to the Zelo, we knew that. They offered to support our tech-development in exchange for removing the Zelo."

"Wha's in it for them?" asked Carter.

"Wiping out the Zelotyr. The Barath'na loses a martial enemy that had already proved to act in its own self-interest. The two races hate each other like you wouldn't believe. They make Belfast look like a model of tolerance." He peered at Carter. "What do you know? Exactly?"

"The virus..." His throat was dry. "They're testing it on the prisoners. John says. I was trying to find evidence." He paused, thinking of John. "But, I's sure. And you're gonna be as dead as I am. Wha' – you think they'd do it to the Zelo and not us?" He tried to nod at the desk. "Audit figures. Prisoners dead."

Downham's eyes narrowed. He got his arm under Carter's shoulder, making him cry out.

"If you're lying to me, I'll see you dead in a ditch," the colonel said.

"Where're we going?"

"Inish Carraig. We'll find out the truth when we get there." A chink of a chance. Carter grasped it, knowing the truth of himself; he didn't want it to end. Not like this. The colonel tightened his grip, supporting Carter's weight. "If you're right, I'll bring the bastards down myself."

One of the Barath'na came back into the room, and the colonel fell quiet, but Carter could feel how tight his muscles were, how much he was holding his anger in.

"Transport is ready." The alien pointed at Carter. "Shall I finish him?"

"No." The colonel hauled Carter forwards. His hands were strong and steady, keeping Carter upright as he teetered. "Take him with us. He could be useful."

CHAPTER THIRTY-SIX

Peters glanced back. "Keep checking behind."

Josey nodded and looked out the back window. The road was dark and empty, the rain leaving long fingers on the window. "No one there." She yawned and leaned against Catherine, who was warm and smelt of something softer than perfume. Apples? Something like that.

"Shhh, close your eyes, I'll watch," said Catherine.

"No." She sat up, watching through the window as they drove on, she didn't know for how long, until the car slowed. Peters turned off the main road, onto a country one. There was a splash as their car went through a puddle and then the longer, slow sound of a flood. He pulled onto a smaller, rutted road. "Christ, this place really is in the middle of nowhere."

Josey looked out. "How far?"

"Another couple of minutes," said Peters. "I'd be better in a boat."

The car stopped, jerking Josey forward in her seat. There was no house in sight. Peters swore.

"What is it?" asked Catherine.

"The road is flooded, there's no way I can get through."

Peters got out and Josey followed, stepping into water beyond her ankles. Her feet went from under her, skidding in the slick mud. Peters took her elbow, and she reached back, letting Catherine grab her arm.

"Come on." Peters set off up the lane, wading through the water, and now she could see a house just ahead, lights shining from both floors. They turned a corner and a figure stepped out onto the pathway, another behind him. Josey stifled a yelp.

"Sergeant Peters, the colonel said we could rely on you to turn up." The first figure nodded, silhouetted in the moonlight. "Take them to the house and get the little ones; the colonel doesn't want any loose ends."

***

The force field buzzed once, loud in the silence. Neeta sat up, her heart pounding. This was it: they were coming for her. She tried to stay composed but she'd never known fear like this, one not driven by the rush of action, but a slow dread building for weeks. She drew in a breath, and then out, in and out. There was no sound from the Barath'na, no whispering bodies, no claws on the hard floor, no movement at her door.

Voices came from the corridor: human ones. She pulled on her boots and crept to the door. A figure passed, heading for the stairs, then another. A yell ripped through the corridor: "Escape!"

He'd done it. John's policeman had only gone and blown the prison open. She stepped out of her cell. The emergency lighting in the corridor just about gave enough light to find her way. The force fields were all open. Adrenaline surged, an old friend, and she merged into the crowd of prisoners, moving easily to the staircase and down, carried in the wave of people going only one way. Out.

She crossed the main hall, staying with the crowd, ready for the Barath'na. Once they appeared, they'd come in numbers; her only hope was to be faster than the others in the crowd, a quicker shadow, like her kids luring the Zelo patrols away. She reached the door to the entrance hall. It was open. The red light above it flashed, as if in warning. The crowd surged forward, shouting to keep going. A first pulse of gunfire sounded. Someone screamed.

Neeta looked behind her. The floor of the prison was opening, the metal melting away. Bodies came from the foundations of the building, flowing like the metal itself. Her hand went to her mouth. There were hundreds of Barath'na, thousands of them.

She ran into the entrance hall, its line of cubicles gleaming softly. Her hand went to her shoulder, remembering the pain of the implant, her fear that day. Fresh sea air hit her face, full of brine and freedom. She ran forwards, wanting that freedom, wanting to get away from the horror in the hall behind her. She was going to get out. When she did, she'd get to the mainland even if she had to swim back to Belfast and the streets she'd made her own. She'd shake John Dray by the hand and tell him he was a fucking geniu....

Hell. John had been in restraints. Was he free, or embedded in the wall as the rest of the prisoners claimed his escape? She paused, torn. Prisoners passed her. Another gunblast tore through the air, followed by a growled instruction, not distinct enough to follow. John might already be out; she'd be nuts to risk herself on a what-if. Decided, she stepped towards the open door and freedom.

Something moved in the entrance hall, low to the ground like a cat or a dog. She stifled a yell, sure it was a Barath'na, but it didn't move like the aliens, sinuous and feral, but hovered as it flew silently forwards. Neeta squinted. It was the kettle-bot, the one that had come to John's rescue in the yard, heading into the prison. As she watched, another emerged from a cupboard: a cupboard whose security seal lay open, obviously triggered by the prison's systems-fail.

"Shit." The bots would only be going back to the prison for one thing; those who'd witnessed the fight had said the bot was focused on John. The sound of firing, and another scream, came from the prison. She ran her hands through her hair, pulling at it. "Shit."

She paused for one more moment and then followed the bots back into Inish Carraig. She couldn't leave John facing the Barath'na on his own. She'd left so many behind: Nani, Niamh, her parents. She wasn't leaving John. She hugged close to the wall, her year in Belfast paying off. The flowing mass of bodies didn't pause to stop her, but focused on the mass of prisoners making their way out of the prison, not in. There'd be plenty of time to catch up with the ones on the inside later.

***

Peters stepped forward. He dipped his head, lit a cigarette and took a drag, the red tip glowing like a beacon. Finally, he said, "Good lads. The colonel sent you?"

Catherine hissed. Josey stayed beside her, close in. What did that mean?

He put his collar up against the driving rain and pointed his cigarette up the drive. "Let's go."

One of the soldiers exchanged a glance with another. "Stop your crap, Peters, and hand over your weapon."

Peters laughed, a soft laugh. "Lads, you're out of date. That turncoat fucker Carter was taken in tonight; you have me on your side. Check with the colonel, if you need to."

Josey shook her head. Demos had said Peters couldn't be bribed, that he was safe. The soldier must be bluffing. But his face was set and stern and when he glanced at her his eyes were hard, flat, not unlike Gary's.

"You can't," she said. "I trusted you."

Peters shrugged. "Next time, you should be more careful." He set off up the path, looking over his shoulder once, and jerked his head at the youngest soldier. "Come on, for Christ's sake. We need to get this done. You want to clear this little loose end, don't you?"

An arm encircled Josey's elbow and she glanced to the side, making out the face of one of the soldiers – he looked very young and unsure of himself. She followed Peters' bobbing cigarette.

She reached the end of the lane and stepped onto a pathway. The house was just ahead, spewing light from its open door down the driveway. Beside her, Catherine was walking steadily. Josey shivered at the rain running down the back of her neck and round her collar. Her trousers were stuck to her legs and she could barely see past the water streaming from her hair. She lifted her hand to push it back, but the soldier tightened his hold on her elbow. She wrenched away, glaring at him, and ran her fingers through her fringe. He was even wetter than she was and appeared just as miserable. He didn't take her arm again.

They reached the house and stepped into the hallway,

water dripping onto the tiles. In front of her was a kitchen, guarded by two soldiers. Their weapons were trained on two sullen female policewomen sitting at the kitchen table. Catherine stopped inside.

"Catherine?" said Josey. "What do we do?"

The lawyer put an arm around her shoulders. She was shaking a little, but she was composed and alert, her eyes scanning the room, missing nothing. "I don't know." She tightened her hold. "Be ready – if you get the chance, run."

Josey frowned. The kids were here – she couldn't run and leave them to Peters and the other men. She ducked out from under Catherine's arm. But the lawyer was right about one thing: she should wait for a chance to do *something*.

"Where are the kids?" Peters said, voice tight.

The two soldiers who had accompanied them up the driveway exchanged a glance. "Peters, we need to check this with the col–"

Peters opened the door beside him and stepped in. A moment later he turned. "Josey. Come here."

She hesitated, but he gave an impatient click of his fingers, and she stepped forward. He had a half-amused look on his face and a part of her wanted to believe this was a trick he was playing. The part of her that had survived the last year knew better, though: he'd betrayed her, just like everyone else.

One of the soldiers put his hand out and stopped her. "We're to get rid of them, that's what the colonel said."

"Aye," said Peters. He tossed his cigarette on the floor and ground it out with his foot, his eyes fixed on the soldier. "It doesn't mean we have to be bastards about it. Let the kids see her; she'll give them a bit of comfort."

Josey stumbled past Peters. The kids were there, right in front of her, with haircuts and decent clothes – actual pyjamas, not her and John's old t-shirts. She looked at them, not quite able to believe it. She'd been so sure they were dead, even after what Carter had said. And now they were here, and everything was wrong, and they were going to be dead anyway. Tears blurred, but she blinked them away. She had to watch and be ready.

195

"Josey, you're here." Sophie's voice was tiny and shocked, but full of relief.

"I'm here, honey," said Josey. She managed not to choke, but crouched down. "I'm here."

Stuart stared for a moment, rooted to the spot, and then he took off across the room, Sophie just behind. Josey opened her arms and they hit her like two cannonballs. The children's heads burrowed against her. They smelled clean, like they'd just had a bath. Josey looked up at the soldiers. She made her eyes big and round – bushbaby eyes, her da used to say. Let the soldiers see what they were going to do here tonight, let them know how much Josey loved the kids, how much they needed her. Catherine's mouth quirked a little, but Josey couldn't tell if it was from understanding of what Josey was doing, or pity, or fear. Peters looked hard and terrifying. She wanted to say something to him, beg for the kids, anything, but he caught the arm of the soldier beside him.

"Right. Get them up, and take them outside. We'll do the wee girl, first."

The soldiers exchanged a glance and Peters pushed past them. "For fuck's sake, if you're going to do a job, at least have the balls to get it over with." He shrugged. "The wee lad then, would that be easier? Choose one of them."

He pulled Sophie from Josey, and the child tried to hold on, but Peters' grip was too strong. Sophie yelled as she was handed to the startled soldier. Peters made to lift Stuart, but the boy clung to Josey, screaming.

Josey tightened her arms around him. "He's mine," she said. "So's Sophie."

"Let him go," Peters said, his voice hard. He wasn't bluffing. No one could bluff this well.

She had to bite back tears; she'd come this far without falling apart, she wasn't going to now. Not with the wee ones watching. She shuffled back. Stuart was buried against her.

"Leave us alone!" she shouted. "You're worse than them. You pretended to help!"

A noise came from the hall – a scuffle from the kitchen. Catherine slammed the front door and moved to block another soldier from entering into the living room. The lawyer had changed, was much more imposing. "Peters!" she yelled.

"Got it." Peters spun on his heel and kicked out at the young soldier, sending his gun clattering. He turned to the one holding Sophie and pulled the child away. The soldier backed against the wall, fumbling to bring his rifle up. A smile started on Josey's face; she'd known Peters was good. She *had*. Her smile faltered. But he'd been very good at being bad.

"Don't bother, lad," said Peters. "Not for orders that are a sack of shit."

Peters raised his pistol. Catherine grabbed Sophie and cradled the child against her, turning her head into her chest.

"Shhhh," she whispered, and the little girl nodded against her. The lawyer backed right up against the front door, blocking anyone from either leaving or coming in, her eyes firmly on a soldier in the hall, who hesitated, took in Peters, and dropped his rifle. It bounced off the hard floor.

Peters grinned. "That's one job done."

Catherine released Sophie, and the child looked around, blinking until she saw Josey. She ran to her sister, hurling herself against her.

"You knew!" said Josey. "You knew he was pretending, and you didn't tell me. I was scared."

Catherine shook her head. "I didn't know, Josey. I trusted him."

Trust. Josey blinked. She used to trust people all the time – her ma, her da, John, Sean's family – and it had got her nowhere. She looked at Peters, how his face was creased into a smile, not hard at all, at Catherine, who'd trusted, and she gave a slow nod. "Will you be able to help John? Can I trust you to do that?"

The big soldier's grin dropped away. "No. They're on their own up there."

CHAPTER THIRTY-SEVEN

The wall drew back and John staggered forwards, onto his knees. He rubbed his mouth, checking the metal had gone, that it wasn't still threatening to choke him, and realised the monitoring screen had gone blank and the door leading to the entrance hall stood open.

What the hell? He clambered to his feet, shaking. Crowds of prisoners had converged in the main hall. John started across to them but stopped when he saw the gaping hole in the metal at the centre of the room. It led down into darkness, and was filled with Barath'na. Hundreds of the bastards. Jimmy had been right: this place was their nest.

A shot rang out, bringing him out of his shock. He ran for the canteen, as far away from the Barath'na as he could, pushing past prisoners descending from the accommodation tiers. He crouched in the shadow of a table, barely breathing. What had Carter done? Surely, he must have known a prison break wasn't the answer?

The biggest crowd of prisoners were bunched by the door to the entrance hall. The report of rifles, followed by screams, cut the air as the Barath'na picked the escapees off. John squeezed his eyes shut; it was a massacre.

The room emptied of prisoners, leaving only bodies behind: some still, some groaning. A group of Barath'na streamed out of the prison after the escapees, others remaining to check the bodies. Every so often, they sent a shot into a body, making John flinch. A further group split into two swarms, one climbing the stairs to the ladies' floor and working its way down the rows of cells. He watched, paralysed with horror, knowing he should get up and do something, but with no idea what. They checked each room, closed it, and moved on to the next. The second group started at the far end of the boys' tier.

198

A small beep sounded behind John. He turned to it, crouched and alert. Jimmy's lights flashed, pleased with itself.

"Jimmy." He felt like hugging the little bot, but settled for a pat on its head. "We have to get out of here."

He stood. His back itched. He was sure something was padding into position to take aim at him. He took a first step. A quick run to the entrance hall, forty-three steps across it, and he was clear. He looked up at the cells. *Taz.* He couldn't leave Taz. They'd come this far together. He ran for the stairs, trying to keep in the shadows. The Barath'na were still working their way down the row of cells; he had a chance.

"John!"

He turned, and Neeta was just a few feet away. Her eyes were bright, her body poised for fight or flight. She was loving it, he could tell by her sharp smile and the way she moved towards him, like a cat, through the darkness.

"Get under cover where you can – they're searching," he said. "Don't try to get out; they're in the entrance hall."

"To hell with that. I came back to help you."

His heart gave an odd stutter. Mad Neeta looked after herself, everyone knew that. Something moved deep down, a twist in his stomach; he'd mattered enough for someone to come back.

"Come on," he said, glad that his voice betrayed none of what he was feeling, and he led the way up the stairs. The swarm were intent on their work; they hadn't noticed them in the darkness. Either that, or they didn't care.

John reached Taz's cell. Three Barath'na were on the opposite side, working along that row of cells, a further group halfway up his side. Not much time.

Taz was lying on the bed, his eyes dazed. Sammy was hovering over him and Jimmy joined the bot, their lights flashing recognition of each other. John knelt beside Taz. "Come on, mate, we have to go."

No movement. John cursed and looked at the door. "Come on, Taz." Nothing. There was no hope of getting out if they had to carry him. "Come on!"

"Don't shout at him, it won't help." Neeta pushed past.

"It's the worst way to get someone moving, shouting. Freaks them out." She put her hands on her hips and lifted her head. "Taz." Her low voice would have had Peters jumping to obey her. "You need to get up and moving."

Taz made a sound, deep in his throat, and started to sit up. Neeta put her hand behind Taz's back, until he was sitting straight.

"Good. John will help," she said. "We're getting out."

John put his arm under Taz's shoulders and pulled him to his feet. He weighed next to nothing, and that shocked John; in Belfast, he'd been skinny, but getting him off the Cave Hill had still taken a fair bit of effort. Now there was barely anything of him. Neeta moved to the other side, taking some of his weight.

"Let's go," said John.

They stepped into the corridor. Below, the dining area was swarming with prisoners, carefully guarded by Barath'na. One of the aliens looked up at the cells, saw him, and bared its teeth. It lifted its gun and aimed.

"Shit!" John wove to the side. A shot hit the wall behind. The metal absorbed the bullet and reformed.

"Any ideas?" he asked Neeta.

"The shower room." She jerked her thumb over her shoulder. "There's a force field door – it's the emergency way out."

"They'll think of that!"

"We don't have time for a committee."

She was right. They set off, half running, half dragging Taz. John checked over his shoulder: a Barath'na was already on its way up the stairs behind them. The room-checking aliens weren't far behind. He glanced at Neeta. "Can you manage Taz?"

"Yeah." She hefted Taz and set off. Sammy hovered above. On the second floor, shadows of the Barath'na moved from room to room.

"Jimmy," John said, and the bot appeared beside him. "Not just me tonight, all of us. We all need looking after. Tell Sammy."

There was a pulse from the bot. John moved to the top of the stairs. A Barath'na was on the flight below. It brought its rifle up. A shot fizzed off the banister.

A weapon; he needed a weapon. There was nothing. He wrenched the iron railing at the top of the stairs, willing it to break, but it didn't give. Jimmy beeped once and a laser-beam spun out, cutting the railing in two places.

"Good job." John took the bar Jimmy had created, hefting it in front of him. It felt good. Safer. He backed down the corridor.

"Hurry!" shouted Neeta. He sped up, half-tripping. The Barath'na from below appeared at the top of the stairs. It was on its hind legs, the rifle clutched in its forelimbs. Jimmy's laser arced out and there was a howl, one that needed no translator unit to understand, high-pitched and ululating; the bot's aim had been good. John backed away, faster than before. A low, dangerous growl stopped him. A Barath'na stepped off the upper staircase into the corridor, its eyes a molten gold of hatred. *The governor.*

"Run!" yelled John over his shoulder. He looked at Jimmy. "I'll take the big bastard. You deal with the others."

The governor came down the corridor and John braced for the attack. The Barath'na sped forward, growling. John waited until it was in range. He took a swipe with his bar, but the governor jumped, not breaking its run. It snarled, diving at John, who was forced back. He slipped and went down on one knee. Instinctively, he raised the bar above his head. His arms jolted as the governor hit it and rebounded off, knocking John onto his back. The governor jerked the bar from his hands and it dropped with a dull clang. John scrabbled away.

"Neeta!" John yelled. "Watch out!" He staggered to his feet. A sharp fizz passed his ear, and growls grew louder behind him. He picked up the bar and turned back to the governor.

Muscles rippled under the alien's fur. The iron bar wasn't going to make much of an impact, but John was out of options.

Sammy fired at the governor, singeing its fur, but the Barath'na pushed on. Neeta let go of Taz, leaving him to steady himself against the wall. She placed herself between Taz and the snarling governor. "All right, you big alien fucker." She took up a fighting stance. "I've taken on worse than you."

The alien crouched. Sammy moved in front of Taz. John

201

closed in from behind, the bar raised and ready. If they stopped the governor, the aliens had no leader. A shot whizzed past his ear and he swung the bar, too early. It glanced off the governor's shoulder. The alien turned to face him, snarling.

"Fuck!" John raised it again. Adrenaline pumped through him, giving him strength.

The governor sprang at him, a blur of matted fur. John yelled as its teeth sank into his arm, and his grip on the bar loosened. The alien's weight came onto him, pushing him against the wall. It released his arm, snarling, and lunged for his throat. John held it back, but his arms were tiring. The alien was too strong.

A laser shot passed him. The smell of burned fur filled the air. The governor howled and Neeta lashed out, catching the alien square on its throat with her foot. It fell forwards, pinning John to the wall, knocking the wind from him. A second laser grazed the governor's snout and it jumped away, howling. John slid down the wall.

Jimmy elevated and sent another laser shot at the governor. The alien backed away. Arms grabbed John, and he and Neeta tumbled into the shower room. Taz was already there, breathing heavily, Sammy beside him. Jimmy moved in front of John and hovered in the doorway, his lights flashing, quick and alert.

John clutched his arm where the governor had bit it. It throbbed in sick pain, and he gritted his teeth. "What now?"

"We go." Neeta was standing by an open space in the wall, where a force field door would normally have been. John stepped forwards to it – the opening led to a fire-escape, its metal steps hugging the wall. At the bottom, at least thirty feet down, the island dropped away to the white surf of the roaring sea.

"Oh, Christ." John faced Neeta. "Get Taz down. Me and Jimmy'll buy some time."

"No, we all go."

He shook his head. "They'll pick us off the stairs. Go!" He grinned. "We don't have time for a committee."

She gave a salute of touché, and started down. John turned, facing the open door back into the prison. It was quiet beyond it, but he wasn't fooled. The aliens might be more careful – John glanced at Jimmy, a little stunned at the bots' effectiveness – but they'd be coming.

"Any ideas?" he asked Jimmy. A laser shone on a shower cubicle door. It intensified, cutting away the hinges.

"You fucking genius," said John. He grabbed the cubicle door as it came off, and hissed at the pain in his arm. He slammed it across the entrance to the shower room, holding it as Jimmy soldered it to cover two thirds of the doorway. The bot finished and moved back, lights flashing.

"Good job," said John. "But it won't hold them long; let's go."

The bot's lights pulsed, but it didn't move. It faced the soldered door. John looked between the little bot and the door and shook his head.

"No, Jimmy, there're too many. You need to come with me."

The bot sank to the ground and beeped, just once. The soldered door crashed as something hit it from the other side. Another hit and it buckled. Jimmy beeped again, surer this time, and John backed onto the stairs. The wind caught him with frigid fingers and the driving rain sent needles against his face and bare arms.

"Come on, Jimmy, we can make it!" he yelled.

The door burst open and Barath'na filled the room, coming one on top of the other. John ducked from a first shot. Jimmy moved off the floor, spinning, a pair of its laser beams firing. One of the Barath'na gave a howl and fell back.

"Jimmy, come on!" John reached forward to grab the bot, but it danced from his grasp. More Barath'na appeared in the doorway. There was nowhere to go but down. A rifle-bolt hit the top of the staircase, inches from him, and the metal banister parted in the middle. John backed away, his mouth dry, until the railings stopped him. If he fell from here, he was dead. Jimmy beeped, insistent and loud.

"Don't," John whispered. "I need you."

Another shot fizzed past. He had to run, he had no option.

He hesitated for just one more second – it was a bot, not a person, he couldn't go back for it – and then ran, taking the stairs two at a time, using the banister to let him half-run and half-slide. He needed its support; he could barely see past the blurring in his eyes. He blinked and told himself it was sea spray.

A bolt passed him, just missing. "Fuck it." He grabbed the banister. It was slippery from the rain and he leant over, sliding down on his stomach, not looking where it was going or at how far he might fall.

A shot hit his shoulder and he yelled at the red pain searing across it, but he kept going. He looked back, half hoping to see Jimmy, and saw a row of dark shapes running down the stairs after him. There was a jolt as his feet hit the floor of the final landing and he vaulted over the edge, dropping the last six feet. He ducked into the shadow of the prison, under the bottom landing. He turned in a half-circle and cursed. Taz and Neeta were gone.

arter was pushed into the back of the GC transporter, the colonel on one side of him, a Barath'na on the other. He struggled to stop shaking. It was the cold, he told himself, but when the doors closed he still shivered. He put his head back and closed his eyes. At least the aliens had stopped hurting him. "Why are we going to the prison?"

"The prison's security has been compromised." Downham laughed, a soft laugh. "Apparently it was your little bots that did it."

He was dreaming this, he had to be. He rolled his head to the side and opened his good eye. "The bots?"

"They decided the prison was attacking your charges. Ergo, they killed the prison's security systems. What the hell did you have put in them?"

It made sense. A low feeling came into his stomach, half-hope, half-dread. If the bots had found the evidence he thought they had, what had he unleashed? He turned to the colonel. There'd be no disciplinary hearing in the morning; no country estate to inherit. His ribs jabbed with every breath, his right arm hung useless at his side, and he still had to face whatever was ahead for him.

"The designer had decommissioned a security-bot, GC compatible. I got him to put the chips in the bots and program them to the boys." He swallowed, and his throat hurt, too. "He falsified the disposal records, and I signed off the bots."

"Very inventive."

"And stupid." But maybe not. "So, quid pro quo. Why did you get involved with the virus? You knew the Zelo had pulled out."

The colonel paused, perhaps still seeking deniability, but gave a short laugh. "You flatter me. All I did was follow orders: make sure the virus was released and the people who

205

did the job were dead, with no link back to the military." He nudged Carter and by Christ, it hurt. "You fucked that one on me, right away. Since then, it's been damage limitation."

"You must know it was wrong," said Carter. "You were killing a whole species."

"The Earth Committee did the right thing. We'd been invaded; it was our duty to repel the invaders however we could."

Carter tried to shake his head, but it hurt too much. 'I followed orders': the weakest excuse in the world. He closed his eyes and floated to a place where there was no pain.

***

John swept his eyes along the coastline. Searchlights cut the night sky at the front of the prison. From above him, on the stairs, came growls and barked orders. Where were Taz and Neeta?

A Barath'na loped around the corner of the prison, its nose to the ground. John cringed back: if he ran, it would see him; if he stayed, he'd be found. His eyes searched the squared-off rock, panic clawing.

A female prisoner rounded the corner, stopping at the sight of the Barath'na. The prisoner started to back away, but the alien jumped, bringing her down. She managed to scramble to her feet, but the Barath'na pounced again. It knocked her against the rocks and sprang back. The prisoner lay still. *Shit.*

Something took the alien's attention, and it turned its back on John. *Now or never.* John dashed to the side. The platform the prison stood on ended in a couple of yards, and he had no idea what lay beyond. There was no time to think, to doubt, to do anything but draw in a breath and stretch his arms and jump.

He hit ground, the impact jarring his teeth. His right knee gave way and he yelled as he fell, but his old rugby instincts kicked in. He rolled to the side and protected his head with his hands. He came to a stop on a gravelled path leading to a small jetty, and waited for a searchlight to pass over. He counted. It flashed again.

Now! He darted down the path, slipping, almost falling,

and scrambled onto some scree and then a rocky beach. He ducked into the shadow of the pier as the next flash came.

"You made it," said a low, familiar voice: Neeta. "Way to go."

Relief filled John like a wave.

Taz managed a thumbs-up from where they were both hidden in the darkness. "You looked like a twat skidding down that path," he croaked.

"You're all right?" He must be: he was joking again.

"Sort of."

The relief left as quickly as it had started. Taz's sort of would be anyone else's half-dead. The light swept over them again. Escape first, assessment later. John looked around, trying to make out any detail, but the darkness was absolute. "We need to get to a boat."

"And then?" Neeta's voice was barely audible over the waves. "I'm no sailor. Are you?"

No. The memory of the trip over to Inish came back. As if laughing at him, the wind rushed around him. If he got off this island, he'd throw up for a year and never complain.

"If there's a boat, we take it." He pointed at the distant lighthouse, its white walls standing out against the darkness. There was a path, he remembered from Jimmy's map. "We'll go that way and stay away from the prison."

Neeta shook her head. She pointed towards the front of the prison. "We go for the main harbour. It's closer."

"They'll see us," hissed Taz.

John looked at him. There was no way Taz could make it around the island. Besides, on a path they'd be sitting ducks. "She's right." He pulled himself up on a rock, and stifled a cry at the pain in his arm.

"Let me see." Neeta felt along the bite. Her touch was light, experienced, but it still felt like a knife running through him. There was a sound of ripping, and she wrapped something around the cut, tying it off.

"If we get to the boats, there'll be a first-aid kit," she said. "But that'll slow the bleeding for now."

She moved out first, taking point, Taz behind her. John brought up the rear. Sammy hovered just above, his lights out.

The absence of Jimmy seemed bigger in the presence of the other bot. They started across the rocks, keeping close to the cliff edge, until they rounded the headland and could see the main pier. About ten boats, much like the one that had taken him across to the island, were moored up, two tied directly to the jetty, the others berthed up against each other. A line of five Barath'na were guarding them. John swore.

"I'll go scout." Neeta moved forward, invisible in moments. John moved forward a little, watching. A hand touched his back.

"John?" said Taz. "We need to talk."

John looked around; everything was still quiet, although he could see the searchlights. Once, as they swept across the front of the prison, he caught a glimpse of a prisoner escorted by a Barath'na. It wouldn't be long until they spread out and started to check the rocks. At that thought, he saw shadows walking on all fours along the top of the cliff, looking down. His pursuers from the prison, no doubt.

"We can talk when we get off this rock. You're okay for now."

Taz grabbed his arm. "I'm not okay." He shivered in the cold air, so badly his teeth chattered. "I'm getting worse." He coughed, covering his mouth to muffle it, and doubled over. It took a few moments before he was able to lift his head. His eyes were wide, scared... and something else. Weary. Taz was tired of it all. He managed a smile. "I'm fucked, John."

A searchlight swept towards them and they lay against the rocks, not moving, huddled in to the overhang of the shoreline, and waited. The searchlight moved on and John whispered, "You're wrong. We can get a doctor."

Taz muffled another cough and drew in a breath; it rasped, loud in the still air. "John, the virus is in me, it's all through me. They were going to move me tonight, they said so. The med-bots gave me more of the virus earlier. I know - I remember the shocks from the first time." He nodded up at the prison. "That's where the proof is, and I bet there won't be any left to find after this."

John didn't answer, remembering Neeta saying the third floor was empty, waiting for the next wave of test subjects. A finger of ice ran down his spine, making him shiver – the Barath'na might get away with this if there was no proof.

There was a slight noise from the darkness. Neeta appeared, right beside him, making him jump.

"Jesus, Neeta, that's not fucking human," he said.

"We need to find another way," she said. "They're just above where we are, and the search is looking pretty organised."

Taz whistled, a low whistle, and John almost punched him to tell him to shut up. Sammy appeared, his lights off, silently hovering. Taz brought him closer and whispered, "Give it to him."

Sammy extended one of his arms, and in it he held a vial.

"What's that?" asked John. If it was the virus, he didn't want to go near it again. Ever. Taz caught his arm and John could feel how weak he was, how his skin was stretched over bone.

"It's proof," said Taz. His voice faded, scaring John. "My blood. Sammy took it."

He closed John's hand around the vial. Another light swung past them, closer this time, and the shadowy figures were highlighted in it, about eight feet away.

"They're pinning us down," said John.

"It's me they want," whispered Taz. "They know I have the virus."

"You don't know that."

"I do." He looked straight at John. "I hurt, like you wouldn't believe." The searchlight swept back and they ducked against the rocks. It moved on and Taz pushed to his feet. "Good luck."

John took a split second too long to understand the words. He reached out with his hand – "No!"

It closed on empty air. Taz was running along the rocks, Sammy behind him. The searchlights swivelled, framing Taz. He flung his arms out, laughing, and yelled, "Come on, you fucking dogs!"

John scrambled to his feet. Neeta barrelled into him, grabbing his arm and pulling him away. He tried to fight, but she held him, her grip strong. "You can't waste the chance he's giving you!"

"No!" shouted John, tugging his arm away. He couldn't lose

Taz. The pulse of gunfire rang out. He clung to Neeta. Taz cried out and fell. The aliens surrounded him, and John was back in Belfast, on a different night, watching his ma fall: not the same aliens, but the same tableau, another loss. He slumped, not able to go on. A wash of hot tears made his eyes sting.

"There's nothing you can do!" Neeta's voice was the one that had kept a group of kids going during the whole invasion.

"I can't leave him!"

"You want him to die for nothing?"

No; that was what the aliens wanted. His father had died for nothing, and his mother. Josey, too, a gang lord's loose end. He saw the set of Neeta's jaw. She knew all about people dying. And about people finding a way, any way, to hold onto life. His hand tightened around the vial. It was the proof that would bring the Barath'na down. If they lost it, Taz's death would all have been for nothing. He turned away, wincing at the sound of another blast, and ran. He didn't look back.

CHAPTER THIRTY-NINE

he colonel nudged Carter. "Out," he said. Carter moved to the edge of the seat and climbed out of the transport. The icy wind caught the remnants of his shirt, pulling it away from the blood-crusted gashes, bringing a hiss of pain. He looked around, trying to get his bearings through the driving rain. Ahead, the darkness was absolute, blacker than the night. It took him a moment to realise the blackness was the prison. Searchlights wove around the rocks surrounding the pier and over the clifftops. The sound of shouts carried through the rain.

Just ahead, a group of Barath'na had gathered around something. He strained his eyes: not a something, a someone. It wasn't moving. The colonel pushed him along the path which ran around the prison, and Carter saw something twisted on the ground beside the body. It was one of the kettle-bots, smouldering and dead, its lights black. *Jesus*. He strained against the colonel's hands, trying to see which of the boys it was, but was forced past the body. He looked back over his shoulder, scanning all round, but there was no sign of another body. Please, let that be a good sign.

"Hurry," said a Barath'na.

The colonel pushed Carter forwards, his grip steady. As they rounded the corner, the pier where Carter had last disembarked came into view. A group of Barath'na converged on it, their movements stealthy. The prison loomed over him as he was led towards the shadow of its entrance. He tried to hold back – if they took him into the prison, he wasn't likely to come out – but was pushed hard. He stumbled forwards, up to the front doors.

He put his hands out, shoving against the doors. He propelled himself back and around, ready to fight, but an

211

alien caught him. The smell of damp fur assailed his nose. He looked in its eyes: one was half-closed, blood crusted around it, a ghoulish match for Carter's own.

"You brought him. Well done," said the governor. "I'm afraid, Colonel, what's going on here tonight isn't any concern for you."

It nodded to one of its pack, and a Barath'na grabbed the colonel, who struggled.

"See," said Carter. Pity he wasn't going to be around long enough to enjoy being right.

"You can watch as we disperse the virus," the governor said. "You worked so hard to get us here, it seems only fitting you should."

"You'll be found out!" yelled Downham. "The GC will attack."

"With what troops?" The governor pulled its teeth back in a growl. "There are no Zelotyr, and the Earthlings can't fight against us."

"They'll know where the virus came from!" The colonel strained forward, his face red with effort.

"There is no proof." The alien leaned close. "Not once we get our last loose end back."

It grabbed Carter and pushed him into the glare of a spotlight. Its claws reached for his chest, making him flinch, and tore the last of his shirt off. Carter shivered as two aliens took his arm and turned him to face the harbour.

***

John stayed low in the fishing trawler, moored at the back of the police transports, and tried to untie a knot that had become stiff in the salt water. If there was a knack to it, he hadn't been able to work it out. It didn't help that his right arm was sluggish and sore. He worked at the knot, keeping his thoughts on that, trying to ignore the vision of Taz falling to the ground, but it flashed each time he blinked. It was his fault. All of it: Taz, Josey; all John's stupid fault. And if he didn't blow open the Barath'na plot, he'd have killed all of Earth.

His hand slipped and he swore. Concentrate on the job. Opposite, Neeta must have had more luck because she'd moved on to her second rope. She'd pulled a dark tarpaulin over her, so she couldn't be seen, and her dark hair hung like a veil.

"John Dray!" The voice came from the island, loud over the hissing rain. He looked up and saw Carter, framed in a searchlight. He took in the bruised face, the blood running down his torso, and swore.

"Who's that?" asked Neeta.

"Carter. The cop." John stayed down; he wasn't sure if they knew he was on the boat – or which one, if they had seen him – but wasn't taking any chances. The island was a mass of skirmishes highlighted by lights. He ducked his head, focusing on the knot. There was nothing he could do for Carter, not from here. If he got away, if he got the vial handed in somewhere, then maybe... he stopped. The only person he had known to go to *was* Carter. Him or Peters.

A scream rang out across the rock. The governor's claw scraped down Carter's chest. *Fuck*. He tried to look away, but couldn't. They'd keep going, he knew they would, and he'd have to sit here and listen to the screams. He bent his head to the rope; he had to get away, or Taz would have died for nothing.

"What are you going to do?" asked Neeta.

"What can I do? I can't go back; they'll just kill him and me then."

She looked between John and the policeman. "I wouldn't go back, no way. My side is untied. We can cast off when you're done."

He tugged at the knot, hurting his fingers. Another scream ripped through the air, chilling in its desperation. John's eyes met Neeta's. "I can't let them..."

She put a hand on his arm. "You know how it is, John. You need to survive every day, however you do it, even if it means letting those who aren't strong enough fall."

John nodded, and swallowed against sick bile. She might be right. He'd tried supporting others to get them through, and it hadn't worked. Another scream cut through the night. He stopped, staring through the driving rain. He'd been running for a year, running in circles, each worse than the last. It had to stop. His father had stayed out of the spotlight, and he'd still died. John reached into his pocket and pulled out the vial.

"Keep this with you, don't lose it," he told Neeta. "You need to get this to a guy called Sergeant Peters, in Belfast." He moved to the side of the boat and grabbed the one next to him, climbing into it awkwardly and not quietly. A searchlight swivelled towards him. He looked back and said, "Stay down, don't let them know you're with me."

He put his hands up, grimacing at the pain, and moved to the front of the boat. "I'm here!" He stepped onto another boat, and over to the pier. The urge to glance back was strong, but he climbed the narrow metal steps to the pier and reached the first of the waiting Barath'na.

"I'm here," he said again. "Tell them to leave Carter alone."

The Barath'na growled, bringing its gun round. It was going to shoot. John's mouth went dry, but he managed to croak out, "Kill me, and you never find the proof that Taz Delaney left..."

The alien snarled and grabbed him, dragging him up the path until he was standing next to Carter. The creepy colonel was standing beside the governor, his shoulders back and proud, his face tight with hatred. Fresh blood ran down Carter's chest, and John heard a drawn-in breath. Carter's good eye met his own good eye. John took a moment to consider everything, and then grinned. "Some fucking cavalry you are."

The cop nodded, looking exhausted. A grinding noise cut through the night, and the door to Inish Carraig opened, inviting them into the hall and its forty-three steps to hell.

***

Neeta undid the last rope and pushed the boat away from the one beside it, just about getting it moving. The Barath'na had started to move through the boats, searching each. At least two other prisoners had been found and taken back to the prison. Quietly, her boat drifted out, carried by the ebbing tide. She started to crawl to the engine room and then stopped, undecided. If she switched the boat on, they'd hear her on the shore. But she couldn't just sit here, either; the Barath'na would notice it wasn't tied up soon. A wave, stronger than before, lifted the boat and carried it towards the harbour's mouth. She had no option now; she couldn't swim back, not in these waters. She sat, the tarpaulin pulled around her, watching; the focus of the search was on the island itself. The boat went out, carried on another wave; it had only been a couple of minutes, yet the shore was far away. She bit her lip, waiting for yells to say she'd been spotted, the flash of a light. Nothing. The boat left the harbour, out onto the open sea.

She crept into the wheelhouse. A light swept across the boat, making her jump, but it passed and she bent her head to the job. She'd have to hotwire the boat. She gave a tight grin; it would be nice to use her hard-won skills. The light swept over again, and she stuck her head out the door to see what it was and swallowed a small scream: it was the lighthouse, much closer than she'd expected. A few seconds later the light swept past again, revealing the sea around her. White horses rolled past her, rushing against the cliffs of Rathlin, not far away – not nearly far enough away – and breaking up. An eddy caught the boat, pulling it into a trough, spinning it in the darkness and she was sucked, once more, closer to the rocks.

CHAPTER FORTY

ohn was shoved through the entrance hall. Carter looked barely on his feet. Ahead, the cubicles stretched, and his shoulder throbbed with remembered pain at the sight of them. Carter was pushed into one, John into a second, but the door didn't close after him this time. Presumably it, too, was linked to the security systems. Instead, a Barath'na stood, blocking each entrance.

A quiet sound, almost a chuckle, made him tense. The governor appeared at outside the glass separating his and Carter's cubicles, pacing down the middle. The colonel followed, held by two Barath'na. Presumably he still had his uses.

"Taz Delaney is dead," said the governor. "His body is being... disposed of, as we speak."

John frowned at the emphasis and the governor licked his lips. John closed his eyes and told himself it didn't matter, that Taz was dead and couldn't feel it. It felt like a lie. It *was* a lie.

"We want to know what the proof is that you claim he left behind. Tell us that and we'll end things quickly."

John opened his eyes, looking straight at the governor. "Piss off."

The alien snarled his disappointment. "We'll see how strong you are." It pressed a button on the external wall of Carter's cubicle and a light blinked along the top of it. Some kind of manual override, John guessed. Clamps came out of the wall, two of them, pinioning Carter's arms at the wrists, pulling them in front of him. The blowtorch extended and Carter paled as it focused on one of the tearing gashes on his chest. Sweat broke across his forehead, and he pulled against the clamps. He looked up, meeting John's eyes. "Tell them nothing."

"What is the evidence?" asked the governor.

The blowtorch narrowed into a needle of blue flame. Carter flinched away. John tried to duck past the Barath'na guarding him, but the alien pushed him back, hard against the glass. Carter's scream carried to him.

John looked away, not able to watch. The governor padded. Another scream. Did it matter if the Barath'na knew what the evidence was? It might buy time. *What use was time?* They were going to die here, anyway. Carter's scream died away, replaced by a muffled choking as the thin line of flame moved down his body. The tip grew thinner; hotter.

"Don't!" shouted John. The blowtorch pulled away. Sweat ran down Carter's face. His lips were bitten against another yell. Across his chest a burn blossomed. "I'll tell you what it is."

Carter rasped and licked his lips. He leaned forward as much as the restraints would allow. "Tell it nothing. Unless it's to shove something painful up its arse. Sideways."

John found himself smiling. Carter may be a pain, but he had solid cojones. He didn't deserve this.

"Tell me," said the governor.

"I have a sample of Taz's blood," said John. "I'll tell you where to find it." The blowtorch pulled away and John gave a sharp nod. "I left it on the rocks, just above the tide line. I'll show you. Just don't hurt him again."

***

Neeta closed her eyes. Imprinted on the inside was the wall of cliffs. She opened them and there was only darkness, as if the nightmare had vanished. The light came round, a great sweep, and there was the cliff. The boat dipped, and she yelled, holding the rail as the prow surged forward, froth hitting her face.

She darted into the wheelhouse. The light swept round, but she determinedly didn't look. If she was going to crash on the rocks, she'd rather not watch it coming. She crouched, working her way into the control panel, reviewing the wires, sure she'd feel the crunch of the cliffs at any moment. Another flash of light enveloped the boat and she ignored it. It would pass in a minute.

It didn't.

A noise could be heard over the boat and the sea: an

engine, overhead. She left the wheelhouse. The sea churned around her, the boat dipped, but still the light didn't go. A new noise boomed over the sound of water and rain.

"This is a GC craft. Prepare to be boarded!"

Neeta paused, the disappointment bitter in her throat. She looked down at the half-pulled-apart control box. She'd never get the boat started in time. She kicked out, enjoying the crunch of the panel, and hoped it was expensive. She'd failed, and she hated fucking failing. There was a thump from the other end of the boat and then a smell hit her, familiar and strong, and her nightmares came to life in front of her.

CHAPTER FORTY-ONE

The Barath'na pulled John out of the cubicle. Carter had slumped against the glass, his lips moving in some sort of whisper.

"Take me to where you put the vial," said the governor.

The door to the prison opened. How much time could he buy? Could he pretend to be lost? That he wasn't sure where he set it? Or claim the tide had taken it? He managed not to look at the boats in front of the prison and count them. Instead he put his shoulders back and stepped out, into the keen wind.

The island was quiet, no Barath'na in sight. He shook his head, not sure what that meant, and took a step forward. A stench hit him, carried on the air, and he wrinkled his nose. The governor sniffed, loud in the quiet, and put his paw on John's shoulder, making him wince.

In the rocks ahead figures stood up, dark against the black night. John watched as one came to its full, impressive height. The governor took a step back. The figures moved forward in formation, passing under a floodlight, and their armour gleamed, golden and alive.

John backed away. *Zelo.* How could they be here... *why* were they here? He gasped as the full consequences hit him. He was dead: they were here to make him pay.

"Governor Distryn," said the biggest Zelo.

The governor barked an order at one of the Barath'na, who dropped to all fours and loped into the prison. The governor moved forward, growling. "What is the meaning of this?"

Barath'na formed up behind their leader. John took a quick count of the combined weaponry; if either side decided to shoot, he was in the middle of it. Not good. He moved behind a Barath'na; it might kill him, but at least it'd be only once.

The lead Zelo brought its gun up. "The prison is mine."

The governor snarled and leapt at the shit-eater, whose gun discharged, knocking the governor back. It howled and fell against the rocks to lie still. The rest of the Barath'na surged forwards, their translator units ignored, the air filled with snarls and growls.

Bollocks to this. John ran. He reached the cubicle where Carter was. A bolt passed, arcing close to him. He yelled and dived to the side, breathing hard. He looked around for shelter and crawled into Carter's cubicle, pulling the final glass door to, shutting them in. God, he hoped it was strong enough.

"The Zelo are here," he said, and the policeman nodded, very slightly, but was too out of it to even ask why.

Another bolt fizzed past the cubicle and John ducked; a thud, and one hit the glass, but didn't break through. Something sounded under him, a rumble that shook the building, spreading and denting the air. A Zelo-smart bomb – he'd know the sound anywhere. The Earth shook: the Zelo knew where to find the Barath'na; the bombs could destroy warrens as well as buildings.

"How can they be here?" yelled John.

"D-don't know." The cop was shuddering, mostly from shock, John decided. He pulled his t-shirt off, draping it over Carter's shoulders, and backed against the glass as another bolt passed the cubicle. Lights passed them and shapes moved in the dim room.

Something crashed against the glass. Hands pulled at the door, wrenching at it. John reached out and grabbed the handhold, keeping the door closed. A flare illuminated the figure; it was the colonel, his hands hitting the glass, his mouth open in a scream. A Barath'na clung to him, its arm around his throat. John backed off cowering, as Downham was pulled away. He turned his head at the spurt of blood that hit the cubicle, obscuring one of the glass panels.

A light flashed on the wall. Red, like the blood: on and off, on and off. The gunfire slowed. He squinted against the darkness. The soldiers – both Barath'na and Zelo – were falling back. John pulled the door open, and a siren shrieked through the room. The smell of smoke assailed him and made him choke.

220

"Carter!" he yelled. "We need to go."

Carter pulled against the clamps holding him. "Get them off!"

John clawed at them. They wouldn't give. He coughed, the smoke curling into his throat. Carter stopped pulling and fell back. His eyes met John's.

"Go," said the policeman. "I can't get out. Go."

John coughed again. He looked at the door to the island. Forty-three steps; he could make that. Even the Zelo were preferable to being burned to death. He took a step forward, ignoring a cough from Carter.

He couldn't go. He'd run from Taz, and from Jimmy, and was no better off. He backed into the cubicle and closed the door, slowing the smoke. He lifted his t-shirt from Carter and ripped it. He tied one part around his mouth, the other around Carter's. The policeman was coughing steadily now. The first finger of flame licked the edge of the cargo door.

It was getting hot. John sank a little, Carter with him, so that the cop's wrists were raised by the clamps. The heat was all around, making his skin tighten. Each breath hurt. He closed his eyes, taking shallow breaths, his strength gone.

The cubicle slammed open. Arms reached in – slippery from mucus, their smell just discernible under the smoke – and lifted John. He didn't fight – he couldn't have – and a breeze shifted the t-shirt on his face, bringing a chill wind. The Zelo carried him to the door, taking him outside. The sky whirled above him, like Earth was about to take off. The island was a crazy cacophony of fire and smoke. It roared in his ears; the stink of the Zelo filled him.

He was set on the ground, and shivered at the sudden cold. Carter was laid down beside him, breathing heavily. He sounded awful, crackling and harsh. John wrenched the t-shirt off his mouth and crawled to the policeman. Carter grabbed John's arm, tried to say something, but nothing came out. The policeman's chest jerked, as if shocked, and went still. The rasping breaths stopped.

"Carter!" John leaned over him, shaking the policeman, but there was no response. He looked up. "Do something! He's dying."

The policeman's eyes rolled backwards and John rocked back onto his heels. This couldn't be happening – they'd made it out of the prison, they'd been rescued. The policeman didn't move.

"Carter, damn you, wake up!"

Carter gave a low groan and opened his eyes. John rolled him onto his side. Carter retched black bile, spattering the ground. He groaned and rolled back, before propping himself up on his elbows and looking at the Zelo. "Christ, it worked," he croaked.

The Zelo ducked its head and said, the translated voice dull, "Inspector Henry Carter, you are free to go."

It turned to John, making his stomach twist. This was it: they were going to claim him and take him back to their home-planet. He felt like he'd died a hundred deaths already – surely he'd paid their price. He swallowed his fear – they weren't going to force him to show it, not after everything he'd been through. "The virus was Barath'naian, I can prove it."

The Zelo said nothing, just nodded, and John waited for the guards to take him, his heart pounding. He wouldn't beg. That'd be good, to hold his silence.

Neeta stepped forward, flanked by two Zelo. She had a blanket wrapped around her shoulders and her hair was lank, barely shifting in the breeze. She was lovely. Her eyes met John's, relief shining from them. He tried to get up and go to her, but even without the Zelo guarding him, he was too tired to move.

She held up the vial, letting the lead Zelo take it. The alien raised the vial.

"The Barath'na will face our justice." It cocked its head. "You did wrong; you must face judgement. That judgement will be your people's to make." The alien nodded at Carter. "Your bots did well: they relayed the viral compound to us. We have safeguarded our people against it. We have returned to see justice carried out on those truly behind our xenocide."

Neeta rushed forward and crouched beside John. "We did it."

Zelo troops swarmed into the nest-tunnels below. They knew where to find the Barath'na, all right. They must know,

222

too, that their real enemy wasn't a lad from the streets of Belfast too stupid and desperate to refuse a job. Please, let them know that.

He glanced at Carter and nodded. "Their cavalry's better than yours," he said.

"Aye." The cop sounded like a shadow of himself. "But at least I did what I promised." He gave a grim smile. "Josey's alive – she's in Belfast with Peters."

She was alive. John had to pause to take that in. He's been so sure he'd killed her. He ducked his head for a moment, determined not to be caught on camera with his eyes glassy, and swallowed the lump in his throat. Finally, he looked up Carter.

"Thanks. You did good." He had at that. And so had John.

EPILOGUE

ohn sat in the dock, looking straight ahead and not at the empty chair beside him. Taz should be here. Today had brought it home to him that Taz wasn't coming back. It was his fault. He knew that. He'd been the one who'd dared Taz to taste the drug. A bitter taste filled his mouth, of regret, of bile.

"It will be okay," Josey whispered from the row behind him. He glanced round. Her hair was drawn back into a high ponytail that made her face pinched and hard. Older. God, they were both so much older. But she'd done a brilliant job, telling the judge all about how Gary McDowell captured her. John had listened, stunned. He'd always known she was tough – he hadn't survived Belfast on his own – but her clear voice and steady description astounded him. She made what he'd done sound like nothing.

Next to her, Sean stood, his parents in the row behind, and beside them, her head up in her best fuck-you stance, Neeta. John half-smiled; he'd have to remind her it wasn't her on trial.

Carter, too, had taken the stand. He'd told the judge about the whole conspiracy. How it had been carried out, and who was involved. He'd been so composed, so sure of his facts, it had been impossible for the opposition to sway him. It reminded John of the day, early on, when he'd stood up to Downham and refused to hand him and Taz over. Cojones, indeed.

Then it had been up to Catherine. She'd told John that he might not get off, that they might still think he was guilty because he'd known that he and Taz were doing something illegal. He'd been so nervous he reckoned he might chuck up, right there in front of the judge, but he'd managed to listen through what she had to say, and keep his head up. He'd done nothing wrong, except be poor and stupid and desperate. Catherine had hoped Carter's testimony about the conditions they were living in, the house's missing roof, might help to mitigate what he'd done. Stuart and Sophie, sitting either side of Peters, were proof of what John had been trying to protect. He listened to Catherine summing up, telling the judge that there had been no intention for John to kill anyone, that he was sorry for his actions. He'd zoned out, just wanting it to be over and to be told what was happening.

"Would the courtroom please stand."

This was it. He got to his feet and the judge walked past him, his face impossible to read. John's heart thumped, but he kept his eyes focused on the front of the room. Whatever happened, it was nothing more than he deserved. But, God, he hoped it would be okay, that he'd not have to be scared anymore, or worried about what lay ahead. And he definitely hoped that death at the hands of the Zelo wasn't on the cards. He glanced back; Josey looked just as frightened. She met his eyes, and bit her lip. Beside her, Carter looked ahead, his face impassive. Josey grabbed the policeman's arm, and he put his hand over hers, still looking forward.

"In the matter of John Dray, the charge of xenocide has been considered." The judge's voice was serious, and impossible to read. John looked at him, zoning everything else out. No matter what happened, don't break down. Not here, in front of everyone.

"It has been accepted the defendant did not know the contents of the tin he was requested to empty." John closed his eyes, and allowed the little spark of hope inside him to bloom. They knew he hadn't meant it...

"Nonetheless, the defendant released the virus."

The spark died. He opened his eyes, waiting, resigned to the worst.

"The circumstances were exceptional. The defendant carried out the crime as an act of desperation." The judge pushed his glasses back. John held his breath. A crime; they were still calling it a crime. He was going to be sent back to prison, at the very least. The idea of seeing the inside of Inish Carraig again, even under human guards, sent a chill through him. He managed to breathe. Just about.

225

"Your actions since have given some mitigation for your actions. Without you, Earth's sentient species would have been destroyed: a double xenocide. *You* are innocent of the charge of xenocide and are free to go."

John's legs were shaking. He wanted to sit, but stayed standing. Distantly he was aware of whoops and cheers and he looked up to see Stuart running down the steps, Sophie just behind him. Carter clapped Catherine's shoulder and congratulated her, his eyes shining the way they always did around her, and then the dock opened and John stepped out and the kids were in his arms, Josey with them. The world shrank to just them and him. He glanced up at the ceiling, and gave a smile. "Well, Da, did I do okay?"

There was silence, but it was enough. If he hadn't, his da would have told him somehow. And his ma definitely would. He grinned and pulled Josey against him. They'd all done okay. More than okay. They'd survived, and nothing else mattered except they were here and safe and together, through the war to the other side, where anything was possible.

THE END

To See Jo Zebedee's other books check out
www.ticketyboopress.co.uk/abendau

Here is the prologue to whet your appetite.

Abendau's Heir Prologue

ater dripped down the rock behind Ealyn. He strained, trying to turn his head to lick the wall, but his chains prevented him, the magnetic binding on his wrists too strong to be broken. His captors knew him well enough to use subtle things to torment him: the sound of water, so blessed on the hot, dry, Abendau; the prism on its thin chain catching sunlight from a small window and sending rainbows darting; the slow build of pain in muscles held firm, a pain that went deep, full of despair.

To hell with them: he was staying where he was, aware of who he was, even if his jaw ached from gritting his teeth and his hands had blistered from gripping his chains. Whatever she sent his way, whatever temptation, he'd take it and spit in her face. He closed his eyes against the dancing light.

Footsteps sounded, clipped, not the boots of the guards. He tried to move back, but there was nowhere to go; he was already tight against the wall. He tensed at the hiss of the cell opening. The footsteps stopped, right in front of him; he could feel her watching him.

Oh, gods. He waited, head down. *Please let her leave.* He clenched his fists, ears alert, his breathing shallow. She was coming so often now, not giving him time to build his strength.

"Tell me a vision of my future," said the Empress. Her first touch whispered its way past his resolve and he whipped his head to the side, trying to force her away. Once he'd been strong enough, he was sure of it, but after his months held in the cell, this time she held firm. Pain built, deep in his head, a white pain that obscured his thoughts and left only the core of him: the power she wished to use.

"*No.*" His wrists jerked in their manacles, the magnets' hard edges rubbing the broken skin beneath. The clean, sharp pain made his mind a little clearer. "No."

"Tell me." Her voice demanded obedience.

His eyes opened to a slit. He fought, willing them closed, but his eyelids were forced up. The prism's light danced across the walls, inescapable, but he willed his focus away and back to the Empress. Her smile chilled him to the bone; she knew he was close to the end, that she was wearing him down. She knew and she enjoyed it, sadistic bitch that she was.

"Give me what I want," she said, "and I'll leave you in peace."

He licked his lips, tongue rasping. She lied: she would come again. He knew better than any that the future was a drug, even for those who only heard it. He shook his head, the effort draining him, and whispered, "No."

"Look at the prism, Ealyn-Seer."

He couldn't stop himself. The light caught his eyes and he fell into the future, moving from the cell, up, up, through the palace to the grand entrance hall. He tried to hold onto the reality of the cell, focus on the pain in his wrists, fill himself with the hatred and anger that had held him to this point, but found himself standing before a stone arch. On a dais to the side a woman and man stood, wearing long acolyte's gowns, like those of the tribal people of the plains. He was forced to his knees before them. Their minds invaded his, their joint powers – greater than the Empress', greater than his had ever been – took his thoughts for their own. Rebel, they said, close to him, echoing each other. He ducked his head, trying to hide. Seer, they said, mocking his attempt: *rebel-seer-father.*

"Look at them." The Empress' voice rang out, and he lifted his head. Their eyes were his green. The woman had the sharp chin and high cheekbones of the Empress, the man dark hair falling over a pale face that could be Ealyn's own. *Rebel-seer-father.* He looked between them and, finally, sickeningly, knew why he'd been taken.

A wave of exultation ran from the Empress, and he could feel life within her, tiny, not even babies yet. She'd got what she wanted: children born of their combined powers, shaped and moulded to further her empire. Who knew how she'd done it, taken what she needed from him – he'd had a whole series of medical tests when he'd first been captured. It didn't matter how, only what it might mean. He watched, helpless in

229

his future, as his children pronounced judgement and sentenced him to the torture chambers of Omendegon.

The vision faded. His head sank forward, drained of all energy. Dimly, he was aware of the Empress leaving and the cell door closing, and could feel only relief. The light danced on the rock ground before him, pin-pricks of promise. It would be easy to focus on it, wander the paths ahead and release himself from the hot, dry cell. It was what the Empress wanted: to trap him, his sanity lost, fit only to give her the knowledge her own psyching couldn't find. To hell with her; he might not be able to stop her, but he was damned if he'd make it easy.

A parrot's screech startled him. The cell became dappled in warm sunlight. He tried to fight the vision but nothing worked: not pain, not the dripping water. He faded into the future, one where he stood on a jungle-encroached path. Holbec, he decided, near the Banned base. He drew in a sharp breath; if he was back with the Banned, there was a chance he'd get out of the cell. Something buzzed close to his cheek and he lifted his hand to swat it, but the chains of his past self stopped him. The sound of laughter drifted up the path. He turned a corner and two children walked ahead, dark heads together as they talked.

"Hey!" His words were croaked from thirst.

They turned, their green eyes meeting his, the girl's smile wide, the boy's fringe dark over his laughing eyes. Ealyn drew in a sharp breath, and spun out of the vision. *His. They were his.* Just as the cold adults in their acolyte's gowns were. Two futures, not the same. Hope flared, from somewhere he'd been sure was too buried to come alive again.

Around him the rainbows danced. He could take another look to be sure. He closed his eyes, fighting temptation. That path, the Seer's path, led to madness; he'd seen it often in others.

But the children had been happy in the jungle, not sad and used and cruel. Somewhere, there was a path to that future. It didn't matter what it did to him; it didn't matter if it drove him to his death or madness: he had to find it, not let the Empress ruin his lost children. Decided, he lifted his chin and focused on the prism, seeking the path he needed. And when he didn't find it the first time, he looked again. And again, leaving the dry cell to walk the paths of time, hope carrying him where nothing else could have.

(ABENDAU'S HEIR, TICKETY BOO PRESS, 2015 – http://ticketyboopress.co.uk)

.

Printed in Great Britain
by Amazon